The Art of Becoming Homeless

Sara Alexi is the author of the Greek Village Series.

She divides her time between England and a small village in Greece.

http://facebook.com/authorsaraalexi

The Art of Becoming Homeless

Sara Alexi

oneiro

PUBLISHED BY:

Oneiro Press

The Art of Becoming Homeless

Book Five of the Greek Village Series

Copyright © 2013 by Sara Alexi

ISBN-13: 978-1492796480
ISBN-10: 1492796484

The Greek Village Series:

Chapter 1

Friday

By the time the plane had landed in Athens Michelle would have given anything for a flat surface and just for ten minutes to close her eyes.

The doors opened and the glorious sunshine startled her senses, momentarily dispelling her fatigue. The heat engulfed her as she hurried down the steps. The sky was an endless blue, lifting her spirits and the caress of the warmth slowed her feet once on solid ground. A man, dragging deeply on a cigarette, used the authority of the airline badge on his shirt to chivvy her off the runway as she lingered, and inside to passport control where her initial joy of having escaped the cold of London ended.

The first air-conditioned hour in the airport could not have been worse, primarily due to the loss of her luggage, but greatly enhanced by her lack of sleep.

'It is not possible,' the airline's representative had argued.

'What do you mean it's not possible? The carousel has stopped, I have this bag and my hand luggage, but my main bag isn't here, so it's missing.'

'No, it is not possible.' At which point he had walked away, leaving Michelle open mouthed.

The staff at the airport help desk, all smiles and welcoming at first, slowly seemed to lose their command of English the more it became apparent her bag had flown to some other destination.

A new face was brought to pacify her. 'Madam, do not upset yourself. You are no used to the heat, you have no slept, maybe you no brought another bag?' he suggested with a smile.

At this, Michelle blinked as the office swam behind welling tears. He handed her a box of tissues.

'Perhaps it will be best if we speak to your husband. He will have a clearer idea I think?' His tone low and solicitous.

The chair almost toppled back as she stood. He stood too, his eyes wide with surprise at her sudden movement. Michelle stepped slowly around the desk and used her height to intimidate him, tears forgotten, to put him straight with the clear enunciation of a few select words.

He'd cowered at her onslaught, and conceded the possibility that she might have in fact lost a bag, and his initial denial was replaced by a quantity of lost property forms which she was obliged to complete. The promises of the bag's retrieval seemed fragile at best.

The relief that her laptop and paperwork were in the case she had retrieved was immense. At least the purpose of her visit would not be thwarted, the meeting could still go ahead, moving the whole claim forward, and going some way to securing her

4

position at work - she hoped.

People entering and leaving the airport kept the automatic doors opening and closing, the heat flowing inside in waves. Outside the taxis were lined up in shiny yellow pairs, even the motorway beyond looked magical in the sunlight, intensely three dimensional, and beyond it the distant hills an unreal hazy blue. Michelle took a step towards the line of taxis, where the drivers on the pavement were in a heated conversation, slamming the flat of their hands on their car roofs to emphasise their point.

Not one to be intimidated, Michelle strode past the group to the car at the front of the line and waited. A red-faced man eventually slid into the driver's seat muttering something in his mother tongue. Presently though, his argument forgotten, he turned his full attention on Michelle, and she wondered if it might have been wiser to sit in the back.

A tinny blare of *bouzouki* from the radio, a cacophony of car horns and a hot dusty smell off the tarmac all served delightfully to remind Michelle that this was not England. Here the view was not dimmed with grey drizzle and the shops' lights not lit all day, reflecting off puddles. Instead the brilliant light gave everything an exciting, vibrant quality. She yawned and settled into the journey, driving through the fatigue of an economy class seat on a night-flight.

The hotel had been momentarily a little more tranquil, but once she had checked in and stowed her suitcase, she came out to find the lobby a sea of tourists all clamouring to speak to the man behind the reception desk, who was ignoring them and yelling into the phone. It seemed that a tour bus had not turned up and the group's travel plans had gone askew.

The hotel's 'courtyard', towered over on all sides by apartment blocks, was relatively quiet. The flagged floor well-scrubbed, the flowers carefully tended. She sank into a soft chair in the shade of an umbrella to revive over a welcome cup of coffee. The caffeine brought enough life to her mind and her limbs to take stock of her situation. Her work days while she is here are accounted for. She should really use her time to read through the paperwork again. But right now is the start of the weekend.

The next two days could be hers, all hers, full of possibilities.

The bright sun makes promises that anything she chooses to do will be full of joy and the heat assures her of deep relaxation to all her muscles and as she sinks in her chair she is excited into motion by an idea.

An hour later, in the back of a taxi this time, trying to avoid making eye contact through the rear view mirror, she arrives at the port of Pireaus, with nothing but a few essentials in a money belt and a small rucksack.

She will island hop for the weekend.

She watches and waits as a man comes out of

the ticket office on the quayside.

His bag is big enough to fit a whole life in.

'Excuse me,' he says as he passes her, his head bowed, concentrating on where his canvas holdall is snagging on the doorframe.

Michelle steps aside to let him by. He shows no embarrassment at squeezing past. The hairs on the back of his neck, dark and soft like a child's, contrast his bright orange t-shirt.

He manhandles the other end of his bag out of the door, patient as it lodges again in the opening, the veins in his forearms bulging in his olive skin as his muscles contract with the effort of lifting it through. These briefest of moments observing someone else's life fascinate Michelle. She squints as her gaze follows across the port in the bright sunshine.

'Can I help you?' The man behind the wooden ticket desk takes a noisy suck on a foam-encrusted straw which is half submerged in something brown and frothy in a transparent plastic cup.

'Oh yes, I would like to go to an island near enough so I can be back by Sunday lunchtime at the latest. Which islands are that close?' she asks. The posters on the walls suggest endless destinations.

'None of them. They are all unreachable now.' He flips over his desk calendar, until it correctly reads 'Friday'.

'Sorry?'

'Boats are all stopped.' He replies.

7

'What, all of them?'

'Yes, everything. Everything stopping: the boats, the train, the bus. Everything to travel. It is stopped for one day, maybe two ... Only the taxis are OK.' He sucks again on his straw, turning the cup as he does so.

Michelle blinks, this is not part of the plan.

'Why?' she asks.

'Money, jobs, pension, everything.' Putting down his empty cup he picks a bit of lint from his crisp white shirt and drops it on the floor, rubbing his finger and thumb together.

Michelle considers this response. 'Oh, a strike?' That could explain all the arguing outside the airport and in the hotel lobby.

'That is what I said, a strike,' he says, checking the rest of his shirt. He has not made eye contact with her yet.

'Oh, but I only have today. There's nothing else?' Her shoulders droop.

'No.' He takes another suck on his straw. 'Only this.' He points out of the window, into the sunshine, to a small, angular grey ship which is rocking ever so gently in the harbour, sandwiched between other, much larger vessels. 'She is private, not union, one day tour.'

'Where does it go?'

'It doesn't matter.'

'What do you mean it doesn't matter?'

'It doesn't matter. It is the only ship. You have

8

no choice.' He glances at her briefly from under bushy eyebrows to emphasise the point.

Michelle sighs in exasperation, feels in her pockets for a tissue to mop her brow, it is so hot.

'If it is not too much trouble I would really like to know where it is I would be going,' she asks, looking around for a bin for her bit of tissue.

'Ah.' He shrugs and stands. He clearly has no interest. 'Tickets on the boat.' He reaches under the desk and pulls out a triangular wooden block with 'CLOSED' stencilled on one face. Placing the block on the counter he pulls down a blind.

Michelle stands for a moment, at a loss, until the sound of a ship's horn brings motion to her limbs.

Stepping out of the office back into the sunshine, she squints at the brightness, shields her eyes with her hand and approaches the boat to which the man had pointed.

A sign hanging from the handrail tells her the boat's destination is Orino Island, a place Juliet suggested she must visit one day. Well today could be that day. The times are scrawled on a blackboard. She can take this boat, have the rest of the day there to explore, stay one night, return on the one thirty tomorrow which will give her Saturday night and all of Sunday to prepare for the meeting on Monday. Perfect.

On board the heat is stale, the air-conditioning barely cooling in the saloon. The room is packed with tourists, bustling to stow their bags, order coffees, arrange themselves on the seats. Michelle finds the outside stairs and climbs as high as she can, to the open top deck. Throwing her head back she absorbs the deep expanse of cloudless cobalt which stretches to the very edges of her vision and finally takes that breath to let go of all her worries. She leans on the rail and watches the activity on the pier as the metal hull judders, the mooring lines are pulled in, and the ship slips out of the harbour.

She experiences a sense of freedom she has not felt for years, which trills in her stomach and makes her feel lightheaded. Responsibility, deadlines, enclosed offices - all echoes of another life. In this second she is the person she always has been.

Once out to sea, the ship's bow cuts through the glinting flat water and seagulls soar silently alongside, hovering on the updraught of the boat's motion. Michelle watches them for some time, leaning on the rail before her tired legs demand that she sit. The slatted wooden benches have been bleached white in the sun, and the green painted deck shimmers in the blaze. Women wave newspapers to cool themselves; men mop their sweating brows with large handkerchiefs.

With only partial shade, there is a choice of where to sit. Most passengers are below in the relative cool.

The slight breeze is deliciously cooling as it picks Michelle's hair off her neck. Leaning her head back, her eyes close against the brilliance of the sun, the insides of her eyelids glowing bright red. Gulls call above her, the hum of the engine vibrates below, the chatter of Greek and English all around. She wants to slow down her time and savour every second, be swallowed by everything Greek, experience the culture to the full.

'Oh for goodness' sake, Josh, put it down.' A south London twang. 'Dirty.'

Opening one eye, Michelle witnesses Josh squatting, dropping a cigarette packet and examining his fingers for evidence of the dirt.

The bench is missing one of its boards. Michelle shifts her weight and opens both eyes. On the seat opposite, a moustachioed man in a black fisherman's cap, sleeves rolled up, swings a *komboloi*, a string of amber beads, which click as they pass through his fingers. He looks directly at her, smiles and nods. Self-consciously nodding back, Michelle shades her eyes with her hand.

It is all so deliciously foreign.

The mainland recedes behind them, a haze hanging over the city, the Acropolis just visible in the distance above the mass of concrete-block houses.

Laughter and animated chatter herald the arrival of a group of girls dragging heavy rucksacks up the steps onto the deck. They are young, tall and slim, in shorts and strappy t-shirts. It could be Swedish or Finnish they are talking. Pushing their bags under the benches they sit, stretching their long legs out in front of them, mopping sweating foreheads with tissues, pulling down the edges of their shorts to get comfortable, and kicking off flimsy flip-flops. The man with the *komboloi* clicks his beads just a little bit faster.

On the seat behind the girls, a man of the church, in a tall black hat and black robe, has spread a cloth over his knees. His hugely round stomach catches the crumbs from his picnic feast that have slipped through the filter of his untrimmed beard. His eyes glassy, his focus seems internal. Beyond, in the shade of one of the lifeboats, two crew-members lean, quietly laughing, furtively smoking, their eyes alert, ready to stub out the evidence.

Michelle fishes into her rucksack to find her guidebook, which she opens, the white pages a momentary blur. She angles the book to put the type in the shade.

The book informs her that Orino Island has not changed in centuries. There are no motorised vehicles, and donkeys are still used for all heavy lifting. Groceries from the mainland, roof tiles and bags of cement for building, as well as heavy suitcases bound for the boutique hotels are all carried by these gentle beasts. It is worth noting, it adds in a boxed section, that the island's strict planning code allows only traditional methods for building, with stone and wood still fashioned by hand. The island works to the old rules, slowly, lost in time. Michelle is intrigued by the idea of a slow weekend, lost in time.

Flicking through the guidebook, the pages fall open at 'Useful Phrases', written both in Greek hieroglyphics and phonetically. It starts with the basics.

'*Efharisto*. Thank you. *Efharisto*.' The word has no link to her reality. Pausing, she looks to the heavens. 'A ferret's toes. *Efharisto*'. It is a technique from her long-gone student days, linking meanings to facts to aid memory.

'*Parakalo, parakalo*, you are welcome, *parakalo*, parrots claws.' Michelle looks about her, suddenly self-conscious that she has just spoken too loud. She runs her hand down the seam to open up the spine of the guidebook as she continues.

'*Mia beera*, one beer.' She turns the page, picking out potentially useful phrases. She hopes she will not be in need of the hospital, nor does she think she will want to buy a kilo of rice.

A seagull lands on deck and patters to a white plastic bag which, after a brief examination, it holds fast with its feet and tears at with its beak. A dark-haired toddler runs across the deck, screeching, arms outstretched for the bird, a man quickly behind him, ready to catch him if he falls, which he does. Michelle smiles. The man scoops the boy into his arms, kissing and soothing in his foreign tongue. She fascinates in people's relationships with their children, an unknown. The seagull flaps lazily away to join its companions, floating effortlessly on the breeze above the ship's side.

The young man she saw leaving the ticket office comes on deck, in his bright orange t-shirt, long legs, and ridiculously large canvas bag. He walks straight up to Michelle's bench, dumps the bag down beside her and flops next to it. She crosses her legs in the opposite direction and looks pointedly at the book.

'Don't I know you?' he asks.

Michelle sneaks a look to see who he is talking to, to find he is addressing her with a broad grin on his face.

'Sorry?' Michelle must have misheard. It's the sort of line she hasn't heard since her teens, of the kind the boys from Bradford Grammar might have used round the back of the pavilion on a Wednesday afternoon, Juliet puffing on a cigarette, school skirts rolled up to make them shorter. Juliet would parry with something like 'you wish' and grind the cigarette out with the toe of her shoe as they had seen in a film once.

'Yes, we have met,' the young man with the oversize bag persists, his eyebrows arching in the middle as he smiles. Beautiful teeth, bright white against his tanned skin.

She calls his bluff. 'No, I don't think so, but if we did, where would it have been?' It's flattering in a way, but she is not sure she wants a hormone-driven youth pestering her. She looks him over; she is old enough to be his mother.

'I remember, but to tell you would be too easy. You work it out.' He runs his hand through his hair, stroking his fringe to one side.

'Oh for goodness' sake.' The words come out as a sigh, but with a smile; he is just a little bit too immature.

A new man sits behind Mr Komboloi, holding a Styrofoam cup of coffee.

Michelle looks around, other people have cups too. She stands and walks towards the back of the ship, where she discovers a little bar selling drinks and pastries.

The Styrofoam protects her fingers as she blows across the top. It's dreadful coffee but in the circumstances tastes like heaven, and Michelle savours the caffeine fix. Now life is perfect. She finds another bench.

She tries to absorb everything: the magnificence of the heat's embrace, the lonely, romantic screeching of the gulls, the deep, beautiful azure of the sky, the animated sparkle of the sea, the possibilities beyond the horizon. It feels as if life has suddenly come into focus.

Balancing the remains of her coffee on a bench near the bar, she stretches her hand to the heavens. Right now life is perfect. Fingers splaying as she reaches up, she yawns and pauses with the sun on her face before opening the guidebook again.

The next sentence in the guide book looks difficult. '*Ti ora fevgi to leo ... leofor ... leoforri ...*'

15

'*Leoforeio*, bus,' a voice helps. 'What time does the bus go?'

Michelle starts and turns to see the young man in the orange t-shirt, who has twisted round to face her from the seat behind, their benches back to back. He pulls at his t-shirt across his shoulders, straightening the neckline, and sips from his own coffee cup.

Michelle wonders if he is going to be a problem. She mutters a 'thank you' and lifts the book slightly higher, turning the page. Conscious now that she is being observed, she takes a drink of her Styrofoam cup for something to do but finds it has all gone.

'You want another?'

Michelle continues to study the guidebook as if she hasn't heard.

'Hey lady! You want another coffee?' Out of the corner of her eye she can see his broad smile, his tight face muscles pulling extra little twists upwards at the corners.

'I'm fine, thank you.' Curt but not impolite. What if she has to call the authorities? Who do you call on a boat? She begins to read about the ancient theatre at Evedaros.

'You are alone?' His hand rests near her arm. Uncomfortably aware of the proximity, Michelle shifts in her seat. He appears not to notice.

Trying to be. It is on the tip of her tongue but she can't bring herself to say it, can't force herself to

16

be rude. Darting a look around the deck she cannot see anyone in uniform who could help her. A cluster of cigarette butts marks the spot that the deck hands have now departed.

'I am meeting a friend.' Keep it polite, best not to upset him. It's not a lie; she will be going to Juliet's house when the meetings in Athens have concluded, and besides, she certainly doesn't want to talk about work. The sun is shining, and she is on a boat in Greece, heading for an island. Work can wait till Monday.

'Ah, you have a friend. Is he Greek?' He hasn't stopped smiling; he is enjoying himself.

Now that is definite fishing. He slips from the 'harmful' category back to the 'annoying'.

'It's a "she" and no, she is English.' There, that should be the end of the conversation.

'Oh English, yes, she lives here in Greece, alone.'

Michelle is not sure if this is a question. Either way this is not a conversation she wants to have with a stranger.

'Do you mind if I just read my book?' She smiles to soften the edge in her voice. He raises and lowers the hand on the back of the bench, a gesture that offers her whatever she desires. 'You haven't remembered yet, have you?' He says it quietly, granting her the choice to ignore him.

The next page displays a photograph of clear sea and sky and endless sand. Why has she waited so

17

long to experience the sun? She continues on the facing page with the language.

She mouths the next words under her breath.

'*Ena Mousaka, mia salata,* one salad, *salata, mia beera,* parrots claws, *parakalo.*' This page is all about food. She flips to the next to see what is to come, and finds another picture, this time of people working in an office, wearing stripy tank-tops, knee-high boots, and miniskirts circa nineteen-seventy.

She lets out a little laugh and leans back. Only a week and she can look forward to spending some time with Juliet, talking, laughing, swimming. Warmth, sun, fresh air, and al-fresco dining. Wine! She should buy some when she goes, arrive with a bottle.

Michelle stands to stretch her legs, wanders past the pecked-at plastic bag, now blown into a corner, and stops at the handrail to look down into the water. The spray the boat creates mixes with the sun, producing glimpses of rainbows that live and die in a heartbeat. Looking up, she takes in the sea, which spans the entirety of her vision.

'The sea is very big, isn't it?' His voice is playful. He settles beside her, like an old friend, and she stiffens. Standing next to her, he is taller than she had imagined, the lithe suppleness of youth apparent in his every movement. She looks down and sideways at him. The muscles in his thighs show through his jeans. His belt buckle is ridiculously large, an eagle with its wings spread, some writing in the middle.

Turning her body slightly, she looks in the other direction. A gull glides past at eye level, so close, it turns its head slightly, looks right at her.

'You still don't remember me, do you?'

'Look, please stop. I am not a fool and you are no longer a boy.' She scans his face. His skin is the colour of a chestnut, his eyes brown, so dark she cannot tell where iris ends and pupil starts.

'OK, I'll tell you,' he relents, chuckling. 'From the village. You were there last Christmas, with some friends. You had chicken and chips at the *ouzeri*. I was with my *baba* on the next table from yours and we all joined as one. We raised a glass to British universities. Remember?'

'That was you?' He nods. Michelle loses her petulance in the delight of the recall. 'That was such a great day. Juliet was being so funny, and her sons. They were the same age as you, weren't they?'

'I remember her sons. One was at university, one in banking, I think?'

'I can't believe I didn't recognize you.'

'You had a few glasses that night ...'

'Oh my goodness, do you remember the fireflies?'

He narrows his eyes. 'I remember,' he chuckles.

The fireflies glowed gently in the grass, the first Michelle had ever seen. She had stared enraptured as this man—*what was his name?*—held one of the tiny insects for her to examine.

19

She pauses. 'So what brings you on a one-day cruise to Orino? Your home's over there.' Pointing, she changes her choice of direction once or twice. He corrects her and she smiles.

'The strike.' He shrugs resignedly. 'You?'

'Like you, this was the only boat going. But then again, the island is new to me. Surely you have been there before?'

'Born there. The village wasn't my home until I was nearly fifteen.'

'Ah, so you are visiting friends?'

'An old friend, Adonis.'

'I am Michelle, by the way, in case you had forgotten.'

He nods and smiles, a carefree youthful smile. 'Dino,' he replies. Michelle extends her hand. He has a firm grip and his hand is cool, but he lingers in letting go just a bit too long for comfort.

It is lovely to see him again, but just a small part of Michelle is disappointed that he wasn't just hitting on her. It's a long time since anyone has.

Chapter 2

They turn at the same time and wander back to the benches. Dino's enormous bag is pushed underneath, the canvas moulding itself around the metal bench legs, folds poking up between the seat slats.

He sits. 'So after the island where do you go?'

'Oh, it's sort of work and play, I'm afraid. I have an important business meeting in Athens on Monday morning, sorting out a shipping claim. Well, I say "afraid", but it's got me out of the office, out of London. And hopefully it will impress the right people.' Michelle smiles and closes her eyes against the sun. Her head rocks forward slightly, heavy, her neck muscles tense. The meeting will go well, surely ....

'And then?' Dino asks.

She snaps out of her negative thoughts.

'And then I go to the village to see Juliet for a week. A real holiday, with sun and wine.' She smiles and tucks her hair behind her ears. The strands curl around her ears and point to her cheekbones. With the sun so strong, she must take care not to burn.

'You've not been many times to Juliet's then?' Dino asks. Michelle listens but doesn't open her eyes. She pictures the bougainvillea that climbs the metal

21

arch of the entrance to Juliet's house, and the gravel drive beyond.

Juliet's single-storey farmhouse, with its terracotta roof, white-washed walls, and blue shutters sits nestled in a garden full of flowers and fruit trees. Split pomegranates that have fallen from the trees litter the ground, and smells of Juliet's cooking drift from her sparse kitchen.

She'll take the holiday regardless of the situation at work. She deserves it. She sighs, then turns her head to look at him.

'I came out at Christmas, and again for a long weekend in February, but the weather wasn't like this. Before that ... well, I always seem to be working.'

'Really?'

'Really. And then there is the house.' She sighs.

'What has your house got to do with your holidays?' Dino chuckles as he speaks.

'Well, yes, I see the stupidity.' Michelle laughs, but then qualifies her position. 'It's a crumbling Grade I listed home. It needs work, which needs money.' At one time it had been her and Richard's pride and joy, something he chose and together they filled, until it became a cocoon of over-padded sofas and thick tassel-hung curtains. The memories feel bitter. It's a place where, in the first few years, Michelle imagined there would soon be the laughter of small children. The bay window for family teas, the fireplace somewhere to cosy around in the winter

22

nights. But the room never delivered on its promises. Now the backs of the sofas are faded from the morning sun, and her dreams dissolved alongside the wasted hours spent in choosing the decor, the whole thing a farce that is physically crumbling into the ground despite the amount of money she pours into it. Most of her salary is spent on the house. It is a bittersweet win over Richard.

She opens her eyes. Dino has slid down the seat, ankles crossed in front of him, hands across his stomach, eyes closed, breathing steadily. She hadn't realised what a nice face he has the last time they met, with long eyelashes, olive skin, very Greek. He needs a shave. Michelle turns her attention to the gulls hovering by the ship's funnel, wings spread motionless, only the tail feathers splaying on the right or left to adjust their drift.

Despite the meeting on Monday and the preparation it will require, Michelle feels as if her holiday has already started. Thoughts of London fade to be replaced with the anticipation of soaking up the sun, chatting with Juliet, putting the world to rights. Michelle imagines pottering in the garden, lazing on beaches, savouring the fresh produce in the street market and drinking wine—lots of wine. There will be no early mornings next week, no negotiating the bustle of the tube or the onslaught of case preparation.

A flutter in her stomach, her shoulders relax. Something exciting is going to happen; she can feel it.

Horizons opening before her.

An old woman in black stands and begins to pull an oversized suitcase towards the stern of the boat, to the bar selling coffee. Her black skirt is almost faded to grey, her black cardigan, the buttons done up, misaligned so it puckers over her stomach. How can she wear a cardigan in this heat? The suitcase runs on wheels, but she has a difficult time guiding it. Something pink and fine, caught in the hinge as the suitcase closed, sweeps the floor, picking up dirt as it moves, invisible when the case is standing upright.

Her gaze wanders over people sitting, reading, sleeping, surrounded by luggage.

In a funny way it's quite nice to be travelling so light. It reminds her of her first visit to Greece, with Juliet, twenty years ago.

Looking out across the blue glassy water, Michelle's gaze follows the thin wake of a small boat. A corridor of white foam.

'You were at school with Juliet?' Dino asks. She starts, she thought he was asleep.

'Er, yes, we met outside the headmaster's office, which I suppose was a bit of a prediction that we were not going to be the best of influences on each other.' Michelle laughs, sitting more upright.

'I don't understand. Oh, you mean you were there to see the headmaster because you had been naughty?'

Michelle giggles, the years falling away, her

feet pulled in under the bench, toes pointing to each other, she sits on her hands.

'Juliet was sitting, waiting, she had been called in for swearing at a teacher. Her parents were splitting up about then and she was so angry. She swore all the time. I was there for truancy, only a couple of weeks into a new term at a new school. Sometimes the teachers would take so long to explain something, there seemed little point sitting in class.'

'Naughty, naughty.' Dino teases with a smirk.

Michelle grins at him and continues her tale.

'"What you here for?" Juliet had said, I remember her as tiny and blonder I think. I replied, "Playing truant, like". I had a broad Yorkshire accent back then. But, do you know, I felt so tall I can remember I slithered down in my seat so our heads were level.'

Dino sits up a little so their eyes meet and smiles. Michelle continues.

'So Juliet said "Was you playing or did you mean it?", or some nonsense like that. Her accent broad Bradford too.' Michelle laughs at the memory. 'We laughed so hard the deputy headmistress put her head around the door, looking stern. We tried to hold back our giggles, we must have sat and whispered, trying not to laugh, for another ten minutes before each of us was called in to discover our fate.'

'And your fate was?' Dino asks, he has slid back down his seat again into a more comfortable position.

'Detention, probably. Yes, that was it, because I remember Juliet was in detention too, that afternoon.' Michelle pulls her hands from under her and she too slides down her seat, leaning back, her legs stretched out.

'After that we were pretty inseparable. For me it was nice to have someone to talk to so I wasn't always coming in second to my sister. Juliet spent as much time as she could at my house to avoid the arguments at home, she was often there at teatime. She would say things like 'Your dad's right nice, never shouts at your mam.' Michelle adopts a Yorkshire accent, which makes Dino smile.

Michelle remembers feeling less enthusiastic about her home life. More often than not she would grab at Juliet's sleeve, pull her back into the street and with a rattle of coins in her pocket would persuade Juliet to stay out, have chips on the street, even missing a meal, anything felt better than going in for tea.

'Coming second to your sister?' Dino asks lazily.

'Oh, what's going on?' Michelle looks behind her, hearing excited voices, to see a little old lady in black wagging a finger at a tall man who is trying to wipe the arm of her cardigan with a serviette. His other hand clutches a Styrofoam coffee cup. He makes soothing noises as the woman becomes increasingly agitated. Dino pays no attention, he

26

closes his eyes.

Michelle wonders if it will come to blows. The woman is beside herself and looks like she might easily whack the man with her handbag. Instead the old lady cackles, the man smiles, they approach the bar together and order something. Her suitcase is left blocking the aisle.

'Completely incomprehensible people,' Michelle mutters to herself. But another coffee is a good idea. She notices that Dino's eyes are still closed, his mouth dropped open slightly, so she slips past him toward the bar.

Dino opens his eyes, just aware that he was muttering in his sleep before he awoke, but he cannot remember what he was saying, or the dream.

'You alright?' Michelle asks.

'Yes.' But he doesn't feel great. He wriggles his body to gain some comfort, but the bench is ungiving. He pushes himself upright and rubs his eyes with the heels of his hands.

'You were talking in your sleep.'

Dino sighs. It is a deep, long sigh. He cannot find his smile. 'It was a nightmare about what is to come. I have to go to see my Baba. It is going to be bad.'

'Oh, that doesn't sound so good.'

'No, that is why I say it is going to be bad. He will kill me.'

'Oh, I got you coffee, one of those cold ones.'

27

'Frappé.' He takes the cup from her, stirs the straw through the ice and then sucks for a moment before adding, 'Too sweet.'

'You're welcome.' She grins.

'Sorry. Thank you, kind Michelle.' He smiles now.

'So, why will he kill you?'

Dino's gaze fixes on the seagulls bobbing on the water. 'Because he has paid and I have studied — English university.' His eyes flick to Michelle's face, she nods. He has no desire to talk about this.

'So?' Michelle asks.

Dino glances at her, her look so compassionate that he continues; 'After I finished my studies I did what he said. I got a job in London. But at the end of each day I would go home and cry. I mean literally cry.' He looks at her to check her reaction. Michelle frowns. He continues, 'All day locked inside walls with no windows. It was sucking out my soul, and then I would go home to a tiny room that I didn't want, that I was paying so much money for, so I quit.' He stops to take a breath. 'But now I must tell my Baba.'

Michelle is speechless for a moment, more shocked by the number of words he had said in one go than the content. He is waiting for a reaction.

'Quitting a job is no reason to kill someone.'

'Ha!' It is short and sharp. 'You do not know my Baba. Years of oranges sold for university, farmhouse not fixed so tuition fees are paid. Now he

28

will kill me.'

'But quitting your job isn't throwing what he has done for you back in his face. You can get another job, one that you prefer, perhaps.'

'Go back, he will say. London, England is good place he will say. All I can see is a life working in a box, with just enough money to rent another box to live in. England is cold. Here is my home.' Leaning forward he rests his forehead on his hands, elbows on knees.

'Ah, so you want to come back here, and he wants you to stay there, you mean?'

He doesn't say anything. He might be crying. Michelle reaches out, her hand hovers over his back, ready to soothe, comfort. He jerks up suddenly; she whips her hand back, hoping he hasn't seen.

'He thinks he can make my life.' His face is set hard in anger, his eyebrows arching slightly, softening the effect.

'So get a job here?'

He sniffs, Michelle hands him the serviette that came with her coffee. 'Thank you,' he mutters.

'You?' he says brightening a little. 'Do you work?'

Michelle looks in his eyes, flecks of gold dancing in the dark irises. She smiles at his resilience.

'Within windowless walls, having my soul sucked out for the last twenty years.' She quotes his words cheerfully, but her chest suddenly feels tight. She hangs onto her smile.

'Is it worth it?' His eyes darken, piercing. He really wants to know.

The heat swaddles her, stealing her breath away in its all-encompassing embrace. In the moment, words elude her. She reaches out and puts a hand gently on his shoulder. His opposite hand raises and comes to rest on her hand, an expression of gratitude for her kindness. He nods as he lets his arm drop again.

In this setting, surrounded by sky and sea, nothing in the world seems more ridiculous than sitting in an office bent over paperwork day in, day out.

'What choice do we have?' she says as gently as she can.

'Oh, I have choice, only it is like the English saying—a hard place and a rock,' he smiles sadly.

'Meaning?' Michelle asks.

'I can return to Greece.'

'And face an angry father.'

'More. And face the army.'

'Oh, yes, of course, they still have national service here, don't they? How long?'

'Two years.' He loses his animation and suddenly looks very young.

'That's not so bad. You'll be out in no time.' Michelle tries to cheer him, then remembers her coffee and picks it up from behind the leg of the bench. Dino does the same with his.

'It's bad, I hear,' he says as he puts his cup

30

down. 'One friend, he goes. The sergeant hates him. "Break the gun," the sergeant says. My friend, he says "no". The sergeant says it is an order, smash the gun against the rock. So my friend, he feels he must do it. The gun is broken. The sergeant has him arrested for breaking army property. You cannot win.' Dino runs a hand across his hair, smoothing his fringe out of his eyes, wipes his mouth nervously.

'But that's not right. He should have reported him.'

'For the army to believe my friend over a sergeant?' He blinks several times

'I can see your fears, but not all the sergeants will be the same.'

'I have another friend who will not go,' Dino says in hushed tones.

'What will happen to him?'

'He will not be able to get a job. They always ask for your release papers. He will not be able to leave the country, what can he do?'

'But your time in the army is not so long. Let's say you did it. What afterwards?' she encourages, wondering if this is anything like being a mother, helping to make such decisions, encouraging the right paths to be chosen. She doesn't feel qualified. Is there a 'right' path?

He shrugs. He locks her gaze. The deep blue sky silhouettes the dark brown of his hair, but his eyes have her fixed.

One minute he was a child with a mother, a family, the next everything changed. One minute he lived on the island and always had, the next he was living in the village where he knew no one. One minute at school, the next on a plane to England to go to university. These days will be the same, one day he will be full of life, the next an old man. He is aware of his youth and it seems so precious. Life makes promises and then snatches them away.

Promises. His mother's eyes when she was happy. The way she threw her head back when she walked. Her arms wrapped around him, her hand snaked so it could hold his head against her shoulder. No words in those moments. He did not need to tell her things, she did not need to ask, she knew everything that was in his head and heart. One minute there for life, the next gone — for life.

And now they ask for him to give up these precious years to the army or some grey office.

'But now? Now you go to the island you were born on to see a friend. The strike has saved you meeting your dad, I presume? Without that, you would be going straight to the village, yes?' Dino nods. 'How long are you staying on the island, or are you just doing the overnight stop?' She hastily changes the conversation, trying to give it energy, to break the spell Dino seems to have fallen into.

He looks at the floor, but when he raises his head his countenance is lighter. He smiles, his

32

eyebrows lift.

'Who knows? Can you really tell what life will throw at you next?'

Chapter 3

The ship's course curves to line up with a streak of grey-blue that smudges the horizon and slowly gains definition, becomes solid, and announces that it is land.

'*Nato*,' Dino points.

'Sorry?' Michelle follows his finger.

'There it is,' he repeats.

Michelle scours the shape with her eyes but can see no evidence of life. It is barren, with no houses apparent.

'Where are the people?' she asks.

'All in the town, together.' Dino smiles.

The island is long and they begin to travel down its length, sailing closer until Michelle can almost make out bushes and rocks. Then a house, white, tall, majestic, not as Michelle imagines Greek houses should be. This one is surrounded by olive trees and a high stone wall that extends all the way down to the sea.

There is another similar house farther along, and one above it, higher up the hill. They are all grand and within walled gardens.

The island is still some way off, and all is misty with the heat. Michelle goes to buy a bottle of water. Even if she has no sunscreen, she should at least keep hydrated.

Dino is standing when she returns. He juts his chin toward the island.

There is nothing to see, just land rising almost straight from the water, no beach, just rock and scrub. Then, without warning, what seemed to be no more than a slight fissure in the rock opens as they draw level with it and reveals itself to be a deep inlet.

As one, the tourists on board, including Michelle and the Finnish girls, gasp as the town comes into sight, a perfect half-bowl scooped out of the hillside. The land, steep on either side, encloses the port. They are close enough to distinguish individual houses that make up the cascade of dazzling whitewashed walls and orange tiled roofs down to the port from the pine trees on the ridge. The town appears small, contained, as ancient as Greece itself. The houses back from the harbour's edge stand four and five storeys high, of solid square-cut stone, majestic, reminiscent of an Italian riviera.

Dino points to the left of the port's entrance at a line of old cannons standing sentinel high on the rocks, their noses pointing out to sea, a testament to the island's turbulent history.

'Once many shipping captains lived here,' Dino says.

Michelle, not wanting to take her eyes off the island, scrabbles blindly in her bag for the guide to the island. The book is more of a travelogue by a

35

journalist than a tourist guide. Michelle prefers the personal approach to the commercial guidebooks, the romance between the words, the extra history. 'The island was the home to wealthy shipping magnates at one time, displaying their wealth in grand houses, three-, sometimes four-floors high, standing to attention around the harbour.' She reads with one eye on the majestic view.

'"Between these solid mansions are nestled one- and two-storey dwellings. The houses behind, packed in tightly, mount the slope like stepping stones, almost to the ridge. Pine trees encompass the town."'

'In old times,' Dino leans into Michelle and talks into her ear, his lips against her hair, his shoulder against her back, 'the people of the island, they put a chain across the harbour entrance, from cannon to cannon.' He points to the right of the harbour, where the rocks bristle with more cannons, long ago rusted and now painted a shiny black. 'The chain, she was heavy and she went beneath the waves, invisible.' Michelle senses he is very close, but her attention is still riveted by the island.

'So the pirate boats, they come and the underneath is caught on the chain. The pirates, they cannot go forward. The islanders now have time to shoot the cannons.' She pulls her ear away from his mouth to face him. He is smiling, the corners of his eyes creased ever so slightly.

As the little tourist ship passes the entrance

unhindered, Michelle leans over the rail and peers into the depths, picturing in her mind's eye the bones of hapless pirates now consigned to the seabed below. From inside the air-conditioned saloon a group of Japanese tourists floods the lower decks. The women are dressed in clean, neat, light-coloured clothing, with white gloves and parasols. The men have cameras out, with lenses trained on the island. A broadside, Michelle muses. The engine's rumble lessens, the speed drops to a calming 'put, put, put'. The wallowing slows to a bob.

The harbour is much busier than when Dino was last here. It seems like mayhem, filled with shouts of people both on and off the boats, the white hulls of their floating worlds moored tightly, side-by-side, along the harbour wall. Tangles of mooring chains knot groups of vessels together. The local fishing boats, wooden, double-ended, brightly painted, are pushed into a corner. An arch through the high pier gives them access to the sea, allowing them to bypass the hordes of pleasure boats. This keeps them safe from the multi-million-dollar yachts and sleek, private, gin palaces that bounce off each other's mooring buoys. The charter yachts dominate, one merging into another in their white and stripes. The harbour is heaving. There are so many boats they are obliged to tie up two or three deep. Those moored up against the pier are in stern-first. The second layer nuzzling in between, bows-in, ties onto the first. Captains and crew of the outlying boats must clamber across their neighbours' decks from their watery holiday-homes to reach dry land.

As the ship manoeuvres with care into a dedicated space, the sounds of the weekend sailors are overlaid by the excited chatter from the harbour-side cafés.

The mooring lines fly through the air onto the pier where hands are ready to secure them to iron bollards set into the stones, and a set of steps is rolled, clanking, up to the side of the ship. The horn is sounded twice. They have arrived.

A wave of people jostles forward to disembark, and Michelle is carried through the ship and onto the harbour with the throng.

All about her is bustle, an unfamiliar excitement. The people sitting in the pavement cafés are smiling, laughing. The waiters sliding through and between them, as if on ice, seem relaxed and in control. Contented cats sprawl and lick their paws in the shade, or prowl the tables for scraps.

She has seen a similar contentment in the wine bar next to chambers at six-thirty on a Friday night. It lasts half an hour, by which time they have all downed double whiskys and the smiles are replaced by grey faces of exhaustion.

But here, joy seems to be a permanent state.

Without the cooling influence of the ship's motion and the sea breeze it created, the heat bounces off the cobbles and the stone buildings, stifling and dry.

'Can I offer you a cool drink to thank you for the pleasure of your company on the ship?' she asks. Dino seems preoccupied and Michelle reminds herself that he is here to see his friends, not to keep her company. She wonders if she should repeat herself or let him go. But Dino makes his way through the outer tables of one the harbour cafés and pulls out a seat, beckoning her over to sit.

The ship hoots again.

Michelle looks around to find out what has caused a sudden stir. The waiter is being called by several raised hands. People stand, throwing coins onto tables. From under the tables, suitcases are wheeled out, people kiss goodbye. The ship's engine stirs back into life. Something hits her leg. Michelle turns to see a box of what looks like water bottles filled with olive oil being pushed, scraping along the floor, by an old lady in black. She pulls her chair in, apologising, but the woman does not look up as she hastens to the ferry.

'The only boat, because of the strike,' Dino explains.

The mixture of excitement and chaos reaches a crescendo and then diminishes to leave a pleasant calm in which Michelle feels she can draw breath again. She sits. Dino orders for them both with a gesture of his hand and one word in Greek to a waiter who is some yards away.

The harbour is roughly square, with a stone

pier on the outer, seaward side, and a wide stone pavement edging the other three sides, covered with tables and umbrellas. The pavement narrows and leads into paths which head along the coast east and west at the corners of the square. Shops and cafés, banks and houses sit behind the harbour front. Between the buildings are narrow, cobbled lanes that lead into the town up the hill. 'Ginnels' they used to call them in Bradford, 'snickets' sometimes. Michelle is not sure there is a southern word for these narrow walkways. If there is, she has never had to use it.

'Excuse me.' Dino stands, manoeuvres his way deftly between the chairs and tables and hurries over to a man, about his age.

He grins from ear to ear.

'Hey, you, villager, where have you been?' Adonis laughs.

'Cut your throat, you peasant,' Dino sneers.

Adonis embraces him, kisses him on both cheeks, shakes his hand vigorously, and pats him heartily on the back.

'So you didn't let me know you are coming? Why are you here? They sack you? Your Baba will be pleased to see you.' Adonis does not release Dino's hand from the greeting.

'Ach, that's because he doesn't know yet.'

'Know? Know what, my friend? Have they promoted you to company director already?'

'Ha, then it would be me cutting my own

40

throat. You wouldn't believe what it is like.'

'Hey Dino.' A serious-faced young man in an open-necked striped shirt approaches, arms outstretched.

'Fanis!' Dino opens his arms.

'So you escape, eh? The English, they threw you out, did they?' Embraces and kisses, and slaps on the back and shoulders are exchanged again. Fanis' shirt is cool to the touch, betraying the luxury of his air-conditioned office.

'Dino was telling me how he was loving the English weather. Look how pale his skin is.' Adonis draws a finger down Dino's face as if wiping off dirt. Dino ducks back and blocks Adonis' hand. They laugh.

'So you are loving it, eh Dino?' Fanis asks, frowning.

'Yeah, like being kicked by a donkey: it is great when it stops.'

'But the money's good?' Adonis asks.

'What comes in is great, but what they give with one hand they rob with the other.' He tells them how much he pays in rent and Adonis grins as if it is a joke.

'But it is a house with a garden to yourself at that price, right?' Fanis says.

'Yeah, good one! It is one room, with just enough space to walk around the bed, a shared kitchen that no-one cleans and a toilet with no light and a window that won't open.'

Adonis is still laughing. Dino gently shoves him back; Adonis bends with the push. 'But you are kidding?' he asks seriously, wrapping his arms around himself.

'No.' All humour drains from Dino's face. 'It is hell. There is no sun, no sea, no one I know, no one smiles. I go to work on the tube and everyone's face is like this.' He drags his hand down his face, pulling the corners of his mouth down. 'You speak to them and they grunt or look at you as if you are crazy.'

'No, you are teasing us,' Fanis says.

'I am not. Let me tell you about the office. It is a big room.' He opens his arms to encompass the entire port. 'The carpet is grey and it stretches from wall to wall. My desk is in the centre; it is so far from the windows I see no daylight. The people near the windows, they draw the blinds so they do not have to look out on the car park or the backs of other buildings. There is fluorescent lighting on all day long in the office. I have never seen it switched off.'

Fanis and Adonis await his next sentence. No one moves.

'So there we are, all working together, hundreds of us. But you know what they do to make this worse? They have built stalls around us like we are animals, each one of us in a different pen so when we sit at our computers, we can see no one, talk to no one, caged.'

'No, this is not true. In China, maybe, but not in England,' Fanis exclaims. 'In England they have wood-lined offices, big wooden desks with green reading lamps, tall windows with heavy curtains, and pretty secretaries. Or shiny chrome offices with floor to ceiling glass walls.'

Adonis nudges Dino in the ribs. 'You have a pretty secretary, my friend?' he leers.

'I wish.' Dino leans against one of the metal poles which support the canvas awnings that shade all the harbour-side cafés.

'So come back and open an office or a shop here,' Fanis says, raising his hand to shield his eyes from the sun.

'Did you never meet his Baba, Fanis?' Adonis asks.

'But you are a man now, Dino. You must do as you please.'

'I wish it was so easy. My Baba, he tells me of the mountains of oranges he has sold to send me to English university, the frugal life he has lived so I can have this opportunity. How I will be grateful for the security that a job in England will offer me when I am married with my own children. He will go on and on and ....'

'Bully you, like he did when you were a kid!' Adonis says. 'Ha! Do you remember that time he went crazy at us? He told you to get his spanner from the work shed. Remember, he was fixing the water pump? So we both went and we looked and looked but couldn't find a spanner and all the time he was shouting for us to hurry. I remember you shaking

43

and I thought you were being silly, acting. But when we told your father we couldn't find his spanner, it was like a volcano erupting. We were only small then, eh? I was scared, I hid behind an olive tree, but you stood there and he bellowed at you and you didn't move. I thought you were so brave.'

'Yeah, brave, huh. I didn't know where you had gone but then I saw you creep from round the tree behind him and reach out to him. My heart was in my mouth. I had no idea what you were doing. The look on his face. He turned on you like someone possessed, and there you were with his spanner in your hand, which was in his back pocket all the time. I had to run before I exploded with laughter.'

'I didn't catch up to you until you stopped at the church,' Adonis answers. They are both laughing.

Fanis smiles. 'Yes, but now he is not such a big man. Age has shrunk him, as it does all men, and we are twenty-four. You must make your own life.'

'Sure. It sounds easy, but he has this way of bending logic, altering the way I think,' Dino says.

'He could argue black was white and make you think it was true. The government should employ him to promote their propaganda.' Adonis' arms are folded over his chest. He leans to one side slightly and raises his hand to his mouth as he laughs at his own joke.

'Hey Dino! Is that you? You are here! Welcome home, my friend.'

'Ilias! How is the water-taxi work?' Dino greets

him.

'Good, good. My Baba's out there now.' He holds up two paper parcels from the bakery. 'Just getting some breakfast, been on the early one. You staying or are you going over the hill?' He nods across to the mainland.

'He wants to stay,' Fanis says.

'Who doesn't? Every tourist who arrives wants to stay. You are a tourist now, my friend,' Ilias teases.

Dino swears at him, calls him a "*malaka*". Ilias returns the insult. Dino throws a soft blow to his stomach, and Ilias grabs him round the neck, still holding his breakfast, and pulls. Adonis pushes them both apart.

'I have to go, but you must find me before you leave.' Ilias pats him on his shoulder but doesn't make any move to depart.

'You haven't said what has brought you. Your Baba, he is not ill is he?' Adonis asks.

'He will be. I quit.' Dino smiles as he says the words but there is no humour in his eyes.

'You quit your job with the green lamp and the secretaries? *Panayia*! Mother of God! Your Baba will go ballistic,' Adonis says.

'But you know, my friend, without joking, things are not so easy here ...' Fanis' brows crease into a frown again. 'Maybe your Baba is right. In Greece now no one is building, and I have no new clients, only one or two construction projects that started some time ago. But when those finish ....'

'Speaking of jokes, I heard a good one!' Adonis is in high spirits. 'You know what the unemployed architect says to the one who has a job?' He waits, and Fanis rolls his eyes. 'Can you guess?' Adonis claps his hand on Dino's shoulder as he delivers the punch line. 'Two souvlaki and a portion of chips!' He dissolves into laughter, but no one else is much amused.

'It's no joke, my friend.' Fanis' countenance is heavy. 'I know many colleagues who have closed their offices.' He makes his excuses and the party breaks up. Ilias lopes off to join his father, who is beckoning him for his breakfast. They all look towards the old man, who waves to Dino with one hand and beckons his son with the other, from one of the brightly coloured water taxis lined up in one corner of the port. Dino nods.

They agree they will all meet up later, and Adonis and Dino are left alone. Adonis the taller of the two, lithe, Dino muscular by comparison, but they could be brothers, with the same dark straight hair swept back, straight noses, full eyebrows. Dino is pale by comparison; the English rain has washed away his tan.

'Coffee?' Dino asks.

'No, work.' He tips his head up a side street towards a little bar with its doors closed, chairs stacked on tables. 'Come.' He begins to walk.

'Actually …' Dino begins, nodding toward the café where Michelle sits. Adonis frowns, and then smiles and nods knowingly.

'Oh, I see,' he says. 'I will see you later then.'

'Can't avoid it, my friend. It's a small island.' Dino grins.

Michelle has finished her drink by the time he returns. They sit a while longer, soaking up the sun and the bustle of life around them. The ship they arrived on gives three sharp hoots and begins to back slowly away from the dock. More of the harbour comes into sight from where they are sitting. Halfway along the edge facing out to sea is a stumpy clock tower with carved stone columns on the corners by the clock face. Opposite, low in the water is a rusty blue cargo ship, strikingly at odds with the sleek white yachts and motor-cruisers that surround it.

Michelle surmises that many of the things needed for daily life must be shipped in to these little islands. She looks around, and the absence of any roads suddenly strikes her. There are many little streets and passages, but they are all too narrow for a car or a truck.

'I did say, didn't I? There are no cars, motorbikes, or bicycles here; just legs and donkeys.' Dino's smile lights his eyes. He seems thoroughly content.

As if to prove the point, a string of donkeys, one behind the other, is led out from a side street to the edge of the pier near the cargo boat. One of the donkeys lets out a braying call. A pair of donkeys

47

follows and these are brought past the cargo ship to the corner where Michelle and Dino are sitting. A man with a flat cap and the most magnificent moustache Michelle has ever seen is holding the reins. He turns to stroke the lead donkey's head. He twists the end of his moustache on both sides before taking out a pouch of tobacco and beginning a well-practised ritual. He cannot be much over thirty. That, or he is very well preserved.

'Donkeys!' Michelle is on her feet. 'I love donkeys.'

Dino slurps to the bottom of his glass, throws some coins on the table, nods to the waiter, and hastens behind her.

The donkeys smell just as she remembers them. She smooths their shaggy coats and pats them.

'Juliet and I once skipped school ...' She briefly turns to Dino but almost doesn't meet his gaze.

'Tell me,' he encourages.

Chapter 4

She pats the donkey. 'We weren't very good at school, really. We kind of egged each other on. She'd come up with the ideas, I'd never think she was serious so I would join in, but she always was and then I would find myself actually doing the thing we had been talking about.' She laughs, realising, all these years later, how petty it really was.

'We skipped school and took a bus to Liverpool. We ate candyfloss ....'

'Candyfloss, what is this?' He nods to the donkey owner, who nods in return, and who appears much younger close up, a little older than Dino, with a sad, distant look in his eyes. The cuffs of his thin, denim shirt are frayed, but he has taken the time to trim them; his boots are soft with wear but no longer polished, the light brown stained and mottled.

'You know, spun sugar you get at fairs.' Michelle looks back from the donkey owner to his animals.

'Ah, "*malli grias*", old woman hair', Dino murmurs.

'Then we went down to the beach where there were donkey rides. We had very little money, but it was a dull day and not many people were around, so we begged and pleaded to have a go on a donkey

49

until Juliet said something like, "If people see you standing here doing no trade, they'll think you're over-priced or something, but if they see people riding, especially girls like us with no money, they'll know you're a bargain and they'll all queue up."'

'Gift of the gab, she had, and the man was talked into it. But after a few minutes, Juliet got bored so she slapped the rump, you know, the bottom, of my donkey and it went crazy and belted off down the sands. The man and Juliet on her donkey came hurrying after, only for Juliet to lose her grip, and she fell off onto the sand. It was chaos; the man didn't know whether to chase after me or help Juliet up and make sure she wasn't hurt. He was livid, but we couldn't stop laughing.' Michelle runs her hand along the saddle before turning back to Dino.

'Can we?' she asks, her hand still on the saddle. Her eyes bright, like Mama when she was happy, but something else too. For a tall woman she has grace, the movement of her hand delicate, as if everything she touches might break.

'Dino?'

He can't help smiling. Inside he feels happy when she talks. He turns to the donkey man.

'My friend, er …?' Dino pauses. He has forgotten the man's name. He knows him by sight, as he knows almost everyone on the island by sight, but he cannot recall if he has spoken to him before. Someone is bound to have said his name at some point or other. Dino twists his hand, palm up, in question.

'Yanni,' the man answers.

'Dino,' he responds. 'My friend Yanni, she wants to ride the donkey. Is it possible?'

'Both donkeys for half a day?' Yanni asks.

'No, I was thinking … ah, OK, why not?'

'I will lead.'

'No need, my friend. I know where I am going.'

'Usually I go where they go.' Yanni's grip tightens on the rein.

'Well, if you insist, but if I were you, I would take the time to sit and do nothing. Life is hard enough. Take what you can.' He grins. If Juliet can do it for Michelle then so can he. Yanni's hand relaxes, and after a moment's hesitation, he hands Dino the rope and they agree a rate.

'Suzi,' he pats the first animal, and bends and whispers something in its ear, 'and Dolly.' He pats the second beast and fondles its ears. 'Be back before two. It gets too hot for them.' And he walks away, hands in pockets, knees facing out just slightly, rolling from one soft sole to the other.

Michelle watches the donkey man leave, twisting his sandy moustache. Dino leaves his big bag at the café. He'll pick it up later.

'*Ela,*' Dino says. 'Come.' He reaches out to take her waist to help her up.

'I can't believe this!' Michelle takes her bag

51

from her shoulder and puts it over her head.

'In Greece we sit sideways.' He points to another donkey man who is sitting side-saddle, his legs dangling, one hand holding the single rein, which he flips onto one side of the neck and back to the other, a gentle tap to keep the beast moving.

'I think I would feel safer with a leg each side,' Michelle decides. Dino offers his hands as a stirrup, and Michelle is surprised at how easy it is to get up, but once seated, her proximity to the ground makes it clear—her feet dangle only a foot or so off the ground.

Dino sits side-saddle, looking like he has never been off the island, never been to university, as if it would be a miracle if he spoke anything but Greek. There is more depth in his few years than in most of the people she works with, their knowledge so specific, their learning all within hallowed walls, remote from the buffeting of everyday life.

Visions of the office bring to mind her desk, sinking into the time-worn dark floorboards with the weight of casework spread across it waiting for her return. But first this claim must be wrapped up before she can move on. This one could be a real feather in her wig. Work's important, but she'll not think about it till Monday. That was the whole point of coming early: to sneak a weekend in the sun. Then get the work done and enjoy a week's holiday after at Juliet's.

She casts work from her mind. The donkeys plod slowly along the path around the port, weaving between the people, past shops selling gold jewellery and linen dresses, past the fishing boats, onto the coastal path. Steep rock and soil to their left, plants and shrubs desperately clinging with exposed roots, and the expanse of the shimmering, island-dotted sea to the right. The horizon ripples with blue whispers of distant places.

Here and there houses seemingly grow out of the rock, overlooking the breath-taking view, some dug into the slope, others low down near the water. The occasional steep track leads inland.

A lizard darts across the stones that form the coastal walk.

They come to a second smaller harbour, on past a shingle beach and slowly the town is left behind, until there are just the four of them. The cobbled stones give way to dusty earth.

'It's so hard to believe this. Yesterday I was sitting behind a desk in a rather damp wood-panelled, crumbling office in central London, and today I am sitting on Dolly the donkey in the sunshine,' she pats the animal as she says her name, 'with a Greek bloke I hardly know looking at one of the most beautiful views I have ever seen!'

'That is life. You can pretend you have control, but really there is no control, for good or bad.'

Michelle wonders if something tragic has ever happened to Dino. He is full of joy and vitality, but he comes out with things that don't fit. Curious, interesting; she is intrigued. The sun is getting hotter. It won't be long before her shoulders are burning. Why did she not buy sunscreen in the port? At least Dino has a bottle of water.

Dino's donkey, Suzi, is the more spritely of the two, and he stops to wait for Michelle to catch up. When Dolly is nearly level, he clicks his tongue to move Suzi on. The donkey's rhythm shakes thoughts from his head until he is lost in the landscape, at one with his surroundings, home. He sighs contentedly.

Michelle has stopped thinking too; she experiences an unfamiliar contentment.

Directly under her right foot, Michelle can see the edge of the path, and far below, the sea. The donkey rocks to the right. Michelle grips the saddle and leans left, inland, and looks forward to where the way widens. Snorting, the donkey throws back its head. A front foot stumbles, its hocks buckle. Michelle yelps as the hind legs sink. The beast whinnies. The ground breaks.

She grabs its mane. The earth slides under them. Michelle hears a rushing sound, the tumble of rocks and dry soil falling outside. Someone screams. She grips with her knees, but the animal's rear legs are skidding backwards down the drop. Its front feet scrabble, but the dirt crumbles and they tumble, the animal falling one way, Michelle sliding the other.

54

Her speed accelerates. She thinks she hears Dino call. Bushes and rocks tear at her. Her shoulder jolts against something immovable. The pain blinds her. She spins onto her back and judders, slowing. Soil and small stones rush past her ears. Her shoulder is throbbing. Everything stops. She opens her eyes to judge where she has landed. Her legs are entangled in a bush, her crotch against its stem, only an inch thick. Past her feet the cliff curves in under her, below are jagged rocks and the sea.

Lungs heaving, eyes wide, she spots a movement. There to the right. Panic in the waves. The donkey's front legs scrabble, its back legs unmoving, the sea turning red, its fore-hooves desperate. Eyes wide at the scent of death. Snorting. The beast's movements become manic, the whites of the eyes showing, teeth bared. The head goes under.

'No!' Michelle hears her own voice.

Its muzzle surfaces, the whites of the eyes more dominant, ears flat against its head, the nostrils flare, the animal whinnies, despairing, an infinitely sad sound. Awareness that the battle is lost. A desperate plea for life. Just one more minute, one second, one more breath. But the legs gain no purchase and Dolly slips, in full consciousness, under the water.

'Noooo.' Michelle shuts her eyes. Still clinging to the bush with one hand, she wraps the other around her face.

'Michelle! Micheeelle?' Dino's voice comes from above.

Michelle's throat is so tight, strangled sobs stutter from her chest.

'Michelle?' Dino calls again.

There is panic in his voice and she twists her head to look up, but the bush hides him from her sight.

'She's dead …' Michelle calls.

'Michelle!' There is such relief in his voice.

'She's dead,' Michelle repeats.

'Are you OK?' Dino shouts. He sounds on the verge of tears.

'Dolly fell in the water.' Michelle's fingers search for roots to cling to.

'Where are you?'

'Below the bush. She couldn't get a grip.' Michelle does not recognise her own voice. It sounds high-pitched, full of sorrow.

'Are you safe?' Dino's voice is deep, shaky.

Michelle looks at the bush that she straddles on the sheer slope, the second bush stem she grips with her left hand, and the root the fingers of her right hand have twisted round. Down by her feet, she can see a grey rock sticking out of the loose, dusty brown soil. She is twenty feet from the sea. She tentatively shifts one foot and tests the rock. It feels firm.

'I'm fine. My shoulder hurts. Dolly's dead. She drowned.'

'Never mind the donkey. You are safe, yes?'

'I'm OK.'

'I am coming down to get you.' A rattle of

twigs, pebbles against foliage, a curtain of dust falling.

'No, Dino, no! It's all loose.' Michelle looks up quickly and feels the bush she is clinging to shift. Her knuckles grip white. The confetti of soil stops.

'I could slide down. How far down are you?'

'Don't. I'm near the sea.'

There's a sound of leather creaking against leather, a rattle of chains, distinct but meaningless sounds.

'Here, catch this,' Dino huffs in exertion.

There is a rustling sound in the bushes above. She can just see the end of a piece of rope hanging down. It looks like Suzi's reins.

'Is it long enough?' he calls.

Michelle yawns and her eyelids flutter and close. She is glad the bush is providing shade, but it is so hot.

'Michelle? Is it too short?'

'What? Yes.' She shakes her head, opens her eyes wide, yawns again, wonders if she could be concussed. 'But if it was longer, the bush would hold it out from the cliff side.' She closes her eyes again.

'You OK?' he calls again.

'Yes. I feel sleepy.'

'Did you bang you head?'

'I don't know.'

'Don't sleep, Michelle. Stay awake. I might have to go for help.'

There is a scuffling sound. The rope end

57

disappears.

'Michelle? Do you have your phone with you?'

'No, it fell.'

'You?'

'No. *Gamoto!*' he swears in his native tongue.

'Just what I was thinking: *Gamoto.*' A strong British accent on a word that has no meaning for her. She tries to laugh but cannot find the wind.

Dino looks around frantically. He has no idea what he is looking for, but there must be a solution near to hand. He cannot leave her.

He pulls the blanket off Suzi's saddle and tests it, pulling it between his hands. He could split it, tie the pieces to make a rope, and shimmy down. At first it doesn't give. He pulls harder to be sure of its strength. The fibres tear, coming apart with feathery dust, crumbling to nothing, the smell of age filling the air. He throws the remains to the ground. The saddle is now bare wood, he pulls it free of the donkey and tries to take the wooden slats apart. Maybe he can wedge them into the loose soil end on, use them as footholds. He slams it against the ground, kicks it. But the saddle is solid; nothing gives.

'I cannot leave her.' He breathes. On Suzi's bare saddle hangs the little shovel to collect her droppings and the sack to hold it.

He feverishly yanks the shovel free. Footholds. He could make a series going down. He cannot leave

58

her to go for help.

'You still OK?' he calls down.

'Yes. Thirsty.' Michelle's voice seems tired.

Dino thrusts the shovel into the loose bank, flings the soil off into the sea, scoops the dust out with his hands. He will not desert her to be told later she has gone. That cannot happen again. He must stay, stop anything from happening to her. The bank disintegrates with every shovelful he takes. The footholds become dusty slides.

The clonk of a goat bell above him tenses his muscles.

He had just gone off with his friend and the goats. Three hours later, his world had changed forever.

'I won't leave you,' he calls down, but not loud enough for her to hear.

The distant put-put of a fishing boat makes his heart beat faster.

Yes! From the sea, maybe they can reach her.

'Hey. *Ela do!*' He calls out across the water with all the power of his lungs. He puts his fingers to his mouth and whistles as loudly and as shrilly as he can, and raises his hands above his head. He stoops, picks up the torn blanket from the floor and waves with gusto.

'Dino.' Her voice sounds tremorous.

'Yes, Michelle, it will be OK. The boat will come, and you can climb down.'

'I think the bush is coming away,' she squeals. There's a sound of breaking twigs.

'Michelle?' Dino stops waving and stares down at the bushes that hide her from his sight.

'It's OK. It's shifted down a bit, but the rock under my foot is still holding.' There is a quiver in her voice.

'Michelle, could you climb down if the boat came?'

He can hear the rustle of dried leaves, a small movement below.

'No, the ground will just crumble. I'll fall.'

Dino feels cold. She cannot climb up, and she cannot climb down.

'How far is the sea? Could you jump?'

'Twenty feet maybe, but there are rocks.'

Dino shivers.

'I am really thirsty,' she adds.

'Shall I try to drop the water bottle down to you?'

'No, I couldn't catch it ...'

Dolly's eyes had looked so scared, like she knew she was going to die. *Just close her eyes for a moment, gain some strength.*

'Hey, hey.' Dino whistles at the fisherman again and waves the half-blanket. The fisherman waves back.

'Yes, yes!' Dino jumps up and down; he can see the fisherman smile. 'No, you idiot, I need your help,' he says to himself. '*Ela, voeithia*, help, help!' he screams.

'What's happening?' A voice behind him brings a wave of hope. A man with a shepherd's crook slows to a halt at the bottom of the steep incline on the inland side of the path, heels digging in the dirt, leaning back to slow his descent. His dog takes easy steps beside him.

'Oh! Please, do you have a phone?' Dino grabs the man by the arm, assuring himself that he is real, that he will not leave.

'No, what is it, my friend? You seem upset.'

'She's down there, hanging on. Quick!'

The shepherd looks over the edge, but all there is to see are bushes.

'Dino, I am really thirsty.'

The man jumps at the sound of the sleepy voice.

'*Panayia*, is she stuck?' The shepherd expletes.

'I cannot leave her; you must go, run to the nearest house, call someone. If she falls, she will die.' Dino's chest heaves with the words, and his eyes sting. The shepherd takes a firm grip on his crook and runs, his dog jumping and yelping around his ankles in the excitement.

The fisherman has moved closer to the shore. He is looking, scanning, trying to see why one man is running and the other clearly in panic.

'What is it?' he calls, standing up in his little wooden vessel, shifting his weight from foot to foot to keep his balance.

'Hey, she is stuck. Can you see her?' Dino calls.

The fisherman shakes his head.

'Do you have a radio?'

The man calls that he does not have a radio, or a phone, but the boat yard is just minutes away. He throttles up and powers off.

Dino watches him go. He looks down the path. The shepherd is still running, just a dot far away. Dino can do no more.

'Michelle. The fisherman has gone for help. Can you hang on?'

'Do I have a choice?'

Dino hears a break of humour in her voice, but his face will not smile.

'I am sorry,' he says.

'What?'

'I am sorry. It is my fault.'

'Don't be ridiculous,' she replies, a little more energy in her voice.

'I put you in danger. I saw the road was crumbling, narrower, I should have stopped us going any further.'

'It's not your fault, Dino.'

'I should have taken better care of you, watched out for you, protected you.'

'Protected me! Ha, I'm not an endangered species.'

'It is still my fault.'

'Dino.' He can hear her shift position. She grunts. 'That's better. Dino? Just shut up. You are not my guardian.'

'Don't die, Michelle.'

'What? I'm not going to die.' Her laugh sounds dry.

There is silence. He doesn't know what to say. He should keep talking, but the words will not come.

'Dino, I've been around a lot longer than you, I'm neither going to die, nor are you responsible. I'll just cling on here until help comes.' She says it with kindness in her voice.

Dino still cannot find his voice to reply.

'Dino?'

'I won't leave you.' Dino's chest feels like it will burst, his breath in short gasps, eyes wide. The last time he saw his mother's face, she had been smiling.

'Go.' She had smiled. 'Go with your friend Zahari and the goats.' She had ruffled his hair and kissed the top of his head. He had smiled and looked into her eyes—such kind eyes. The eyes that looked into his soul every morning, looked into his heart after school. To be separated so abruptly, and to be given no time to mourn. From having a mother to no mother is harsh enough, but his father made it into something much worse than having no mother. The anguish, the guilt, the fear that what his father said could be true. And the anger. Anger at his father for the words he spoke, anger at his mother for leaving him. But no soft place in which to mourn.

'I am coming.' The words explode from deep in

63

his chest. He throws himself on his stomach and slides off the path down the sandy bank towards the sea, grabbing at grasses and roots as he goes, the speed building.

Chapter 5

The dust clogs his nose and he screws up his eyes. His t-shirt scrapes up to his armpits as he falls, his bare chest tearing against rocks and twigs.

Someone calls his name.

'Mama,' he shouts and digs his fingers deep into the loose soil. His pace slows. He grabs a root, a branch, a bush stem. His toes kick into the bank and he brings his fall to a grinding stop.

'What the ...?' Michelle exclaims.

He shakes the dust from his hair and opens his eyes. Michelle is less than a metre away, down to his right. The bank is slightly less steep here. Below, the loose earth turns to rocks that jut from the soil before a sheer drop to the sea. Michelle is balanced on one of these rocks, the last stable place. Dino reaches down and across with his foot. His hands scutters over the soil, scared to let go, eager to find a better hold, roots to cling to. He pulls himself across, so both feet are on the ledge, and finds his balance.

Breathing heavily, snorting out the debris, he dare not let go to wipe his nose or eyes.

The soil and dust stop falling. The pebbles cease splashing into the sea. The scene becomes still, the air clears. He has a good hold of a bush stem and a root. Gingerly he eases his head in Michelle's direction and raises his eyes. She is motionless, her mouth agape, her eyes wide.

'I am not leaving you.' His eyebrows arch in the middle. He is a little surprised that she is not expressing her pleasure at seeing him, not even a smile.

Dino is flat against the bank on his stomach, Michelle flat on her back, their faces a foot apart, sharing the same rock to stand on.

'I am not going to die,' Michelle says, her voice firm.

'I am not going to let you.' His neck cranes and he kisses her fingers, dusty and grass stained, clinging to a tuft of roots just centimetres from his mouth.

They lie eye-to-eye, silent for a moment, then a seagull screeches overhead.

'I don't suppose you brought the water, did you?' Michelle asks. He blinks. He has lashes so thick it almost looks as if his eyes are outlined in kohl. Michelle considers this an odd observation considering their predicament.

Dino presses into the earth, hesitantly lets go of a root and slowly reaches down to feel his back pocket. 'It's fallen out.'

Michelle doesn't answer.

'Just a thought—if people come to rescue us, how will they know where we are now you are here with me?'

The colour drains from his face. His square bottom lip bows as he sucks it in and chews on it. Michelle cannot imagine what possessed him to follow her down the bank. How did he expect to rescue her? If she is not able to climb up or down, does he think he can, and even if he can, how does that help?

'I don't think we can climb down from here,' he states.

Michelle sees no point in answering.

Dino looks up, reaches for a short trunk of one of the sparse bushes that is slightly higher, and pulls. Michelle watches, the orange of his t-shirt torn, his underarm close to her face, the hairs fine, wet but not matted, his ribs visible through his thin skin and three long muscles following the line of his ribs. He begins to shift his weight; the muscles swell and then relax again as he releases his grip.

'OK, so you could pull yourself higher up on that branch, I can provide support for your feet until you get your foot on the root over there.' He points.

'I've hurt my shoulder. There is no way I can put any weight on it.'

Dino frowns, then turns to look out to sea.

'What is it?' Michelle asks. She is hidden by the bushes. She cannot see or be seen.

Dino twists his head and shoulders round to get a better view.

'It's the fisherman. I think I heard voices above, too.'

'Hey, the radio at the shipyard wasn't working. Is it best I go to the port for the port police? Or can you reach the rope?'

Dino looks up but can see only leaves. He calls back in Greek, 'Who's up there?'

'They have a donkey. It could be Flessas. Hey, yes you, who are you?' shouts the fisherman from below.

'It's Yanni and Flessas the goat herder.' The voices come from up above on the path. Dino recognises the monosyllabic tones of the man whose donkeys they hired.

'Hey,' Dino calls up.

'Whereabouts are you?' Yanni calls down.

Dino takes hold of the stumpy bush trunk above him and performs a one-handed chin up. He gets a glimpse of the top of two men's heads high above him before he lowers himself back down. The leaves shimmer, pinpointing the location.

'Here you go,' Yanni calls. There is a disturbance in the branches, and the bushes above them quiver. 'Got it?'

'Got what?' Dino shouts.

The leaves above them rustle again. A twig snaps, then a moment's silence before the leaves are disturbed again.

'Can you see it?'

Dino tries to move to his left to see around the bush. He glimpses something red and follows the line, a rope, with a rock on the end. The rope lies over some bushes, the rock pulling it taut. It is too far away to reach.

'Try again,' he calls. The rock is hauled up, bouncing on the rocky terrain as it ascends, and then whips into the air above the bushes. 'Try a heavier rock,' Dino suggests.

Nothing happens.

Dino turns to Michelle and smiles.

Michelle wonders at him. Is he enjoying himself? He seems much more certain on the cliff face than she feels. She hasn't once thought she might die, though it has crossed her mind that she might be stuck for a few hours perhaps, waiting for a helicopter to air-lift them off. But after the initial slide, she was never in real danger. These sorts of situations are so often publicised. Airlifts are commonplace, aren't they? She tightens her grip. It's no big deal. She inhales deep into her lungs to calm her breathing.

'You all right?' Dino asks. 'You are breathing heavily.'

'Yes, fine. Just feeling a bit dizzy.'

The leaves rustle again and there is a sound of rock hitting rock. Dino looks to his left. He can see the rope. He traces it down, the heavy rock on the end pulling it through the twigs of the bush. Delicately he lets go with his left hand and reaches for the line. He stretches to the point where he is about to topple, but the rope is out of reach. He inches along the rock he is standing on.

69

'Careful,' Michelle breathes.

Dino balances on one foot and stretches as far as he can, the rope teasing the ends of his fingers. He pauses, his limbs sagging.

'What now?' Michelle asks.

Her pupils have dilated; her voice sounds calm, but Dino senses she is scared. He thinks for a moment and then unbuckles his belt. His trousers slide onto his hips.

Turning back to the rope, he uses the belt's buckle to extend his reach. His supporting leg shakes with the effort, and he exhales and sucks in air noisily.

'Ha!' he shouts as his belt falls, bouncing off the rocks below them, splashing into the sea. 'Got it!' He hears Michelle breath again.

The makeshift stretcher cuts into her hips.

'I can walk. Let me.'

'Lady, be still,' the donkey man says. He is strong and solid. His hands near her head are thick-skinned but fine-boned.

'Nearly there,' Dino soothes. 'I'll go and get a handcart.'

'I am not going in a handcart,' Michelle cries, but he is gone.

'Stay awake.' Dino nudges her. The handcart is bumpy and uncomfortable compared to the stretcher. They pass the stumpy clock tower. Whatever happens, she must catch that boat tomorrow at one-

70

thirty. Perhaps coming to the island had been foolish, considering the overall situation at work.

'Juliet, he was amazing. He took the rock off the rope, which I know sounds like nothing, but if you could have seen where we were balanced you would be amazed. He passed the rope to me, to tie around myself, but I couldn't, my shoulder was so painful.'

'Have they x-rayed it yet?' Juliet asks.

Michelle tucks the hospital phone between her good shoulder and chin, and pours a glass of water. Her rucksack with phone, guidebook, and toothbrush are somewhere at the bottom of the sea, or floating off to Crete. Thankfully her passport and purse are safely in a money belt.

'Yes, I'm waiting for the results. Dino is in the room next door, apparently. They have been cleaning up his chest, full of tiny stones scraped under the skin. It sounds horrible.'

'So Dino tied it for you?'

'Yes. Which was also not as easy as it sounds. We could either stand too far apart so he couldn't reach me or so close we could hardly move, depending on which rocks we put our feet on. Such a hero.'

'He is a nice guy. One of life's sweethearts,' Juliet agrees.

The closeness of him had felt safe, the life in his eyes reassuring, his breath on her skin comforting.

71

He had his own particular smell, earthy and young. His arm around her as he tied the rope was commanding, sure, older than his years. But then he had to let go.

'The next bit was scary, after I was tied to the rope. He called to the donkey man, who got the animal to pull me up. I was not sure the rope would hold, and then I was even more worried about the branches of the bush spiking me, but they did it slowly. The really embarrassing part was, by the time I had got to the top and caught my breath, Dino had already climbed up, without any help. Goodness knows how. He was caked with dust and soil. His hair and eyebrows were white. The fisherman was cheering and clapped and shouted, "Bravo!" It all became a bit comical at the end ....'

'I'm just glad you're safe,' Juliet says.

'Anyway, listen, I didn't want to worry you with this call. I could have told you all about it when I come, but I have a problem. The donkey man,' Michelle drops her voice. 'You should have seen his face when he realised what had happened. I think he thought Dolly had run off, at first.' Michelle pauses, holds the phone between chin and shoulder and reaches for a tissue from the box on the bedside locker. 'When we told him what had happened, his back straightened up; he just stood, so erect and still, his eyes not focused on anything. He was like that for so long I wondered if he had fallen into shock. Then he turned slowly, went to his other donkey and put his arms around her neck, whispering to her. I swear I saw him wipe his eyes, but he tried to hide it. He was devastated.'

'I imagine he was. It's his whole living.' Juliet's voice is calm.

'It was more than that ….' Michelle swallows and pats under her eyes with the tissue.

'I'm just glad you're OK. Will they keep you in?'

'Oh, I don't think so. I feel fine apart from the shoulder.' She takes a deep breath. 'Apparently there are only four rooms in this tiny hospital—a staff room and three beds. They can't really afford to keep me in.' Dropping the scrunched up tissue on the bedcovers, she takes a drink of water. 'But Juliet, what should I do about the donkey man? How much is a donkey? Do I need to compensate him?'

'The donkey man will probably not expect anything,' Juliet says, there is a slight crackle on the line.

'But surely, it was my fault his beast died. Oh it was horrible, Juliet, the poor thing was fighting for its life. And then its life suddenly gone … I feel so guilty and sad. She was such a lovely animal. What does the Greek law say I should do, do you know?'

'It is very sad,' Juliet exhales slowly, 'but life happens, and that is how the donkey man will see it, I expect. Just how life deals the cards; no one's fault. It wasn't as if you wanted it to happen or took the animal onto an extreme path. This was the main path

73

along the coast to the boatyard, right?'

'Yes. But even so, I was the one riding her. What's the law? What would you do, Juliet? In England, I would expect to pay, but then in England I know the law and I am sure the owner would have become very angry as well. It feels very different here.' She sighs. 'It was so sad.'

'In England the donkey man would sue the person down the cliff, the person down the cliff would sue the council for not maintaining the path, the council would petition the government for more money, the government would tax the worker to get it, the donkey man would pay more tax to the government, who would pay the council to pay the person on the cliff, who pays the donkey man.' She laughs dryly. Michelle does not join in.

'Yes, but what would you do?' Michelle asks.

'I'd pay the donkey man.' Juliet does not hesitate.

'Yup, that's what I thought. I don't know what I am legally obliged to do, but it is the only option that feels right. How much is a donkey, and how do I pay for his loss?'

'No, you can't pay for his loss. Just let him see your heartfelt sorrow. That's all you can do, really …'

A man in a white coat walks into the room, an x-ray in his hand.

'Got to go, Juliet. See you in a few days?'

Juliet wishes her well and says she has plans for a lot of eating and drinking for the next week when they will be together.

The doctor tells Michelle that her shoulder is not broken, and as the swelling goes down it will feel better. She may, however, have a concussion, so he needs to keep her in for twenty-four hours.

'What time is it?' Michelle leans back on the pillow. She has been put in a white gown for the x-ray. She would like to put her clothes on, but they are nowhere to be seen, just her wallet on her bedside table.

'One-thirty.'

'I have to be on the one-thirty boat back to Athens tomorrow, concussed or not. I have an important meeting. Can you have me discharged by half-past twelve?'

'Yes, yes, of course, do not worry. The best thing now is rest.'

The door closes solidly on her room which is part of an old stone building, with high ornate ceilings and tall windows. It is a large room for just her one bed. The hospital was probably once a fine home. Now layers of white paint mask the former grandeur.

Muffled voices drift indistinctly from the next room. Michelle wonders if it is Dino's room. It is in the direction the nurse had pointed when she asked after him. Maybe the doctor is in with him now, tending to his cuts and scrapes. Dear Dino, what a foolhardy thing to do. No one has ever dived down a cliff for her before, nothing even close. Visions of

75

Richard diving off a cliff in his wig and gown to rescue her amuse Michelle for a moment. It's a most unlikely scenario, however; for a start he would remove his gown and fold it carefully, find a safe place to put his wig, brush imaginary dust from his robe, and even then he would not likely leap to save her. He might roll up his sleeves and order someone else to do it for him. Her eyes flutter and the lids close. She will just rest a minute and then go and see how Dino is.

Michelle feels for Dino's arm around her. She reaches for him, but he is not there. Panic closes her throat, no breath passes. The cliff gives way. He is not there to cling to. She begins to fall. Richard plunges even faster beside her, his gown flying behind him, his wig taking flight by itself, until, with a splash, his cape is splayed like moth wings on the sea's surface. His wig floats away, his arms scrabble. The water turns red.

Her eyes open, she gasps for air. The curtains are drawn but the moon peeps between them, a slice of night cutting the bed diagonally. The room is unfamiliar in greys and shadows and, for a moment, Michelle has no idea where she is. She pushes herself up to a sitting position, and the pain in her shoulder reminds her.

There is no buzzer for the nurse. Slipping her legs from the bed and holding her gown together behind her, Michelle pads to the door and into the hall, which is lit by a dim bulb dangling bare from the high ceiling. The next door, Dino's room, stands open, dark and empty.

'Do you need something?' A nurse comes from behind a screen pulled in front of the permanently open staffroom door.

'Has Dino gone?'

'Dino? Yes, he was discharged earlier. He went in to see you, but you were sleeping.'

'Oh.'

'What can I get you?'

'No, nothing, thank you.' Pattering back into her bed, the hospital seems cold and empty. Shadows play in the room. The flicking of the curtains in the soft night breeze cools the warm air and makes the greys dance and ripple, shimmer and slide, crumble and cascade. The donkey's hooves clatter on the rocks, her whinnies become more frantic. Dolly's eyes wide, her tongue protruding.

Michelle wakes again with her heart pulsing, the images still in her mind's eye. There is no one she can call on to soothe her, so far from friends and familiar places. It takes time for her to slip once more into sleep.

The sun jolts her awake. Once the curtains are fully drawn, a new nurse busies herself with the chart at the end of the bed.

'What time is it please?'

'Six.'

Michelle groans and turns over to sleep again.

77

'Time to wake up.'

'Hmm? Er? Oh! What time is it please?'

'Just after twelve. Your friend Dino came in, but you were fast asleep.'

'Twelve! I need to go! Please get my things. Will the doctor be here soon? I have to catch the one-thirty boat …' She flings off the sheet and steps onto the cold marble floor. 'Can I have my clothes please?'

'Doctor must see you before you go.'

'I know, but if I am fine, I must go immediately. I have to catch the one-thirty boat.'

'Doctor coming.'

'Can I have my clothes please?'

'Yes, yes.' The nurse leaves the room.

Michelle walks to the window, from where she can see a square, partly covered with grass, planted with orange trees. Two old ladies passing with heavy shopping bags have paused to rest on a bench. One shakes a walking stick at a prowling cat. Michelle wonders if there is fish in her shopping bag. How long will it take to get to port from here? She cannot remember the route from yesterday.

She must get the one-thirty. If she misses this meeting, things could become difficult. Not only for the firm—although Michelle no longer really cares how the firm is doing—but since it has been made clear that 'belts need to be tightened', and that this may involve job losses, everyone feels a bit jumpy.

The downturn in the economy had prompted

78

the decision: someone must go. Michelle thought getting this claim in Athens back on track would be an easy way to prove her performance, and it will be, as long as she can get to the meeting. She has no qualms about her ability.

There is no clock in the room. The door to the hall is open, and Michelle can see past the screen into the staffroom, where the clock on the wall says twelve-fifteen. Surely she can still make it, if someone can tell her the way. How big is the town anyway?

The familiar London pressure reaches all the way out here. It is not only her, it is all the salaried partners who are on trial, putting them all in competition with their colleagues. The powers that be decided it was the only fair approach.

How will she find the way to the port? Surely it is just minutes to the harbour, but she cannot recall the journey here.

'Excuse me, could I have my clothes please?'

The nurse looks up from her desk. 'Yes, yes, one minute.'

At twelve-thirty the nurse comes in with her clothes.

'How long before the doctor comes?'

'He is coming.' The nurse leaves.

Michelle waits. Her breath shortens until she becomes aware that her shoulders have tensed up around her ears.

'Relax, relax.' she whispers, but if she doesn't make it to the meeting, it could result in her pulling the short straw. Then what? Unthinkable. How would she be able to pay the bills, keep the house heated or dehumidified, to stop it crumbling? The place would dissolve.

She peeks out of the door, no sign of the doctor. The nurse is typing.

'I really need to go,' Michelle calls. Twelve forty-five.

'I will phone him again,' the nurse replies, but she does not pick up the phone.

'Could you do it now please?' At her age, fifty this year, she would be sunk if the firm lets her go. Who would employ her? She would be the last in the line of employable lawyers, behind the eager young things and the self-assured forty-year-old men. Even if there were jobs, no one would touch her. Then what? The law is all she knows.

'Now?' Michelle cringes at her own tone of voice, but it does the trick; the nurse picks up the phone. Nearly one. 'How long to the port?'

'A minute, down here.' She points with her pen as she dials. 'Or straight and left.'

The house. How could she let the house decay? It is her safety, her symbol of success, her impenetrable fortress.

Her mouth drops open. What if she has to get rid of the house? What if they take it from her? Homeless. She would be homeless and unemployed.

'I have to go. Tell the doctor I waited.'

'No ...' The nurse stands.

'Ah, good morning, is the patient better today?' The doctor from yesterday walks through the main door into the hall, casually, no hurry.

She runs lightly and quickly down the hospital steps. They could not have discharged her more slowly if they'd tried. Turning toward the port, the way is blocked where a handcart full of bottled water has tried to pass a second handcart of breezeblocks, and their wheels have become interlocked.

An old woman in slippers, laden with shopping bags, points an alternative way. Michelle marches in the new direction. The ship's horn vibrates across the blue sky, calling all aboard. If she can keep up the pace she will catch it. Down the narrow alley, left toward the port a corner and . . . into someone's backyard.

'No!' Michelle retraces her steps twice as fast.

Back to the alley farther along, each turn left to the port could be another dead end. She tries another, a whitewashed alley that ends at a solid wooden door, a single round brass handle in the middle.

Perspiration is running into her eyes, the ripped edge of her dust-encrusted t-shirt is rubbing her slightly sunburned shoulder, and her linen trousers, creased, stained and torn, are hot and clinging. Turning another left, she can see the sea. Her feet break into a trot. She wipes the sweat from her eyes, down the widening path, shops on either side.

A man is pulling the mooring rope off the bollard.

'Wait!' Michelle cries, but he is too far away to hear. Another man is dragging the landing steps away from the ship on the harbour wall. Michelle waves at him. He stops and waves back.

She slows her pace, her heart pounding, relieved he has seen her. She keeps her gaze fixed steadfast on him. He leans against the steps and lights a cigarette.

But the ship begins to draw away. They have not stopped the departure. Michelle begins to run again, shouting and waving. She rushes along the quay. The ship is two feet from shore, four feet, six. Michelle bends double to breathe, staggering the last few feet to the man at the boarding steps.

'Please stop them, I must board.' She takes hold of his smoking arm.

'She is gone.' He gently pulls free to take a drag.

'I have to be on her, please!'

Chapter 6

Her chest caves in, her shoulders droop. She is conscious of someone watching her. The man leaning against the ship's boarding steps inspects her clothes, head to toe. She half glances down at herself to see what he sees: the results of yesterday's disaster. But it is a minor detail. The boat's propellers spin, the water churns: today's disaster. Michelle watches as it slowly pulls out of the harbour.

She remains motionless, her heart sinking, waiting for the wave of panic that is sure to overwhelm her. She tries to control her breath, but the wave surges and crashes down on her and her throat contracts ... Curiously, the greatest sensation is one of relief!

Across from the pier is a stone step in the shade. She sinks to a sitting position, her hands to her eyes, all resistance gone. A frown flicks across her forehead. Relief floods through her body. Relief at what?

'You always think you are about to lose your job,' Juliet had said on the phone, shortly after Michelle was made a partner in the firm.

'I don't think you know how tough my world

is.' Michelle deftly took the cork out of yesterday's wine and poured a glass, carrying it through to the sitting room, the phone wedged under her chin.

'Yes, but you do this every time there's a glitch at work. A small problem and you build it into a big one, which ends in you losing your job and then losing your house.'

'Do you know how much that house costs to maintain?' Michelle had sunk into the sofa and stared at the black, lifeless grate.

'Then why did you fight for it?' She had heard Juliet take a sip of her own wine and had imagined her sitting out in the warm evening, not facing a trek into the cellar for coal. She'd sighed.

'Because I am stupid. Because I wanted to take something he valued. Because I wanted to hurt him.' The wine had gone too soon and she'd put the glass down on the hearth and returned to the kitchen for the bottle. 'I should have realised when he gave in so easily.' She'd settled back on the sofa.

'You weren't to know though.'

'He slipped the paper in with all the rest after the settlement, just like it was any other paper. I can't believe it has taken me two years to find it.'

'Have you had a second opinion?'

'Yes. Definitely deathwatch beetle, and the whole wall will have to come down, new timbers, tens of thousands. Richard knew exactly what he was letting go of.'

'Anyway, that's a separate issue. You're

digressing. You are not going to lose your job over forgetting to copy in your boss, so relax. You know, sometimes I think you want to lose your job, and the house, to give yourself some breathing space.' She had hated Juliet at that moment, hated that Juliet could not see what the house meant to her. The time she had lived with Richard there in security and comfort, a proper home guaranteed. A haven after years of couch surfing as she worked and saved the money to put herself through college and the bar exam. She had repeated her early childhood of instability and no roots.

'Yes, that's right, Juliet, I loved those years of my family moving from job to job and me from school to school, never having friends for longer than six months.' She had changed hands with the phone, releasing her clenched fist, the blood rushing back to her white knuckles.

'Ah, you just hadn't found me yet.' Juliet laughed. Michelle had wanted to slam the phone down, but there was something in the way Juliet had said it that started her giggling, which set Juliet off. And she was right, Michelle had reasoned. Life had changed for her after she had moved to Bradford and befriended Juliet. Right from the beginning it had been clear she could rely on Juliet to be there for her.

So maybe Juliet was right. Maybe it would be a relief to get rid of the house. It has already eaten up two years' money to keep it warm and dehumidified, treating mould and pinning back panelling.

Coming across the paper about the deathwatch beetle had been the last straw.

But to move out? Pack up everything she and Richard chose together, box it up, sell it, donate it, make decisions about each piece? It would be so painful. Move to a house for one person, with no history, just her? After eighteen years, the house is where she lives, it's home. It's her place. How can she move?

The sad truth is that, at her age, she is unemployable if she loses her job. No job means no money. Room by room the old place will decay, the mould will spread its way along the hall, the panelling in the library will split and crack, the chimneys will no longer be usable, and the beetles will eat and eat until the wall collapses. She can see she will end up in the scullery with an electric fire to keep her warm, until the money in the bank is gone and the house falls down around her, leaving her in the street in her dressing gown and slippers.

Homeless.

Flopping into the nearest café chair and ordering an *ouzo* will solve all her problems—if that one *ouzo* is followed by another, and another. It's tempting. No matter how many deep breaths she takes no energy returns. The ship has gone, leaving her to drown. This mess might really lose her her job.

Despite all this, that feeling of relief remains, a feeling she has never allowed before when thinking about the house. And a part of her really does feel like this relief is, well, a relief.

'Hey lady, you all right?' A waiter addresses her. 'You need some water?' He is carrying a tray, drinks lined up. With his free hand he passes her a glass of water.

'Thank you.'

'You had an accident?' He looks her up and down.

'No ... yes ... no. I am fine; it was yesterday. Do you know where there is a phone please?' She must not give up.

'Public phones up the third street by the post office.'

On the corner there's a shop with a dummy outside draped in linen and cotton, white and beige for the heat. Michelle dips under the low door and reappears minutes later in a clean, new outfit, noting to herself that things could have been worse—she could have lost her wallet as well as dropping her rucksack and missing the boat. But it is a small consolation. Now she needs a phone.

The phones are mounted on a wall and covered with transparent plastic hoods. Michelle cannot imagine for a minute that they will not be vandalised. She approaches the first, ready to be disappointed, and is surprised to see that not only is it intact, but a phone directory sits on the shelf below it.

'Hello, I am just calling about the meeting tomorrow. Sorry, no I have not been able to pick up my emails … Oh, I see. No, no, I understand. No, sure, fine, if that suits you better. No, of course. Yes, yes, yes. OK then, next Friday. Yes, and by the way my phone has been mislaid so I will call you nearer the time to confirm. Emails, yes of course I will be available on email.'

She exhales heavily and hopes there will be an internet café.

Her new clothes get a brush of flaky whitewash from leaning against the wall. She needs some help in standing, if only for a moment. A reprieve, a stay of sentence. The Greek lawyers have requested a postponement until the following Friday, and they have emailed her chambers proposing the change of date, saying that they would be contacting her. She must get in touch with London, if for nothing else than to bring her some feeling of normality, assure herself that her job is still there.

Energy returns to her limbs. The Gods seem to be smiling on her—for now, at least.

The job is still intact, but the following Friday is the day she was planning to go to see Juliet. She should call and explain there is a chance she won't make it now.

She could cry. This reprieve, on top of everything else, is all a bit much. And now her planned week with Juliet is defusing into the melodrama of work. Tears threaten to fall. She still feels shaky from yesterday. Where's Dino?

She cannot find the strength to call Juliet to let her know of the possible cancellation. It would make it too real.

The need to sit drags her back to the port, where she subsides into the first comfortable chair she comes across.

She lets her head rest on the back, her hands loose in her lap, eyes closed. There is too much to process. Part of the reason for taking a break with Juliet was to discuss things that were causing her disquiet in the first place. Now a hundred other worries have been dumped on top. Where to even start!

Juliet may be a bit wild, a bit of a knee-jerker in her reactions, but she always had the ability to cut through to the nub of situations. She would have unveiled the source of Michelle's disquiet and revealed its underlying causes in a heartbeat.

With Juliet, Michelle finds a place where she can shed Michelle-the-lawyer. Juliet hangs no labels on her. At most she is Juliet's accomplice again, reverting to her teenage days and losing her sense of responsibility. Such a relief.

Michelle opens her eyes. The three-sided dock is no less full than when she arrived. The halyards of the yachts rattle against the masts, a rhythmic slap, slap in the slight swell. Black and white cats line up on the quayside by a rough-looking vessel full of nets and occupied by men in rubber trousers, their faces sun-burnt and smiling. The sun blazes upon the scene, the sky a sheet of blue. Tourists enter and leave her field of vision, young girls in bikinis and matching sarongs; more mature ladies in cottons and linens, gold dripping from their wrists, ears, and necks; men in summer suits, with matching hats and designer sandals, next to the grinning donkey men, their work shirts rolled up at the elbows, caps pulled over their eyes and their jeans wearing out at the knee and the seat. The locals seem content, relaxed. The tourists here are wealthy. This island seems to attract a moneyed crowd.

Michelle knows that to reach the kind of wealth these people are displaying requires hours of toil: weekends in the office, evenings spent working, day in day out, until the concept of there being anything other than work becomes alien. Is it worth it for a fortnight in the sun every year?

There is no sign of a waiter, so she pulls herself to her feet and wanders back to the public phones.

She fishes for change.

'Yes, of course I have been in touch with them. Yes, I know it has been postponed. No, I am not quite in Athens. Nearby. Yes, I will look out for that email. OK, yes, OK, right. Will do. No, I still plan to get the same flight back, in the office on Monday. Yes. Bye.'

Wandering back to the port, the idea of an *ouzo* sneaks back to her, but the necessity of finding an

90

internet cafe comes first. She must check her emails.

'*Ouzo*, beer, cup of tea.' A waiter offers as she passes.

'Internet?'

'Yes, we have free internet.'

'No I mean, like an internet café, with computers.'

'He is here.' The waiter's hand lands in the small of her back and he guides her to a better vantage point. 'This street here. You must go to the green door, turn left, first right, under the arch. The door on the right will be open.'

'Left, right, arch, door on right. Thank you.'

It doesn't seem so desperate now. She had overreacted as usual. Looking around her the world continues, her part in it so small. The sunshine is heavenly. A tiny shop displays a rack of sunscreen outside. A minute or two later she emerges feeling protected, smelling nice and just a little bit like a tourist.

The street off the harbour is very narrow, the whitewashed walls on either side undulating slightly, set back here, protruding slightly a little further on, following the line of the individual houses. At one point it appears to come to a dead end, but as she nears the blank wall ahead, the lane turns sharply and opens up again, even narrower than before. The path begins to climb, with broad, shallow steps, and then there, ahead, is a green door.

The directions amuse her, she takes a left, and

the first right but this leads into someone's back yard. Retracing her steps, she takes the next right and finds the first building spanning the path with an arch, its front door in the shade beneath. Beyond, out in the sunshine on the right, a door opens into a darkened interior.

'Hello?' Michelle knocks quietly and enters.

It takes a moment for her eyes to adjust. There are shelves of wires and buckets and pipes. She had been expecting tables in a line, each with a monitor and keyboard. She steps back into the sunshine. This must be the wrong place.

'Hello, hello,' a cracked voice calls.

'Hello, I am looking for the internet café?'

'No English.' She can make out his outline, short, bent with a stick to lean on.

'In-ter-net?' Michelle breaks the word down.

'Yes. *Nai*, yes, come here.' He has a tweed jacket on, which is sliding off his shoulders. He turns his back and retreats further into the gloom. He takes longer steps with his right leg than his left. Their progress is slow.

How can a business be run like this, with no light, no sign, and at the speed of a snail? Michelle tries to imagine London made up of such places. It would grind to a halt.

But it would be less pressured.

'*Nato!*' With the word and the flourish of a hand, he delivers up the computer. It's a big grey machine with a large bulbous monitor and a grimy keyboard.

The old man tries to rest his stick by the chair, but it slides first one way and then the other and Michelle offers to hold it.

He then eases himself down onto one knee with a pained expression and clicks on a switch. The journey back up is even slower, and Michelle steps forwards several times to help, but he waves her aside. Once more or less upright again and back in charge of his stick, he presses another button on the computer, which produces a loud whirring. He pulls the chair out and shuffles away.

The screen is still black, though, dimly reflecting Michelle's face. She scrabbles around at the back of the machine and finds a cable that has come loose. This does the trick, but now there is a message asking her to enter a password.

Michelle closes her eyes momentarily and takes a deep breath. The old man is out at the back of the shop in a tiny courtyard where he is attending to a pan balanced on a camping gas stove. There is a smell of coffee. The courtyard is littered with electrical appliances in varying states of disassembly. There are washing machines, microwave ovens, a toaster, and not a few computer screens.

'I need a code?' she asks.

'*Ti?*' He shakes his head.

'Code, password?'

The man frowns deeply and shakes his head again.

'Son.' He declares finally.

It takes a minute for the meaning to become clear.

'Ah, where is son?' She knows she is shouting and she knows this won't help, but it seems to be a natural consequence of speaking Pidgin English.

'*Ti?*'

'Where?' That was definitely a shout. She coughs to compensate and cover her embarrassment.

'Ah, ah.' The man wags his finger; he has understood her. 'Athena,' he says proudly.

Michelle raises her eyebrows, breathes in, and exhales as slowly as she can. Even if she could make herself understood, it seems pointless asking when the son is likely to return. It won't be before the strike ends.

Back out in the narrow lane Michelle's shoulders slump. How, how, how, how! How can a country operate with businesses like that? How can anyone on the island get anything done? Everything must take forever. Do they still rely on snail mail? It is absolute madness.

A cat turns onto the path in front of her and meows. It winds around her ankles as she nears, begging to be petted. Its coat is soft, as if a hundred hands have smoothed the way before her, every hand on the island taking the time to flatten the fur. The island lost in time. No kidding!

But with no internet and no boats, that's that. There is no rush. She can take the time to stroke the cat, smile at the old lady, walk casually back to the port, stop and look at the bougainvillea, the geraniums in pots on either side of someone's front door.

The port seems lazier than when she left. The locals happier, the tourists more out of place. The flagged walkway must have been there for hundreds of years, trodden smooth by countless feet. The grand mansions tower solid and immoveable, witnesses to history. The man with the donkeys, the men with the nets may all be descendants of the builders of these fine houses. They must have been to school with everyone else of their age on the island, and their fathers before them, and their fathers before that. They must know every stone and every alley, every house and every face.

No single house is their home, but rather the whole island is.

So lucky.

Chapter 7

But right now she still needs to get online, check her e-mails, and buy a new phone. Tomorrow she will take the boat back to Athens, catch up with correspondence, and get this whole thing back on course. It had been a bad idea to take a day off to sightsee.

As she considers this, her attention is still held by the scenes unfolding all around her. Everyday life for the locals, but foreign to her eyes. A cargo ship has come in, its heavy steel bow door hinged down flat on the pier, the metal grinding against stone as the hull slides to and fro on a gentle swell. Coloured lines where the paint shears off the hull have become embedded on the quayside next to the indentations left from previous visits. Men with handcarts busy themselves around the boat, stacking and pulling, the deck crew unloading and shouting, cats waiting, donkeys, laden and heehawing, swishing at flies with their tails.

'Lady, hey lady?'

Michelle almost collides with a tray of Greek salads.

'Oh sorry, I didn't see you.'

'Lady, sit down. Here is not a good place to stand … here.' Balancing the tray on one hand, he pulls back a chair and invites her to sit before winding his way between the tables to deliver his tray of food.

It's tempting—a coffee and some breakfast. Michelle realises that she hasn't really had anything to eat yet today. The food in the hospital had been sparse. The nurse explained that with the island being so small, anyone staying overnight would have food brought in by their families, and consequently a kitchen had never been considered. She hadn't been tempted by the bitter Greek coffee and half packet of biscuits on offer.

On her last stay with Juliet, Michelle had been introduced to both *spanakopita*, spinach pie, and *bougatsa*, a cream-filled pastry eaten at breakfast.

Her stomach rumbles. A donkey clicks its hooves on the flags, a cargo-man shouts, something falls, accompanied by laughter.

The waiter returns, his tray now empty. He scrutinises her face and pulls the chair out farther.

'Are you OK?' he asks, putting the tray down and wiping his hands on his apron.

'Yes, why, what?' She breaks her stare. The men on the cargo ship are fishing a bundle of mineral-water bottles out of the sea, using a pole with a hook on the end. It's clearly not the first time it has happened and appears to be a big joke.

'Ah, you seem to be ... I don't know, worried, perhaps. Pressured.'

'I am. Actually, I need to get online.' She

97

glances at him.

He tips his head, his greying hair is white at the temples. 'You are here on this beautiful island for how much time? A day, two days, a week? Come off line for a while. These days everyone is online all the time. Does it make them happy? I don't think so. Look!' A pair of tourists, Americans perhaps, sit huddled over their laptops, excluding the world and each other. 'The tourists sit and look at their computers, lost in an online world, instead of the reality of the sea, the sky, the boats.'

'It's work; I just need to get online and check my emails.' Michelle's voice is more shrill than she expected. She feels her face flush hot. He looks at her oddly.

'I'm sorry, I didn't mean to be rude,' she says. Her stance relaxes a little.

'Ach, don't worry, people are rude to me all day long. But seriously, you need a coffee and to sit down. After all, I have the best coffee on the island, freshly ground, and each cup comes with a biscuit my wife made this morning. Come.' He pats the back of the chair, smiling, and maintaining eye contact.

'You aren't going to tell me where I can find the internet unless I buy coffee, are you?' The muscles around her mouth twitch, a smile forming, his relaxed attitude infectious. Liquid brown eyes, their intensity a contrast to his soft grey hair.

'Aha! I had not thought of that, I will use that in the future. But also beautiful ladies should not be running around burying themselves in emails. They should be sipping the best coffee on the island and being entertained by attentive, handsome Greek men.'

Michelle would like to say, 'cut the crap' in a really cool, worldly way. It would fit, and maybe he would laugh.

'You are talking nonsense.' The words come out with a giggle, partly at him and partly at herself. 'OK, I will have a coffee, on condition that you will then tell me where I can get online.'

He pushes her chair in as she sits and walks away. He nods to a passing man crossing his route, smiles at a lady with a shopping bag and two children, and stops to stroke the cat that sits by the café door.

Until she gets to Athens, it is going to be like wading upstream to get anything done here. She should have brought her laptop instead of leaving it at the hotel. The hotel that she has paid for but probably won't be sleeping in tonight. Thinking of which, where is she going to sleep? That's yet another thing to do—organise accommodation. But for now, she sighs. The weight is off her feet, and the sun is bathing her in its gentle caress. There is much to watch: the cargo men; the donkey men; the group of German tourists two tables away, who are clearly in disagreement about something; the little old man, bread tucked under his arm, coming out of the bakery, his trousers held up with string, and odd shoes on his feet. She closes her eyes and drifts, soaking in the sounds of the island, the buzz of the port life, children laughing somewhere behind her, in between the houses, a bell ringing up high on the hill.

'Here you are.' The waiter has returned with his tray and two coffees.

'Oh no, I am alone.'

'Which I will remedy if I may?'

He pulls out the chair next to her so he too can survey the port's activities. His tall and lanky frame seems to become boneless as he sits.

'So tell me, have you not heard the tale of the hare and the tortoise? The two little creatures who decide to race?'

'I don't really have time for fables.' Michelle says this casually, having never much cared for them. The coffee really is pretty good, though.

'Exactly my point. You see, you are the hare. No time to stop and listen to a tale, no time to take a breath, rushing, rushing. And is it really achieving the perfect life? Or is the perfect life that of the tortoise? Look at that old man over there.'

The man in question, his face weather-beaten, craggy and dark brown, stands in his fishing boat, his shirt thin, his trousers old, slowly pulling little fish from his net. The cats are lined up on the dock waiting patiently. When he comes across a fish of the wrong kind or too small to sell, he throws it to a cat. Michelle watches as each cat is fed in turn. As he feeds them, he talks to them and laughs at what he says.

'He is the tortoise, but a more contented man than Constantinos I have never met.'

'Well he's a lucky man then, but I don't fish for a living, and you don't do the work I do, so you would not understand.' There is a biscuit on the saucer, which reminds her of her hunger. She nibbles at it to make it last.

The waiter laughs.

'Tell me, what do you see when you look at me?' Michelle turns to face him and opens her mouth to speak. He puts up a hand. 'No, wait, I will tell you what you see: you see a waiter. A waiter in his white shirt and black trousers and short apron with a pocket for change. Not even a young waiter, who may break away and do something with his life, but a mature waiter, life's decisions made, the dice cannot be recast.' Michelle opens her mouth to object, but he raises his fingers and shakes his head. 'I know what you see. A man who has grown up on an island, probably ill-educated, with no money, in a dead-end job: an island boy. Maybe you are right, maybe not. You see that hotel over there?'

Michelle shuffles in her seat to see where he is pointing. It is one of the mansions by the water's edge, four floors high of solid stone, with windows and balconies overlooking the harbour. A four-faced pitched orange roof tops the warm orangey-cream stone.

101

'Actually no, first I will tell you a story.' He takes a sip of coffee, and a moment to really taste the flavour, smacking his lips and rolling his tongue.

'You know, I think I am a bit hungry.' Michelle says it quietly.

'No problem, what would you like?' He raises his hand and one of the other waiters comes over. He speaks a few words, they laugh, and Michelle feels a little uncomfortable.

'We will have a choice. Now, where was I? Oh yes, a story.' The second waiter quickly returns with a tray of spinach pies, *bougatsa*, toast and butter, and new coffees.

'Once upon a time—you are comfortable, yes? I can begin?' Michelle has just taken a mouthful of the *bougatsa* and is struggling to free the bite from the pastry, icing sugar all round her mouth. She nods and smiles as best she can.

'OK, so once upon a time, a long, long time ago, when I was a boy, I thought I knew what I wanted to do, what I wanted to be. I took the time to do the things necessary to make this come about, and the further down the path I was the more convinced I was that I was right. I have strong opinions and with these opinions came an arrogance in the belief that my way was the right way, the only way, and that everyone else was too blind to see that they were taking the wrong path.

'My Mama tried to tell me that my single-mindedness was not necessarily a good thing, but

102

her words fell on deaf ears. I continued on my way, but she did not give up. She tried many times to tell me that perhaps there are other ways to live life, that the choices I was making did not necessarily lead in the direction I was hoping to go.

'But with the arrogance of youth and the feeling that my time on this planet was endless, I battled on, determinedly thinking I had all the time in the world to change my mind.'

He takes another sip of coffee, looks at the food but doesn't choose anything, then sits back contentedly.

'Eventually I received my prize. I went to Princeton to study Astrophysics. I was young. I wanted to do amazing things.' He speaks casually as if it is insignificant.

Michelle stops eating and looks the waiter up and down. There is no sign of humour. Could he be serious?

'Several years I stayed, lost in my studies, you could say.' He laughs briefly. 'Never any time to come home to my beloved island, but I still kept the vision of it in my heart, an ideal version of my life "back home".'

He pauses, his eyes focused inward.

'I came home eventually, here to the island, after I graduated. My mother was pleased to see me, and I was delighted to see her and all my old friends, but after a few days I grew sad. The island seemed to have lost its charm, the people seemed slow and

103

stupid, the methods antiquated and pointless, the traditional ways no longer made sense. I felt like an alien in my own home. I told my Mama of my sadness, and I also told her that for these reasons I had to leave again, live the rest of my life in America. It did not feel like I had a choice, and it made my heart heavy.'

The *bougatsa* is gone and Michelle absent-mindedly picks up a piece of spinach pie. Her attention is fixed on the waiter.

'The day I was due to leave, I had said goodbye to my father. My cases were packed and I was very stressed by the decision I felt compelled to make, and very sad. Mama called me inside. She said, "Come, son, let us have a coffee together," and she made coffee in her little *briki*—that's the Greek coffee pan, just big enough for one cup. She waited for the coffee to boil. The mixture came bubbling to the top, and she snatched it off the heat just before it boiled over. She poured it into her little cup, then she put the *briki* back on the stove to make a cup for me. When it was just starting to boil over, she took it off the heat, the froth subsided and she waited for the grounds to settle. Whilst they were settling, she filled my little cup with rich goat's milk that she had just brought in from milking. Not just a splash—she filled it to the brim. And then she began to pour the coffee on top.

'I watched, astonished, as the coffee overflowed into the saucer, filling that too and spilling onto my Mama's clean white tablecloth. I could not believe what she was doing. I sat there with my mouth open, unable to move. But she just kept pouring, the coffee and milk mixing together and becoming cold and dilute. Into the saucer it went and all over the table, and still she didn't stop until the *briki* was empty.

'Finally I found my voice and I said, "Mama, what have you done? Have you gone mad? The coffee's spoiled; it's all over the table. What are you doing?"'

'"Why did it overflow, son?" she asked me. Well, at that point I thought she must have gone senile and I looked at her with love. "Don't pity me, Costas Voulgaris," she snapped. She always used my full name when she was cross … "I am enjoying my coffee," she said. "It is you who is not."

'I didn't leave the island that day, and, as you can see, I am still here. What can I do with astrophysics? Sure, I wanted to do something amazing with my life, but here everyday life is amazing, not by doing but just by being, and it is available for everyone to taste, just as long as their own cup is not so overfilled nothing else will fit in.'

Michelle looks at him side on. She feels sure she has heard a variation of this tale somewhere before, but he has taken the time to adapt it for the moment.

'Did you really go to Princeton?' she asks. He doesn't answer her. Instead he returns to what he had stated earlier.

'You see that hotel over there? That was the first one I renovated. When I started, it was nothing but a shell and full of rubble. Now the tourists can come to stay and experience for a few days what I experience every day. If I had stayed with astrophysics, would I have achieved amazing things by now? Maybe, or I might still be waiting. But with the choices I have made I don't have to wait to do amazing things. Now I see every day is amazing, everything on the island is amazing, everyone I meet is amazing, and instead of living in the future I live right now. It is perfect.'

Michelle wonders how he is going to wind up this thought-provoking piece of entertainment.

'Today, for example, it is amazing to be sitting drinking coffee with a lovely lady from England. And look, today's work is finished as I have made her smile.'

She could applaud him; it is so beautifully delivered, so nicely rounded. She is flattered that he took the time to present this piece of philosophy to her.

'The loss is to the world of astrophysics, I think.' She smiles. 'Princeton should be proud.'

He smiles but he does not grin. He is watching an Asian lady being lifted onto a mule that is baring its teeth.

'How did you know, though? I mean, know that you wouldn't regret such a decision, to stay here?'

'It was easier than I expected. All the time I was away, I was just that—"away". The work was "work

106

abroad", the people who loved me were here, the people who knew me were here, the people who cared about me, here. The people I worked with over there did not really care about me. They cared about the work, the working relationship, and the project. So really when I thought to make the choice, there was only one place that I could live happily, for the long term anyway.

'It is not bricks and mortar that make our home, it is people who love us.'

A group of rather red-looking English people enter the port.

'If you will excuse me.' The waiter stands, and in two easy strides he is talking to them.

'Tea and toast, or maybe you have had breakfast already, in which case you must try our crab. It is the best on the island. Constantinos there catches it for me.'

The old fisherman stops folding his nets to wave. 'Every day he goes out, the most content man I have ever met. Now, who wants some of the best coffee on the island?'

Michelle looks over the café door where the proprietor's name, 'Costas Voulgaris', is painted by a rather shaky hand. Owner, waiter, astrophysicist, she muses.

Michelle lets her back curve into the chair; she, too, feels boneless, melted by the sun. Her mind is blank, washed clean by the waiter's stream of words.

She considers letting go of consciousness just

enough for a quick snooze when she sees Yanni the donkey man walk into the port, his one donkey behind him.

She must do something about him. She leaves some money on the table and stands.

Chapter 8

Yanni's loss is apparent in the way he walks, lifeless, slumped.

A girl in the office in London has a horse, talks about it like it is human, and seems to spend more time with it than with her boyfriend. The whole chambers knows about its schooling, its learning progress, how some things it learns faster than she does, and she feels she is holding it back, and how, over other things, she has to be patient, repeating them again and again.

Until listening to her, Michelle had never considered what sort of bond a person could have with a horse. It seems it can be pretty intense. This is confirmed by the look in Yanni's eyes.

'Er hmm,' Michelle coughs her introduction.

'Ah, nothing broken then?' he asks.

'No, just painful.' She is not sure how to approach the subject. It is not going to be a straight compensation discussion. 'Can I buy you a coffee?'

He loops Suzi's rein around a post. 'I don't drink coffee, thank you.' The thank you comes as an afterthought.

'Look, there is no way I can express how sorry I am about what happened.' The image of Dolly's last breath brings a lump to her throat, she squeezes a tear back. 'I am truly really sorry, it was a terrible thing to have happened.'

'You are alive.' Yanni has taken out a tobacco pouch. He twists his moustache before beginning his ritual. His moustache seems odd on one so young, but most of the donkey men have them, and Michelle presumes it must denote status.

'Yes, I'm alive, thank goodness, but this doesn't detract from your loss.' She wonders if he will understand the word 'detract'.

'She is gone. I will miss her. Suzi will miss her.' He pats his remaining beast. 'Last night, in the dark, she cried out her loneliness till nearly dawn. This is life, is it not? Life and death.'

'Well, yes, but for you it is also your living.'

'True, things will be a little harder this winter coming; we will not have so much to fall back on.' He pauses to lick his cigarette paper before the final twist. 'So maybe this winter we will make things stretch a little further.'

As he uses the term 'we' Michelle has a sudden horrible thought that maybe there is a wife and children at home who will suffer.

'You have a family?'

He looks at her strangely.

'Of course I have a family; every man has a mother and father.'

This gives Michelle a small amount of relief, but she knows that doesn't really make any difference. If someone suffers, they suffer, old or young.

'I hope your parents will not suffer too much …' This is her opportunity to lead into offering some compensation, but he rejoins with:

'The only hope I had was to finish building a room, so my parents would no longer need to sleep on daybeds.' He picks some tobacco from his tongue.

Michelle tries to digest this information. She is not sure what it means, what a daybed is in Greece. Nothing comes to mind. It seems to imply they do not have a bedroom, but surely that cannot be right.

'Well, what I was going to say was, I would like to recompense you for your loss.'

He looks at her as if she has switched languages to Chinese.

'Oh, sorry, I mean buy you another donkey.'

He looks at the floor and shakes his head. 'No,' he mutters.

'Sorry?'

'Why would you buy me a donkey?'

'Well, I was on her when …' She cannot finish the sentence.

He shrugs and adjusts Suzi's bridle, running his hand under the nosepiece so it fits without chafing.

'You left her in my hands, you trusted me.'

'No, I left her in your boyfriend's hands. So is it his fault?' Michelle begins to protest, but realises Dino not being her boyfriend is not the point of the matter. 'Or maybe it is the fault of the *dimos* for not

111

paving the path, or maybe mine for renting her out to you and not going with you to keep her safe.'

Michelle finds his logic incomprehensible. She had the loan of the donkey, so it was clearly her fault, her responsibility. She is not sure how to explain to him the reasons why this is so, on his terms.

He drops his cigarette end and grinds it to nothing with the toe of his cowboy boot.

'If you had died, who would buy me a donkey? Because you are lucky enough to live you must buy a donkey? This is strange thinking.' With this he has finished the conversation.

Michelle has not.

'In England my job is to see who is at fault. I am a lawyer.'

'Ah, *dikigoros*.' He nods as if all has become clear. Michelle bristles.

'When things happen, it is someone's fault, and that person is responsible for making good any losses.'

'When things happen it is not always someone's fault. Last winter a rock fell onto one of my goats. Whose fault is that? If you had been sitting on that goat would it have been your fault?' He doesn't wait for an answer. Instead he asks a question. 'So what is the difference between rocks falling up or falling down?'

'In my work, someone is always to blame,' Michelle defends limply.

'It is unfortunate work; you must never feel

112

satisfied,' Yanni replies.

Stroking Suzi's neck, Michelle struggles as pictures of Dolly swim in her mind's eye. She feels guilty, but what could she have done?

'Yanni, I would like to buy you a donkey. I have pictures in my head of the accident.' She stresses the word 'accident'. 'It would make me feel better if I could give you a gift.' Yanni's face remains unchanged. 'Please,' she adds. He still does not respond, but his eyes flicker. He is thinking.

'One minute.' Nipping back to the café, she uses one of Costas' receipts to write her phone number and email address on the back, but then crosses out the email address as she imagines it will be of little use to a donkey man on this island. She writes Juliet's number instead, as a backup.

'Here, this is a number in England where you can reach me, and I have also put a Greek number where you can leave a message. Please, please think about it.'

A rather large man sweating in tracksuit bottoms and a white vest rolls up to Yanni and babbles in Greek.

'I have a job, I must go.' Yanni says.

'Please call me,' Michelle implores. He looks her in the eye for just longer than is comfortable before turning on his heel. Michelle watches him go, and as she is about to give up hope, he raises a hand and gives a stiff wave without turning around.

The Greeks are growing in mystery. Their way

of seeing is at such a tangent. All the people Michelle can think of would have taken the money and run, even if they didn't want to replace the donkey, wouldn't they? He could have taken the money to build this room for his parents, or just to help live through the winter. How can someone living so hand-to-mouth be so choosy? If his parents sleep on daybeds, he is not secretly wealthy like Costas Voulgaris the waiter. But perhaps the people she comes into contact with through her work are the sort who would resort to the law to settle their difficulties or even use it to their advantage. Perhaps there are scores of people, the majority even, who are like this donkey man? A whole world of people who don't complain or try to make a profit from accidents.

Michelle frowns. She was about to do something—what was it? The heat is delicious but seems to be sapping her ability to think. She shades her eyes with her hand and looks up. The sky's blue is deep, no clouds, not a wisp. High up, there is a ragged line, a vapour trail, the plane no longer visible.

She leans against the post Suzi was tied to and looks out to sea.

'Michelle, here's a new case to cut your teeth on. It's a small claim, but he is a regular customer, so keep him happy.' Arnold Braithwaite, head of the Yorkshire branch of Dulwater & Marown, grinned as

114

he passed her the folder. This was in the days before she transferred to the London office. Grasping the folder, she returned to her desk, eager.

'What ya got?' drawled William, who sat opposite her and liked to make a point of being her senior, although he'd only been at the firm a month or two longer than Michelle.

'Cyril Buttershaw.' Michelle read the name at the top of the file.

'Ha, Septic Cyril! Bad luck!'

'Why bad luck?' she asked, but William wouldn't give anything away.

'You'll see,' he laughed.

The next day she went to visit the place where Cyril Buttershaw had tripped on the upturned paving slab. He had made the same claim against the council three years in a row. He lived in a small, one-street village that looked like Yorkshire had forgotten about it, the houses set back from the road with a narrow strip of land in front that one or two had planted with flowers, nothing surrounding the houses but fields across which a single-track lane curled, flanked on either side by dry stone walls. For the most part though, these front yards were bare soil or a dumping ground for household refuse. There was a cluster of children's bikes rusting on one, a mattress on another. The offending paving stone was near the end of the row of houses before the road turned a corner and disintegrated into the overgrown front gardens of the last two houses.

There was not much to see. Michelle made some notes on her clipboard, holding down the paper against the keen wind that was blowing. She took a photograph as an aide-mémoire and then turned to go.

'Are you from the law firm?' The voice had the trace of a lisp.

'Er, yes, hello. Michelle Marsden, can I help you?' Michelle tried to tame her hair, which was blowing either side of her face, her back to the wind.

'I'm Cyril.' He did not offer his hand, and Michelle retracted hers awkwardly.

'Ah, Mr Buttershaw. I take it this is the offending paving slab?'

'Yes it is; I fell over it last year and the council still hasn't fixed it. France this year, I think. Last year was me first cruise in the Bahamas with me claim money, but it's a long way; won't do that again. Didn't like the food, neither.'

He used both hands to hitch up his trousers. Michelle noticed they were a thick-weaved pair of suit trousers held up with coarse string tied in a bow, his shirt a dirty cream with a multitude of vertical thin coloured stripes and a large collar dating it back to the seventies, a typical charity shop bargain buy. The collar was pulled onto the outside of his jacket, a rough, shapeless tweed worn smooth around the inside of the neck with drooping baggy pockets. Nothing fitted—the trousers and shirt too big, the jacket too small.

116

His wire-rimmed glasses did nothing to improve his distinctly old-fashioned look. There was something very grubby about his general appearance. The name Septic Cyril seemed more than appropriate.

Michelle looked around her. There was a very bad smell coming from somewhere, but there were no bins to be seen.

'Cup of tea,' he announced cheerfully. 'This way.'

The porch outside his house looked at once oddly familiar and rather out of place. It was made of an old wardrobe, a wooden one just like her Grandma had had, which had been pushed up against the front door, and the back taken out to allow access. Michelle's mouth hung open.

As she stepped through and into the one downstairs room she heard the words, 'Mind your step,' and she refocused to see Cyril grinning back at her.

Passing through, she could see that one corner of the wardrobe housed a collection of Wellington boots. The remainder, apart from a central walkway, was piled high with plastic bags, the contents of which were not clear. This trend continued into the house, with all manner of jumble lining either side of the remaining walkway. Tables were stacked on tables, chairs on top of that. Beyond was a large, double-fronted fridge with a big dent in one door, the plug hanging lifelessly over the handle and the broken shelves stacked on top. Michelle wondered briefly how he had managed to get it in the house, it was so big. A dead plant in a plastic pot crowned the top, on the broken shelves. What looked like an Edwardian wind-organ with two rows of keys, many of which were missing, provided a shelf for a plastic suitcase bulging with grey-looking clothes. Objects piled in front of the windows shut out most of the light. There was a large bookshelf, a long-case clock, a tower of radios and televisions the likes of which Michelle had only seen in junk shops. A bare bulb hung in the centre of the ceiling, which too was grey, especially around the edges. The bulb was not lit and seemed to have something hanging from it, which swayed slightly in the otherwise still air.

Michelle cautiously stepped over the threshold to find the carpet raised by some four or five inches above floor level. Now out of the wind, the origin of the overpowering stench was apparent, not only from Cyril, but from his house in general.

The further she stepped inside, the more furniture she could make out, stacked in every corner, leaving nothing but a passageway through the front room to the lean-to kitchen at the back, the door of which was flattened against the wall by another large bookcase supporting endless plastic bags, swollen with unidentifiable contents. Michelle preferred not to speculate on what was in them. Instead she held her hand over her nose and mouth and tried not to breathe in, reminding herself that all smells are particulate. Very little light filtered in from anywhere. The smell was insufferable, and she stuck her nose into the crease of her elbow, hoping to mask the stench with the aroma of fresh laundry, but the lavender mixed with Cyril's own smell and she gagged.

Moving forward but wishing to retreat, she pulled herself in tightly and tried not to touch anything. The kitchen was a little less cluttered, but filthy. Oddly, the carpet extended into this room, and the cooker leaned back at an unusable angle, its front feet lifted by the carpet's unusual thickness. The smell in here made it almost impossible to breathe, and Michelle began to feel a slight panic.

There was movement in the corners, and two or three dogs slunk out of the open back door as she and Cyril entered. As Michelle's eyes began to grow accustomed to the gloom, stains running down the walls became apparent, and the abstract pattern on the carpet revealed itself to be comprised mainly of dog mess.

'Actually, Mr Buttershaw, perhaps I could stop by for tea another time,' Michelle gasped, 'only I've just remembered something very important, and I must return immediately.' Cyril turned to face her, a rather grubby cracked teapot in one hand and a dish of used teabags in the other. Something that looked alarmingly like raw liver clung to the inside curve of his ear. She felt her stomach turn and retched involuntarily as she turned to run from the house.

William had laughed out loud. 'What do you mean, it "looked like" liver in his ear? It almost certainly *was* liver. He works one day a week in an abattoir.' He held his sides and rocked back on his chair. 'You didn't go in his house did you?' Michelle could not help herself; even now, safely back at the office, she retched again.

'Ha ha, you did! You know why the carpets are so thick? Six dogs he's got, all shitting in the house, just lays another carpet on top. Tell, you didn't drink the tea, did you?'

At this point Michelle threw the file at him.

'I don't want it. I've dealt with the last three claims. It's your turn now, as the newbie. My wins have financed one trip to Spain, one to Disneyland, and last year a cruise in the Bahamas.'

'Why the heck don't the council just lay the paving stone back down!' Michelle exploded.

'They do, after every claim, but somehow it sticks back up, ready to trip poor Cyril again. It's his living: one day a week in the slaughter house; Wednesdays down to claim his disability benefit, and once a year a claim so he can go on holiday.'

No, the system has many faults and a lot of people take advantage. It isn't quite as bad as that now, but still, some of these big claims she is involved in are not providing compensation for any real suffering or hardship; they are just business, one business suing another. Yanni is right, it is most

120

unsatisfactory work, and it is work that she no longer really agrees with. It makes no one happy, and there is no thrill in winning, as you know the next case will just be a variation of the last, a flow of money. It produces nothing. Society makes no progress because of it. It is just a game in which she is trapped. It's what she knows, what she has been trained for, what she understands. Personal opinion plays no part.

'Michelle, you are here!' Dino bounces in front of her and grabs her into a hug from which she breaks free to take a breath.

'Oh my God, I thought you were gone.' Just half an hour before he had rushed to the port to see her ship pulling out of the harbour and turning towards Athens. His legs did not stop at the sight. He had kept running, faster even, up to the cannons, hoping to spot her on deck, running along the coastal path trying to see into the port holes, one more glimpse, a chance to … to do what? The most important person who had walked into his life was on a boat just a few yards away but completely unreachable and he had nothing, no phone number, no email address. He didn't know the name of the firm she works for. He didn't even know her surname.

He had stopped running and shouted at the top of his lungs, but her name ricocheted off the rocks behind him and became lost over the open sea. He stood forlornly, wondering how it could have happened, how she could have left him, how such a calamity had occurred, how he could right this life-shattering wrong.

His legs had moved before he was aware, stumbling back towards town until, with a flash that lightened the weight in his chest, the notion occurred that she was a friend of Juliet's. With that reality, returning to his home no longer brought the fear of facing his father, but rather the joy of being reunited with Michelle. In a single thought, a bounce returned to his step and a plan formed until this moment when he spotted her sitting here and the whirlwind of emotions evaporated, leaving only contentment that she was near.

'Dino!' She gasps once her breath returns.

'You are not on the boat.' He pulls a face. 'So no Athens?'

'I missed the boat, the fuss just to get discharged. You? How are you?' Without thought she puts her hand on his chest where the stones and branches had cut and ripped. She can feel something soft, gauze probably.

Dino's heart races under her touch. The unexpected relief that she is still here is immense. His chest releases, he can breathe again. His hand spontaneously covers hers.

'I am better now. It is good you have not gone.'

'It's luck that the case is postponed.' Colour rises in her cheeks and she breaks eye contact as she pulls her hand away.

'I came to see you in the hospital but you were sleeping. I waited on a bench outside, just around the corner from the front door, in the shade. The nurse she promised to tell you I was there.'

'Oh, well she didn't, but never mind. We would have found each other again at the village after the meeting.' Her face pales. 'But actually, yes, you're right, with this postponement I might actually not have made it to the village.' The thought raises tension across her shoulders, but she looks at him as he smiles, and her muscles relax.

'The postponement is until when?' He is shifting his weight from foot to foot, unable to stay still in the excitement of seeing her again.

'Next Friday.'

'That's great news. Stay here, let me show you my island.' Does he imagine it, or is there hesitation? Perhaps there is a reason that she wasn't looking for him, but then again, how could she? She doesn't know the island, she lost her phone … but if she had really wanted to, wouldn't she have found a way? He senses something slipping away. The sky seems to darken. 'Or, well, maybe you are busy?' As soon as these words come out he regrets them. What was it Adonis says? 'Act as if it has already happened ….' No, not that. 'A woman is an empty vessel?' No, definitely not that. Adonis would have told him to presume she is interested, take the lead, make it happen. But then, what are Adonis' motives?

123

'No, I would love that.' The hesitation is gone, the sun a little brighter. It is a surprise to see Adonis is not always right. Dino stands a little taller, his shoulders back.

Memories of the warmth of her hand linger. He wants to feel her skin again. He grabs her arm to lead her toward the coast road. 'No donkey this time.' He grins. A wave of concern crosses her face but her smile soon returns.

The time on the cliff-face seems to have altered his perspective. He feels he has known Michelle all his life, that he knows her as well as he knows Adonis even. Her grace, her height, and, OK, her age, do remind him of his Mama, but these are not feelings he would ever have for a relative. There! When she turns her head, the jut of her chin, the way her hair swings.

'What, is there a bug in my hair?' Her slender fingers reach and gingerly touch the area he is looking at.

'No, no bugs. Come on, I will show you something.' He still has her hand and they walk around the harbour to the start of the coast road. The path is wide enough for a couple to pass side-by-side. She pulls her hand free. They have not gone far before he takes her elbow and guides her to the right, down a narrow rocky path that leads to the sea. Near the water, someone has tried to concrete steps into the rocks. The path flattens and they leave the face of the rock behind on a small natural jetty.

124

At the end of the jetty, Dino turns to look back, and Michelle follows suit. The sign is still there: 'No jumping.' The sign he and Adonis ignored as boys, and other boys are ignoring even now.

He watches her face as she takes in the sea cave with the hole in the roof that boys are leaping through into the shade below. The cave's interior sparkles as crystals in the rock reflect the blue of the water in a magical display. It is one of the most beautiful sights he knows, filled with some of his best childhood memories. He wants to tell of the times he was here with Adonis, breaking free from the restraint of clothes on hot August days, the thrill of the cold water on his skin.

Her hand is in his again but she hasn't noticed. He looks down at her cuticles, the ones he kissed on the rock face after he had slid to save her.

'Amazing,' she whispers, in awe of the cave. A young boy jumps through the hole in the roof, tucking his knees to his chest, the splash as he hits the water sending ripples to the rocks they are standing on. They watch as a few more boys jump.

Michelle puts her arm up to shade her eyes and begins to turn, taking in the whole view—the cave, the harbour, the yacht cruising out between the cannons, the sea opening up and the mainland beyond. Seagulls hover overhead calling out their song of freedom.

'Perfect,' she breathes.

Dino nods.

'What?' Michelle asks. Dino is looking out to sea with a frown.

'I am not sure what to do about Yanni, the donkey man.'

'Oh. Me too, I feel so bad, but he won't let me do anything.'

'You've spoken to him?'

'Yes, just before you found me in the harbour. I offered to buy him a new donkey but ....'

'I should buy him the donkey, really. I can already feel peoples' eyes on me in town.'

'What do you mean?'

'Unless I make things right with him, I will be known as the man who drowned his donkey. It is a small island. The people get bored, gossip is their entertainment. And I suppose it is the right thing to do.' Dino's hand goes to his mouth and he chews on the outside edge of his thumb.

'Do you have the money to buy him a donkey?'

'No.' Dino chews harder.

'Fine, so let me buy the donkey. You would do the same for me if it was the other way round wouldn't you?'

Dino smiles with a look that says, 'How can you doubt it?'

'As long as he has a new one from us, I don't suppose the gossip will last long. But I am not sure how we can get him to accept. He was adamant he wouldn't take my offer.' Michelle takes Dino's hand from his mouth and holds it for a while, patting it

126

gently.

'He's a bit of a loner, has lived up on the ridge all his life, has his own way of seeing life. Oh, by the way, where are you staying tonight?' Dino's face brightens at the change of topic.

'Do you know, I hadn't actually thought about it? Mostly I need to get online.' Some of the muscles in her face tighten and her voice drops.

'You don't sound happy about that.'

'Work.' But she is more interested in the view.

'I know about that.' Memories come, but he pushes them away.

'You know, being here, looking at all this makes work seem very unimportant.'

'Adds perspective,' Dino agrees.

'If I could snap my fingers, I would make everything in England disappear.' She turns wide-eyed to look at Dino, her hand to her mouth, shocked by her own words.

'Really?' He pauses. She stays with her hand over her mouth searching his eyes. 'Do it,' he adds quietly.

Another boy jumps, there is a roar of laughter from his friends.

Michelle's hand uncovers her mouth.

'Unfortunately, I live in the real world. Come, let's go find me a place to stay. You are staying with Adonis, right?' She leads back the way they came.

'No, his place is too small.'

'So where are you staying?'

'Same place as you?' He grins.

Chapter 9

Is it wrong?

As they climb back to the coastal path she glances behind. He sweeps his fringe from his eyes and smiles at her. His skin has tanned an even deeper brown in just a day. He has on a new t-shirt, not quite as orange as the last, with 'Greece, the Experience' written in small letters across the front. The colour accentuates his skin tones. Every step is a bounce, so much energy. She lets him pass, and he holds out a hand to help her up. Bitten nails.

The last few steps seem steeper than they appeared going down. A lizard runs across the path, she jumps and lets go of Dino's hand. The lizard stops on a rock, flicks out its tongue, motionless, sunbathing.

Dino keeps going, but then he'll have seen lizards a hundred times before. He looks so Greek, so foreign to her eyes and yet so familiar. His kissing of her fingers on the cliff face seemed so natural. But then how can these things be judged? It was a very unnatural situation. Does the situation make such a difference? Would someone else in the same situation have done the same thing? Is it a cultural difference? After all, Greek people kiss even passing acquaintances on both cheeks when they meet.

Perhaps it didn't mean anything. Clearly there is no logical conclusion to this argument, but the questions continue to invade her thoughts.

Dolly's last moments flicker through her mind's eye again. One minute so alive, the next . . . It could have been her.

There is bound to be a well-known psychological response that explains these feelings she has for her rescuer. Some syndrome or other. Yes, she has read about it somewhere, White Knight Syndrome. Everything is a syndrome these days. It doesn't mean that her feelings are reciprocated, or appropriate. He is the same age as Juliet's boys, for goodness' sake!

Blinking, she shakes her head at how embarrassed he would be if she were to act on her feelings, only to find she had misjudged his. Her cheeks grow hot at the thought.

He reaches behind him and offers his hand for the last few steps. The dark hairs lie flat on his forearm, his fingers explore her palm as he takes her hand. Little actions like that make her feel almost certain she is not misreading the signs.

But his age. There is a word for people like her in England.

'Adonis' aunt, Kyria Zoe,' he states, not even slightly out of breath with the climb. 'She has a place that she used to run as a pension.'

He leads the way along the coastal path, away from town.

His arm slips around her waist for the final step, but once they are on the flat he lets go.

Not far along the path they cut up past a house overlooking the sea and climb long, low steps that take them inland. The path flattens and houses appear either side, replacing the barren rocks. Soon they reach a meeting of ways, a small square at the bottom of a very long, steep flight of steps, with cats sprawling in the shade of a majestic eucalyptus tree half way up. In this heat, the steps look insurmountable. Michelle stops walking just at the thought of the exertion that will be necessary.

'Here we are.' Dino takes her hand again to gently direct her to a gate near the bottom of the steps. A grand house stands behind a walled courtyard. Tall metal gates offer entrance.

The courtyard has hardly changed at all, although it does not seem as tidy as he recalls. Some of the brightly coloured floor tiles are cracked. Potted plants line the perimeter and play sentinel on every step up to the grand double doors. Jasmine covers the walls, flowers explode with colour everywhere.

On the ground floor, the several doors into the building look as though they are no longer used. Ornately carved, with the paint now peeling, the hinges rusty. Wooden boxes lean against one, a fishing net is hung over the handle of another, which clearly functions as a storage area now. The main house is centred around the double doors at the top of the steps, the veranda leading away from this in either direction to less ornate doors that have been painted fairly recently.

Dino bounces up the steps and knocks heartily on the grand double door, turning to smile at Michelle.

'Yes?' A voice calls from inside.

'Kyria Zoe? Have you a room for me?' Dino can hardly keep himself from laughing. Kyria Zoe would give him biscuits, olives, oranges every time he and Adonis used to call on her. She would praise him whilst shooting disapproving stares at Adonis.

'Who is it?' The voice asks. A creaky old voice, but then how long has it been? At one time she would have hundreds of guests every year supplementing her pension, helping to support her family.

'It's Dino.'

The door opens a crack, releasing a faint odour of antiseptic.

'Who is it? I am feeding my mother.' Kyria Zoe's hair is a white halo, like candyfloss, but lighter, like clouds.

'And how is your mother?'

The door opens fully and reveals her familiar smile, her kind eyes, a soft face no less beautiful for the loss of colour in her hair. She takes a minute and then her face lights up and she grabs him in an embrace that is strong for a lady of her age. She kisses him on both cheeks, then stands back so she

132

can look at him, hands still clutching his shoulders. Her questions tumble out in a continuous stream, with no pause for an answer. Where has he been? Is he too clever to talk to her now? Is his English perfect? Does Adonis know he is here?

Finally she looks at Michelle and holds out a hand to shake. 'Girlfriend?' she asks with a sly fleeting look.

'This is Michelle, my friend.' Dino can feel colour rising to his cheeks, and he is glad, for some reason, that Michelle does not understand Greek.

'Ha! I know what you boys are like.'

She gives first Michelle and then Dino a long hard stare.

Dino explains that the strike has kept them on the island and that Michelle needs a room for a few days. He will stay too, but he doesn't know for how long.

'In separate rooms.' She does not ask, she states. She returns indoors without inviting them in. There is a sound of wood scraping on wood and the tinkle of metal on metal. Dino can hear voices inside, a girl's voice, high and shrill, and someone who is grunting. Zoe is addressing her mother and Uncle Bobby, who is really her deceased husband's brother. A typical large Greek family. Dino sighs, and not for the first time wishes for his own family, but there is only his Baba. Zoe returns with several keys on different bunches.

'Uncle Bobby has not been well,' she mutters.

She addresses Michelle, 'You can be here.' She says it emphatically, but with a smile, as she opens the blue door nearest to her own.

'This one is for you,' Dino translates.

'And you ...' she marches Dino to the end of the balcony to a yellow door. 'Can be here.' She glances at him before opening the door. He looks past her into the cell of a room, takes in the narrow bed with a sheet pulled tightly across it and an icon above the headboard. A jug sits on a three-legged table, and apart from that it is bare. Zoe steps across the room and pushes open the shutters and sun floods the space, the dust motes dancing in her wake.

'It's lovely, thank you, Kyria Zoe.' He feels he should bow or nod his head or something—she is one of those people who commands respect—but he refrains. She ambles back to her door, deadheading the geraniums in their pots along the way, pocketing the petals in her apron. After Zoe has returned to her own rooms, Michelle's head pops out from around her door.

'Is the coast clear?' She is giggling.

'She is, how you say, "old school".' Dino feels some rough skin on the edge of his thumb and chews at it.

'I gathered by her looks what she was thinking!'

Dino watches her mouth as she speaks, the way her tongue moves behind her teeth. Maybe he is just like Adonis.

'What is your room like, or are all the rooms the same?' Michelle asks, breaking his stare.

'I think you have to take vows to enter mine. Yours?'

'It's charming.' She steps back to let him in. She has opened the shutters in this room, too, and French windows lead onto a small balcony with two chairs.

From the balcony the view is of the island's interior, across to the convent where a solitary nun resides. It might be possible to see the larger, neighbouring monastery up on the ridge. He stares up to the skyline and can just make out the orange-tiled roof through the trees. He had thought of becoming a monk at one point to try and find his salvation, gain some peace, after his mother died.

At the time he really thought it was what he wanted. It's amazing how at one point in your life something can seem so right, exactly what you want, and then just a short time later it is the last thing in the world you desire.

'There's a guidebook here. It says the monastery was founded in 1704.' Michelle peers out beyond the trees. '1704. That was the year they tried to pass the Act of Security in England.' Looking back to the guidebook she muses. 'Unbelievably hard on Queen Anne.' Dino has no idea what she is talking about, but her knowledge impresses him. 'The Scottish and English parliaments were quarrelling about who should be the royal successor. But Queen Anne! At least seventeen pregnancies, they think.

Gave birth at least twelve times, but only five survived the birth. Can you imagine?

'Poor lady. Four of them died before they were two, which left Prince William. And he, bless his cotton socks, died at the age of eleven. I'm sure Queen Anne couldn't have cared less who succeeded her after that. She must have been beside herself.'

Like a bolt of lightning the thought strikes him. She is here alone. Her friend Juliet is single, but that does not mean Michelle does not have a husband back in England. And children, perhaps. He feels slightly sick.

'You all right? You've suddenly gone pale.' Michelle asks him.

'Are you married?'

'No. I was, not now.'

The warmth returns to his cheeks.

'What happened?'

'Too tacky for words. His secretary. Just walked out with one bag. No fight. I even got the crumbling old house.' She laughs briefly, but it seems to be unrelated to her words.

He must have been crazy.

'Mind you, she was Lady Philippa Someone-or-Other, with her own crumbling house, so I guess he didn't need ours.' The same laugh.

'I am sorry.'

'I'm not. You know, it wasn't until he left that I realised how much he set it up so we were permanently competing. I mean, we had no reason

136

to. I was employed in chambers, he was independent, but every conversation, every case I took, it was all compared, demeaned, in relation to his work.' She pauses, a far-away look. 'Anyway, he is gone. Let's forget about him.'

'Was she as clever as you?'

'Who, Lady Home-Wrecker? No, not very bright. I've met some secretaries who are astoundingly bright, but she wasn't one of them.' Michelle looks back up to the monastery.

'Maybe that is what he preferred.'

'What? Someone who wasn't bright?'

'No, someone not capable of giving him competition.'

'Huh! I had never thought of it like that.' Up on a high path, a figure leads a donkey, the pace steady, no rush.

Does she have children? What age will they be? His age?

'Children?'

'No.' She returns her attention to the guidebook, the conversation closed.

During his days at university, he had studied and crammed to pass the exams, learnt by rote even when he hadn't understood, all of which he has now forgotten. He pulls at one of the chairs on the balcony and sits down.

'Ah. It says here that the monastery that stands now was built at a later date. A Giorgios Felos built it for his daughter, who chose to become a nun.'

137

She might be single, but what about her family? Who are they? Are her parents still alive? Does she have siblings? Does it make any difference? If they were Greek it would, but in England everything is different. People are separate from their families. She is too independent to be considered in any way other than in her own right.

'… Don't you think?' Michelle concludes.

'What? Sorry, I missed what you said.' Dino breaks free of his thoughts.

'I said if we walk up to look at the monastery it would be best to go early morning before it is too hot.'

'Oh. Yes, definitely.'

Looking up, following Dino's line of sight, she spots the figure leading the donkey, climbing higher and higher up a path that hairpins back and forth and into the trees near the ridge. Michelle is struck by a thought.

'I met a man today who was a waiter, only he wasn't. He's been to Princeton and now he owns hotels.'

'Costa Voulgaris.'

'You know him? Yes, I suppose you would. Well, what hit me was this island is full of huge stone houses and rich tourists, and yet the locals look as poor as church mice, like Costas Voulgaris.'

'It does not mean the same here.'

'Sorry?'

'Money doesn't have the same status here. You can be standing by a goat-herder in his rags, and an Athenian. The goat-herder might be financially wealthy, the Athenian paying a heavy mortgage for his summer house here.'

'Ah, so that's it. Their wealth has come from selling off property. A bit silly to leave yourself homeless just to make some money, though.'

He laughs. 'When they built these big houses there was water here, wells everywhere.

The water dried up, the people left. Those who remained inherited the worthless land, the property with no value.'

'So what brought it back to life?'

'Some artists came in the sixties, bought some of the houses. Their friends followed.'

'I have heard a few celebrity names being linked with this island.'

'They like it that no one knows them here.'

'It also sounds like their wealth is not held in awe.'

'Money is not wealth.'

'Sometimes you seem ridiculously old for your age.'

'How old do you feel?' He grins at her.

The sun is still hot. Dino leans his head back against the wall. The heat overcomes him, and after a few minutes she hears the gentle rhythm of his breathing. The sun has sapped her energy too. She tries the bed, which is a bit on the hard side, but that

139

is better than being too soft. She drifts off, watching a fly trying to find its way out of the room.

He is not there when she wakes. The door is open. His voice mingles with Zoe's in the courtyard; they sound like they are arguing, but then all Greek sounds like it is an argument.

She swills her face in the washbasin, and it is almost dry before she picks up the towel. The heat has not decreased. She closes the door behind her and then feels for the key. Her stomach grumbles.

'No need to lock it,' Dino calls up to her. Zoe is nowhere to be seen, the flowers dead-headed, the courtyard swept.

'I can't anyway, there's no key.' She skips down the stairs. He steps towards her. She can feel her grin stretch her skin just at the sight of him. Her hand reaches up to touch him, almost forgetting herself. She turns the movement into a smoothing of her hair.

The air is still warm, but the light is soft now, bathing the whitewashed walls and houses in a pink glow. Dino takes the lead, down narrow alleys, some with steps, some on the level, branching off at odd angles at the intersections. Each new corner reveals a subtly different part of town, with a tiny church tucked in a corner, or a colony of cats feasting on scraps, or perhaps a little grocery shop set into one of the walls, with produce spilling out into the street, all making up the fabric of the island.

They turn a corner, and the whole town, along with the view down to the port, is displayed before them.

'You see that land up there, between the house with no roof and the one with green shutters?' Dino stands behind her, his chest against her back, his arm over her shoulder so she can see down its length and along his finger. His breath is in her ear.

'Yes.' She breathes in, his skin a mixture of warmth and a trace of salt.

'That's Adonis' land. He is clearing it so he can build. He is not rich.'

'Oh, where does he live now?' Hopefully he does not hear the tremble in her voice. Is she doing wrong just being here so close? Would leaving be the right thing to do?

'With his mother, but they have only one room.'

'Crikey. It's one extreme to the other. So when am I going to meet this infamous Adonis?' He has moved to one side. Normality returns.

'You haven't met? Oh no, of course. He had work.' He picks a sprig of bougainvillea from a vine that is spanning the alley, giving brief shade as they pass underneath, and hands it to her. It is a casual move, but he makes eye contact.

Now that is definitely not something one Greek would do for another as passing acquaintances. Perhaps she needs to let him know she recognises his gestures. Maybe she can ask him to put it behind her ear ... No, that would be too tacky.

'Here we are.'

At a corner a sign above a stone arch announces the *'Taverna tou Kapetaniou'*. 'The Captain's Tavern', Dino translates.

The courtyard is a cool haven, with vines growing up three walls and across a wooden frame, providing a ceiling of leaves that flutters with the evening breeze. Crude paintings hang on the walls, and in the corner is a boy picking out a tune on his *bouzouki*. Dino chooses a table up by the door of the building, from which wonderful smells drift.

The waiter takes his time, and he eventually ambles over to their table. He wishes them a good evening in English and says something to Dino in Greek, which makes him blush. Then he lists from memory all the food that is ready or can be prepared quickly, first in English and then again in Greek till Dino assures him there is no need.

After a brief discussion, Dino orders for them both. Greek salad of cucumber, tomatoes, feta and olives; stuffed vine leaves and *saganaki*, whatever that is. Michelle wonders if everything the *taverna* prepares gets eaten every day; the list seemed unbelievably long.

A jug of chilled red wine is the first thing to arrive. When the vine leaves come, Dino squeezes lemon over them, adding to the light lemon sauce into which he dips her bread and hands it to her. After this he feeds her *saganaki*, the melted cheese running in strings, some of which trail from her chin.

Being with Dino is as comfortable as being with herself, but not as lonely. Actually, it is nothing like being with herself. With him she feels interesting. He encourages her to talk, listens to all her boring details about life and work in London. There is some admiration even.

The *bouzouki* boy, who was making progress with his piece, is called inside, and returns with a pile of books, which he spreads out on one of the tables and pores over, the end of his pencil in his mouth. The resulting silence makes the conversation between Michelle and Dino falter and they laugh because of it. He pats her hand that is resting on the table, sending a little shiver down her spine. The wine jug is empty, and Dino calls for a refill. Michelle, already rather light-headed, wonders if it is wise to drink more. It would be a shame to ruin such a lovely friendship with a drunken action, even though his kohl-rimmed eyes seem to be looking right into her soul.

Taking a toothpick from the holder, Dino pushes his chair away from the table and leans back. No sooner has he done this than a black and white cat jumps on his knee, reaching up with its nose to smooth its fur under his chin. Smiling, he strokes the cat and feeds it leftovers. Together they sit back and start on the second jug of wine, the candle on the table and the moon now the only source of light.

It is going to be very tricky saying goodnight

tonight.

Chapter 10

Kyria Zoe is sitting on the balcony at the top of the steps watching the sky.

She wishes them both goodnight and watches as they go to their rooms. Michelle feels like a naughty teenager, a mixture of indignation and thrill. She decides to enjoy the feeling, and it becomes all thrill.

Once in her room she reasons that things might have become a little clearer if Zoe had not been there, that their goodnight might have been more than just the briefest touch on her shoulder as he walked past to his room.

The very fact that Kyria Zoe is sitting there makes Michelle want to sneak past to Dino's room, just to be naughty. The idea makes her giggle. Dino would find it funny. She puts her hand on the doorknob, imagining herself and Dino peeping around the door to watch Zoe snoring, his hand slipping around her waist, him whispering close to her head, his lips touching her ear.

Shivering, she shakes her head and lets go of the doorknob. She is getting carried away, and not in a suitable direction. It must be the wine and a mix of being tired and the heat.

How long will Zoe remain sitting out there?

Michelle watches the fan on the ceiling of her room, mixing the night's heat to an even temperature, giving the illusion of cooling. The sheet is sticky against her legs. The heat, even in the night, is unrelenting. Thoughts of Dino sneaking to her room tease her. Maybe he is waiting for her, his door not completely shut, lying on his bed, hand behind his head. She could go and see if his fan works more efficiently than hers, perhaps the temperature in his room is more pleasant, he might have some water left cooling in his fridge …

The cool of the morning and a chorus of birdsong wakes her. There is a delicious chill to the air which will be snatched away as soon as the sun gains any height.

Kyria Zoe is no longer in her chair, and the chair itself has gone. Michelle giggles to herself. Fancy this Zoe woman seeing her as a child that needs to be watched. Or maybe it was Dino she was mostly watching, trying to protect her.

She laughs out loud, but there is a feeling of relief too.

'What's funny?' Ruffle-haired Dino pops his face around his door, a bare, smooth, hairless shoulder visible, just as tanned as his face. Her breath hangs in her lungs momentarily. She exhales to hiss: 'She's gone.'

'She doesn't want me to become Adonis.'

'Is he really that bad?'

'You can meet him.'

'Not sure I would feel safe.' She laughs again. Dino smiles, the skin around his eyes creasing, his dark eyes shining. He almost has a dimple on one side, but really it is a crease when he smiles. Everything about him speaks of his gentle nature, his controlled masculinity, almost as if he thinks he will harm people if he is not restrained. 'Are you up and dressed?'

He shakes his head and retreats into his room, closing the door behind him.

Splashing his face, he tries to bring some life to his eyes, which just want to shut. Kyria Zoe's vigilance last night was misguided. Sitting there, bolstered by her morals and ideals. Who is she to sit in judgement? Not all men are Adonis.

On the other hand, it might well have saved him from an embarrassing situation.

But Kyria Zoe sitting there was not so much a deterrent as a highlight to the possibilities. What else was he going to think of once shut in his cell with Kyria Zoe all but waving a flag outside his door?

It had not occurred to him to go to Michelle's room at night—until Zoe sat barring the way.

He shakes some of the creases out of his t-shirt and sniffs before putting it on. The reality is that Michelle is not likely to be attracted to someone as young and as poor as him.

Back in London she will be surrounded by expensively suited men with neatly cut hair and letters after their names. People who thrive in the rat race, who love to sit behind desks waiting for their bonuses, their promotions, who drive expensive cars to their big houses in the country at weekends. The truth is her life is sorted and he is just a kid in her eyes; the most she could see him as would be a toy, a distraction.

Glimpses. That's all he seems to ever get. Glimpses of a life that feels complete, warm, full. It may have been fourteen years of his life, but his time with Mama had also seemed like a glimpse, something special snatched away. The closeness he had had with his tutor at University was snatched away too. A sabbatical, she said.

On the cliff-face another glimpse. So close to her, all he could do for her, all he could give to her, if she would let him.

Maybe he is destined to be alone. Maybe that is his lot. Well, if so, that is his discomfort, but he will give her nothing but joy. He will give to her all he can so she will never know the emptiness of loneliness, at least not while she is with him.

'It's a hot one.' She greets him and smiles as he shuts the door to his room behind him. The smile that makes the world seem brighter.

'Breakfast?' He smiles, as many fears fall away simply by not thinking about them.

The shop has so many lovely things. The handmade dresses are beautiful in soft, flowing

148

fabric, but she would never have the chance to wear them. England is too cold, and besides, she lives in her suit.

There are wickerwork bowls of trinkets displayed on coffee tables in front of the clothes rails. A very large and extremely fluffy longhaired cat sprawls on the chair next to Dino's.

'Look at these.' She admires a display of handmade ceramic doorknobs. They would look great on her bathroom cabinet. Then every morning she would remember this moment, in this low-ceilinged front room that has been converted into a very personal shop. Beautiful Dino lounging, waiting for her, his long legs crossed at the ankles, his sleepy eyes watching her every move. This self-indulgent mindset is very enjoyable, she smiles to herself.

'OK, come on, long enough in here.' Michelle pays for the knob.

'No rush.' Dino shows very little inclination to move, but once she is handed the small rope-handled bag with the ceramic 'find' wrapped in tissue inside, he is on his feet offering to carry it for her. Their fingers become intertwined in the passing and Michelle does not hurry her escape. Dino gives a nervous laugh.

He leads the way through the maze of houses like it is a child's game, up three steps, along, down two, back three, across the small square, third on the right.

She can imagine him as a child, with the same

149

haircut, perhaps a little shorter, his limbs a little more gangly, in shorts, not jeans. It is unbelievable he doesn't have a girlfriend. Or maybe he does!

'Dino, you have a girl?' she blurts out, and immediately regrets her lack of subtlety.

'Yes,' he replies.

Her stomach drops and her knees lose strength. She puts her hand out to steady herself around the corner. He turns and grins at her.

'You.' He winks.

Michelle's smile returns, and with it a ridiculous spasm of hope that he means it. She stops for a minute to catch her breath. Dino walks on a few steps, oblivious. As she watches his back, his easy, youthful stride, she considers how ridiculous she is in allowing herself to get so emotionally wrapped up in this boy. It can only lead to pain, and certainly not to anything long-term. And yet, she knows she is not likely to do anything to protect herself—or him.

He leads up some wide steps that culminate in a double door, one leaf of which is open. The courtyard beyond is broad and is paved in large black and white marble slabs, worn around the entrance. He pauses at the door and turns to look back, motioning Michelle to do the same. The view is down towards the harbour, the panorama of houses, boats, and the sea curving away on each side, bright in the sun.

Michelle wipes her forehead on the back of her arm. The heat is intense out of the shade of the alleys and in the glare of the sun.

The town is a perfect 'U' around the port, like the pictures of the ancient Greek theatres, only this one is stepped with houses instead of stone seats. It is so perfect she tries to forcibly take in every detail, save the moment forever.

When she turns around, Dino is nowhere to be seen. The mansion's front doors stand open, and beside them is a notice. It's in English, too, and it announces that the house was built by a wealthy sea captain, and that it is now open to the public. Michelle doesn't stop to read the history or dates. Where's Dino?

Inside is cool, with no one at the entrance desk in the vestibule. The inner doors lead to a long hall, also tiled black and white, with heavy wooden furniture placed here and there between internal doors that lead off to rooms beyond. The first room on the right is labelled 'The Admiral's Office', and it has a fine, high ceiling and windows overlooking the port. She steps in.

'Ah, there you are. Quick, take this bag of gold and drop it down the well, I see pirates coming.' Dino stands by the window with a brass telescope to his eye. She stifles the urge to tell him that he should not touch the artefacts.

'Down the well?'

'The pirates never looked down the well. They say the gold has plugged all the springs and that is why the island no longer has water. A punishment for greed.'

They turn to leave the room, and Michelle jumps at the sight of a curator sitting passively behind the door. She looks back at the telescope, which Dino has replaced on the desk.

They wander from room to room. Dino is the admiral, and Michelle tries to be a domestic servant of some sort. Game-playing was never her forte.

In the kitchen the wellhead stands in the middle of the room, a carved stone ring, standing to knee height from the floor, and topped with a wooden cover. Dino lifts off the cover and they peer in, but there is nothing to see but blackness.

'Did they really drop their gold down there?'

'Yes.'

'How did they get it out again?'

Dino shrugs, lithe and supple.

'Some say it hasn't all been retrieved, that there is still treasure down some of the wells.'

'Do you believe that?'

They are both leaning over looking down the well, heads close together. Dino puts his arm around her. She dare not move. He pushes her forward. She loses balance. Heels off, falling. His arms around her waist, pulling her back. Letting her free.

'Saved you.' He grins.

'So childish,' she blurts. She slaps her hand to her mouth and turns away, but he just laughs.

As the day cools into the evening, Michelle

feels a certain relief. Her skin continues to glow as they stroll to the *taverna*.

Dino picks the table nearest to the path overlooking the harbour and pulls out a chair for Michelle.

'This *taverna* has the best view in all of Greece,' he announces.

As well as the view, he wants her to experience the food he has grown up with, to taste the '*moschari kokkinisto*'—veal in a tomato sauce. Hopefully the dish is still as good as it always has been, as good as his own mother's always was. He wants her to try the '*briam*', the perfect mix of roast vegetables. He will order a selection of side dishes, too; she must try everything.

A woman comes to the door of the *taverna*, wiping her hands on her apron.

'*Kokino krasi*.' He gently calls his order for red wine. His hope is Michelle will have the perfect dinner, which will be followed by the most perfect sunset, as it always is from here. The sky will turn orange, then deeper into red, and the islands dotted in the sea will hover before turning purple and then black, along with the water.

The woman brings a jug of wine and two small glasses.

'Hello,' she says in English to Michelle. The "h" is guttural. Michelle smiles. The woman leaves them in order to go to one of the terracotta pots, where she picks a flower and returns to give it to Michelle, who gasps and smiles again.

'How do I say thank you?' she asks Dino. 'Oh no, hang on. I remember.' She turns back to the lady *'Aferritstoes.'* She smiles, the woman tilts her head and smiles back.

'Efharisto,' Dino prompts.

'Oh yes, *Efharisto.*' She grins; the woman smiles and nods.

Dino orders all the dishes he has missed whilst being in England: peppers stuffed with feta, *pastichio*, and *'gigantes'* —butter beans in a tomato sauce. He is aware he is ordering too much for two people and asks for each to be a half-portion. The woman dismisses him. She has seen it all before, she knows how it works, 'All Greeks order too much,' she says to him. 'The tables groan under the weight of food and they sit there for hours after they have finished eating, picking over the remains. It's good.' And she bustles away.

Dino pours more wine and sits back to gaze at the view.

'What do you think of the island so far then?' he asks.

'It's really quite odd there being no roads and no cars or bikes. I love the grandeur of the mansions next to the island houses.'

'Nice feeling, isn't it?' Dino sips his wine, lounging on his chair, legs crossed at their ankles in front of him.

'It's amazing. Part of chasing the whole

154

"Lawyer in London" bit for me was to get away from the places we lived in, such as Bradford, which I saw as being really old-fashioned. There are mills everywhere from the days when it was a centre for the wool trade, and tiny, terraced houses close to them for the mill workers.' She pauses to admire the view.

'It's so quiet.' She sips her wine. 'There was one mill still working when I was a kid. If you walked past it you wouldn't believe the noise of the machinery, shuttles slamming back and forth, the whole thing run on leather straps turning wheels, all powered by a waterwheel outside. You had to shout as loud as you could to be heard.' She sighs. 'It's a museum now.'

They sit in silence for a while.

'That's what made me hate all things old: the mills, our tiny mill house, Bradford. Richard had to talk me into that house in London, I wanted something modern. Old meant dead—or dying. But this …' She waves her hand across the sea and the little harbour, the *taverna*, and the silence.

Dino says nothing; he is thinking of what old means to him. Old was like his Baba, old in his head, old in his way of thinking, old in how rigid his beliefs are.

One very good reason to not want to grow up was the possibility of turning out like him, but that wasn't going to happen.

155

He would never shout at a child as his Baba had done.

His Baba had raised his voice on several occasions after Mama was gone, shouted that Dino had to grow up, screamed that he couldn't sit and cry, that he had to face life like a man. But all Dino could think of was losing his Mama. His Baba trying to force him to 'man up' was just another way of saying 'let go', and he could never do that. His schoolwork had suffered; there seemed little point. Planning for the future was just a false sense of assurance that life could be controlled, when it can't. He only worked after that to keep his Baba off his back; the joy, the interest in learning was gone.

He looks down at the table. Michelle's hand rests there. He wants to pick it up, feel the soft flesh, the bones beneath, the life it represents.

He puts his hand on top of hers.

'I am very happy it makes you happy,' he says. Michelle looks down at her hand.

'*Ena stifado*.' The woman pushes between them and all but drops the hot dish on the table. '*Mia gigantes.*' She jostles back inside. Dino cannot look at Michelle, but he can feel she is looking at him. He wills her not to say anything. Whatever she says, he cannot answer. If she asks why his hand was on hers, he cannot answer. If she asks what they are doing here this evening, at a *taverna* together, he cannot answer. He concentrates hard on looking out to sea, but she has not taken her attention from his face. He

156

takes the knives and forks from the basket of bread that the woman had placed on the table, and passes Michelle her cutlery.

'Here you go. Stuffed peppers, bread, *tatziki*, and I bring you some olives from our trees.' She places a dish of olives by Michelle and smiles as she speaks, the words bubbling in her chest.

The table is laden, and Dino is relieved that the focus is elsewhere.

Michelle helps herself to a little bit of everything, piling it onto her plate. Dino picks up the empty wine jug and holds it out to the woman, who is resting on a very fragile-looking wooden chair by the door of her *taverna*. She scrambles to get up; a cat at her feet runs behind one of the plant pots. The woman loses one of her slippers as she stands, and she huffs as she tries to push her toes back in, the slipper sliding away. She corners it against the pot, and once it is firmly back on, she strides over to take the jug.

'The other thing that made me become a lawyer was safety.' She looks out to sea, the feelings rather than the memories so fresh.

'Tell me,' Dino prompts.

'I was just remembering how wild Juliet became.' And she tells him how she and Juliet skipped off school one day, and how that one day turned into two.

'Come on, let's be bunking off school, it's

boring. You tell your Mam you're at mine, and I'll tell mine I'm at yours.'

Michelle was horrified, said she couldn't do it. It didn't faze Juliet one bit.

'OK, tomorrow, I'll sort your Mam,' and they went in to tea.

'Hello, Mr Marsden.'

'Hello, Juliet, Michelle. How was school?'

'Good, thanks. Sausage rolls, brilliant. Hey Mr Marsden, is it alright if Mich stays at mine tomorrow night?'

'You mean a sleep-over?'

Juliet was always braver than Michelle.

The next morning Michelle found herself reluctantly on a train to London.

'I can't wait. They're right good, come all the way from Sweden.' They didn't have tickets, but Juliet felt sure she could wangle them at the gate.

'Wembley stadium, bloody huge. Did you see them on Top of Pops last Thursday?' and they began to sing: 'Take a chance on me...' into imaginary mikes.

King's Cross was positively overwhelming, busier and more full of people than anything Michelle had ever seen, and she hung onto Juliet's coat so they wouldn't be separated. They spent ages trying to make sense of the underground map until Juliet gave in and asked a stranger to explain it. He was very patient and took his time but finished by saying, 'Ought you two not be at school?' and then his eyebrows had risen in the same way that Mr Eldridge the geography teacher's did. Quick as a flash Juliet retorted, 'It's alright Mister, it's orienteering day,' and squeezed Michelle's hand so as not to laugh.

They spent a good few hours getting lost on the tube, and when they finally found Wembley Stadium it was closed. 'It's next week,' said a man sweeping leaves, and he pointed to a poster. Juliet had argued, as she always did, but he just shrugged and carried on sweeping.

The milkshake they bought in a little café nearby had been like nectar. They were so hungry, but there wasn't enough money for food too.

'Go on, take the drinks to the young ladies,' the man behind the counter had urged his son. Juliet had winked at him just as he was lowering the glasses to the table, and one shot forward, covering her with pink froth.

'What ya do that for?' She laughed, but the boy, not much older than them, couldn't stop apologising and tried to wipe down her jumper with a damp cloth.

'Hey!' Juliet pushed his hands off her chest. The apologising began again and Juliet started to giggle.

'They gave us a fry-up on the house,' Michelle tells Dino, 'by way of apology, and more milkshakes.'

Back out in the cold and grey of a London

afternoon, the girls felt suddenly tired and homesick, and made their way back to the train station.

'What do you mean we don't have the money to get back?' Michelle almost screeched.

'Have you got any?'

'I had a quid for my lunch.'

'Well how did you think we were going to pay for it?'

'I didn't. How much have you got?'

'Mum left her purse in the kitchen, but I couldn't hardly take it all, could I?'

Michelle felt all the fried food turn in her stomach, but Juliet didn't even blink.

'Come on, we'll hitch.' And with that she ran off in the direction of the underground, Michelle straggling behind. No one seemed to care that they ducked the barriers. They surfaced at Watford.

Everything with Juliet used to happen in a whirl back then.

They walked for a bit, but the light was fading, and soon it was dark. No cars stopped to pick them up. Juliet had not batted an eye at finding a doorway out of the wind, and together they huddled up and spent, for Michelle anyway, a rather sleepless night. In the morning they got a lift from a trucker who told them they were going the wrong way and took them to a transport café where they were faced with a room full of burly men, their sleeves rolled up, tattoos exposed, tucking into egg and chips and huge steaming cups of tea. Michelle sat and pulled her

160

school skirt down as far as it would go, but Juliet grinned as they drank their tea, bought and paid for by the truck driver.

'Oi, listen up.' The truck driver stood at the counter and called out into the room. 'Got two young un's here, need a lift home to Bradford. Anyone going?'

'Pair of skivers,' someone had shouted, and laughter rippled round the room. Michelle felt heat in her cheeks, and looked at the floor.

'What, and you were Einstein?' came a reply.

'I'm going to Sheffield,' another barked.

'I'll take them, got a delivery for Grattans in Bradford. They'll have to sit back though; not meant to have passengers,' said a third man, from the back of the room.

'Sitting back' meant cross-legged on the sleeping bunk behind the seats.

'Cool.' Juliet climbed straight in. Michelle found it a bit more difficult as she was taller. Before they were far out of London she must have dropped off, as the next thing she recalled was Juliet pulling her sleeve and telling her, 'We're home.' Literally, as the truck driver had made a small detour right to Juliet's house.

They waved him off. Juliet's parents were out, so they raided the cupboards and feasted on a packet of biscuits, a lump of cheese, and a jar of pickled onions, and watched the late film—*Roman Holiday* with Audrey Hepburn—after which they cut each other's hair so they could sport *Roman Holiday* fringes for school the next day. Most of their classmates laughed at them, but Juliet walked with her head held high, arm in arm with Michelle. Michelle felt so proud of her friend and quite forgot to be embarrassed by her own Hepburn fringe. Her parents had voiced their displeasure at the haircut at tea that night, and Juliet was banned from the house for a week.

'But you know, the overriding feeling it left me with? The fear that still stays with me to this day? In the dark of that night, other homeless people had passed and tried to make conversation with us. Not young people like us but middle-aged people. People who had lost their jobs and ended up homeless, people who had no mums and dads to return to, people who lived that way night after night.' Michelle recalls the dread, the real fear of being homeless, of being lost in that situation, devoid of hope.

Dino looks as if he is about to say something but changes his mind and holds out his glass. Michelle picks up the full wine jug, and as she does so she looks out to sea. Dino follows her gaze. The sky is darkening and the most distant islands are turning purple against a pinking sky.

'We are both in the same place, you and I,' Dino begins. He feels that perhaps he should have eaten something before drinking half a jug of wine.

But Michelle replies before he finishes what he was going to say.

'Yes, in a perfect *taverna* on a perfect island with a perfect view.' Michelle raises her glass.

'With perfect company.' Dino smiles and touches his wine glass to hers. They look at each other for a moment, listening as a donkey on the hills brays, a soulful lost sound that dwindles to a wheeze.

Kyria Zoe is not sitting outside. Tonight her lights are off and the pair are alone outside Michelle's door.

In the light of the moon she is stunning, regal, her back straight even though she has had a good deal too much wine. Poised. Maybe she did ballet? Maybe she still does, there is so much he doesn't know about her.

But there is something he does know. She is way too special for a clumsy manoeuvre of the type Adonis would try. She deserves far more respect than that.

Maybe he should use words, or just a kiss, on the cheek perhaps?

If he kisses her hand, will that be too smooth? She has opened her door, now is the time. She is looking at him, expectantly. Or is that the wine and his imagination?

He brushes his fringe across, out of his eyes, looks at her, but cannot maintain eye contact.

'Goodnight, Michelle.' It comes out all of a rush. His cheeks feel hot. He has drunk too much

163

wine. He marches to his own room and shuts himself
in.

Chapter 11

Sunday

The next day passes like a dream. They drink coffee in the harbour, go to a *taverna* under a huge fig tree for lunch, while away the afternoon. Michelle doesn't care where she is or what she is doing. Inside her head, she is having an affair with Dino, a cerebral romance until she has to return to Athens. She is soaking up being with him, delighting that she has his company. All the feelings of love, but with a switch-off time and date, so no one gets hurt or embarrassed. He need never know. She will not one day lay on her deathbed regretting she never lived; from now on she will allow every feeling that comes her way. She just might not share them.

'You want to meet Adonis tonight?'

'OK.' She doesn't mind one way or the other.

The bar Adonis is working in is playing soulful jazz, the interior lit with red bulbs, the decoration dark, earthy hues. It is very bohemian.

They sit on the rush-seated wooden chairs outside. All the traditional Greek wooden sofas with their curvy backs have been taken, their ample cushions drawing the early birds to lounge in the open air and watch the people walking up and down the alley.

A waiter comes to serve them, and Michelle instinctively knows it is not Adonis. He smiles when he sees Dino, shakes his hand, argues in Greek, slaps him on the shoulder, and goes back inside, throwing his circular tray up in the air, end on, and catching it.

When Adonis appears, he is exactly as she imagined. Taller and leaner than Dino, he walks like a model.

Dino covers his mouth with his hand and whispers, 'He's done modelling, can you tell?' and sniggers.

Adonis has the straightest nose Michelle has ever seen.

And then he smiles.

All the stars are extinguished, the world recedes, the girls from several of the tables around them turn his way, his hips respond by rolling as he walks. Michelle groans inwardly at the sight of him.

The same graceful arrogance of Richard, the sort of charm that makes women flirt even when they don't want to. An unforgivable sense of superiority based purely on the looks he was born with. She takes a drink of wine and braces herself.

'Hey Dino ...' and then he speaks in Greek. No arguing tones here, a slow drawl, words continuing into each other seamlessly and without breath.

'This is Michelle; Michelle, Adonis.'

She tenses. He scans every laughter line, the length of her hair, the size of her breasts, her unpolished fingernails, her shaved legs and then back to her lips, which she licks in nervousness and then wishes she hadn't. See! Men like this always make you flirt. Until they know you and then they expect you to pick up their dry-cleaning and compete with you on the work front, and all that charm disappears.

It was Richard's father who brought about the marriage. She had dated Richard on and off, when he was free, and then, one lunchtime, he had come up with the idea of cohabiting, out of the blue it seemed. Their joint salaries could afford a much better place to live than the flats they each rented at the time. As soon as she returned to her office, Michelle did a brief, but excited, online search of some practical places near to work. She was thirty and old enough to know better, but up until then her life had been all work and no play, and her clock was ticking, as they say. She e-mailed her finds. He was uninterested in any of her suggestions and after a few days she began to think maybe he wasn't serious. But the following Sunday he had turned up in his Jag and took her for a drive. Lunch, he said, at a country pub.

She skipped lunch that day. There was no pub, but there was the crumbling Grade I listed house he had lined up to see. To Michelle it had looked like a castle after all the council houses she had lived in with her family, sharing a bedroom with Penny, fighting for space. Richard said it was the sort of place they deserved, considering the hours they put into work, and besides, with a house like this they would never have to upgrade.

But it was too far from work, needed lots of attention, and in any case, they could not afford the deposit. So that was that, or so she thought.

The next weekend they went up to Richard's family home for lunch, which was a rare occurrence and not one to which Michelle looked forward. On her last visit the entire conversation revolved around a monologue by Richard's father about his personal experience of trap-racing and horses until, fearing the onset of rigor mortis, Michelle excused herself on the pretext of finding the toilet. To her delight, she got lost and spent the only pleasant half-hour of the day talking to a girl from Barnsley in a maid's uniform, who was having a quick cigarette in what she told her was the original pantry. This room, the girl had said, in a broad familiar accent, hadn't been used since 1915 when the family had bought one of the first fridges to be imported into the country, from America she thought, or was it Germany? Michelle had almost been on the point of sharing her last cigarette with the Barnsley girl as the whole situation reminded her of being in the pavilion with Juliet when they had played hooky from assembly.

Eventually she pulled herself away and returned to the drawing room to be greeted like a long lost child by Richard's father, with the words:

'Isn't it about time you two settle down?' His arm around her, his fingers exploring the little bit of extra weight she kept around her middle back then.

On the next visit the same topic was brought up but this time, to Michelle's surprise, Richard replied, 'Talking of which, Dad, I have found the most perfect house,' and he poured himself another whisky.

'Well there you are. Time to make an honest woman of this girl.' His fingers moving up to her ribcage trying to find their way further around the front.

Michelle pulled free and reached out a hand on Richard's forearm as his words were already slurring and he always insisted on being the driver on the way home.

'That house is way out of our league.' She smiled, mostly glad that she had established herself by Richard's side at arm's length from his father. Richard's mother had helped herself to yet another sherry and sat down again without a word.

'We could afford the mortgage payments if we only had the deposit.' Richard had put his own arm around her shoulders at that point, his hand limp; she was a resting post.

'Well come on then, how much is the deposit? I am happy to splash out for a wedding present.' His father had laughed from his belly, refilling his own tumbler. 'Mother, there's no ice,' he announced to his wife. Richard's mother had gone to the door and opened it to quietly call someone called Brenda, who turned out to be the cigarette-smoking maid, and who was dispatched to bring ice.

'My God, Richard, this is a day to celebrate, bridling a good, level-headed, down-to-earth girl like Michelle here. You have asked her then?'

'Well not exactly but hey, you are up for it aren't you Mich?' He didn't wait for an answer. 'So, is that a deal then, Dad? Actually, it would be a lot more useful to have the deposit as an engagement present.'

'Ha! You think I don't know you're a slippery pup.' He cast a brief glance at Michelle before patting a guiding hand on Richard's back. 'Let's go into my office, my boy. We can smooth it all out in there.' The two of them, disarmingly similar in height and build, sloped off, with the same gait, into his file-lined office and closed the door.

Richard's mother had offered her more sherry whilst filling her own glass. Michelle had declined, and they sat in silence listening to the voices behind the polished wooden door laughing and bantering until, eventually, the money was agreed. Father-in-law-to-be added a proviso on the gift, giving Richard five years to be properly wed. Richard came out with a signed contract.

'Congratulations, my dear,' Richard's father had said before turning to Richard to say, 'You have a good settling influence now; you will be a better man for it.' His head jerking in her direction to indicate what, or rather, whom, he meant.

Michelle had searched her feelings and her

motives, but each time there was the seductive promise of stability. Richard's excitement over the house that soon became their home was contagious. It really all had had the promise of happy ever after.

They married five years later to the day.

Adonis takes her hand and raises it to his lips, maintaining eye contact. Michelle wants to snatch her hand back but Dino is looking on, and for his sake she bears it. He grins as he releases her hand and Michelle, quite spontaneously, tells a lie.

'Oh, you seem to have something green between your teeth. Lettuce perhaps?' She smiles innocently. If only she had ever been brave enough to say such a thing to Richard. Ha!

He colours in a second and puts a hand over his mouth as he sucks his teeth. Michelle is a little shocked at her own deceit.

Adonis is at the end of his shift, and the three of them stroll around the harbour and up to the top of the hill that flanks the far side. Here a remote single-storey mansion had been turned into a disco, but the shutters are closed tight, the place looks dead.

The noise jumps out at them as they open the door, the *bouzouki* in a refrain that the locals are singing along to, a line of people arm over shoulder snaking around the dance floor, flicking their feet out in front of them every so often, following the steps.

'Ah, Adonis.' Dino laughs. Michelle casts him an enquiring look and he points. Adonis has already joined the line of dancers, his head thrown back, lost

171

in the music. Dino leads her to a table and orders a jug of wine from a passing waiter.

As he holds out a chair for her to sit, she can feel herself pulled in the opposite direction. She stumbles as she is dragged bodily into the line, Adonis' arm around her shoulders to support her, a girl in a blue dress on her other side. Michelle trots to avoid falling over her feet, performs a remarkable full twist, freeing herself from all arms, and slides smoothly back to the waiting chair.

Dino applauds her manoeuvre.

Once seated and with her glass filled, she watches the dancers' feet. To her surprise, the steps look quite easy. The girl in blue is English, and each time she passes she makes comments in an East London twang as she gets the steps. As Adonis passes, he looks at Michelle and smiles, beckoning her with a head movement. She rolls her eyes; his slick moves lack sincerity. And yet, there is still something charismatic about him. She looks away. She labels him dangerous but only half thinks these thoughts and soon she is not thinking at all. It's still hot and the wine flows down her throat like water. She watches the dancers snake out of the nightclub doors, each in the line looking forward, past Adonis, to see where they are going. There is a fumbling behind her and she sees Dino has risen from his chair and slid his way between a waiter and a large lady.

He is grinning. They snake out into the night sky, through the open door, then weave between the olive trees. Adonis pulls into the line a man who is tethering a donkey for the night. He takes the lead for two or three steps before breaking away back to his work smiling, and the line snakes its way back inside. The musky aroma mixes with the wine in her system until Michelle is completely lost in the moment. Just conscious enough to feel carefree.

By the bar the line breaks up, the dancers laughing, falling into seats, and the *bouzouki* player takes a well-earned rest. He downs a full glass of water and two shots of *ouzo* before lighting a cigarette.

Adonis drops himself into a chair at their table, grinning, languid, smooth. Dino is chatting to a man of about his own age.

Another *bouzouki* player joins the group of musicians: a younger man, shirt open down his chest, a medallion completing the cliché. When he begins to play, there is a different feel to the music.

'*Opa!*' Adonis expels. He stands again and takes to the centre of the dance floor, his arms wide, stretched out, at shoulder height, his wrists limp, fingers clicking, his head bowed. One by one, the other dancers shuffle to prop up the walls as Adonis commands the floor, his passion, his grace, his vitality entrancing all around him. He stomps and kicks, slaps his ankles behind him and slaps the floor in front of him. He spins and throws his head back, observing a tradition of generations past. His energy grows as the music gains momentum, his movements

173

more aggressive. He is no longer Adonis the waiter. Instead he is a hunter, a barbarian, a Greek warrior, and proud of it.

The hypnotised cheer as the music comes to an end. Adonis is spent, breathing heavily.

The transformed crowd settles, wandering off to replenish their glasses, regain their seats, talk about what has just happened. Adonis rejoins Dino, and several people pass him shot glasses, which he slams back one after the other, sweat running from his forehead. He passes the shot glasses to Dino and Michelle. They both accept. She tips her head back and her throat burns pleasantly. Looking around the room, she feels satisfied with everything in the moment.

The music fades a little. Adonis slaps Dino on the back and pours them all more wine. He tries to make eye contact with Michelle.

'So you are loving England really, eh Dino?' Adonis asks, she can tell that his English is good, and Michelle wonders if the accent is something he cultivates.

'Hey Dino, that you? You are here! Welcome home my friend.'

'Illias, hey! How is the wood shop going?' Dino greets the newcomer.

'Work is not so good, but I am married now.' He pulls his hand from Dino's grasp and holds up his fingers to show a ring to prove it. 'Florentia.' He nods to a pretty, tiny girl standing by the bar with a group of friends, who Dino vaguely recognises from school. She clearly only has eyes for her husband, her head swivelling like a bird's every few seconds to smile over to him.

'Congratulations, Illia.'

'Thank you. Are you staying?'

'He wants to stay,' Adonis says.

Ilias spits on the ground. 'What do you want to come here for? There is no work. Stay in England, don't make a mistake … find an English girl. Marriage is a wonderful thing, you should try it Dino. Don't end up a lonely bachelor like our friend Adonis here.' He grins at Adonis, expecting a rise, but Adonis tuts and turns his head away. 'Seriously, Dino, it is amazing. Life feels settled, content. We have no money, but …' He trails off, and then breaks into a broad grin. 'Ah!' he shouts into Dino's ear, above the music, 'I heard you have been taking riding lessons in England. But you have forgotten how we do it here in Greece ….' And with this he pats Dino on his shoulder and leaves, almost hurrying, with long, easy, light strides. Dino scowls in the direction of the bar where Ilias is now embracing Florentia.

The club is smoky and dark, the music a fraction too loud. There are mirrors on the wall, and the walls are painted black. The bar is all mirrors, but somehow it all looks a little homemade, not the cosmopolitan place it is trying to be. Flashy by island standards but slightly funny compared to anything in London.

Michelle tries to picture Adonis in London. He would be lost, not just geographically but in his style, a lamb amongst wolves. They would undo his cool and eat him alive in seconds.

Dino would fit in more. He may be an island boy, but there is more to him somehow.

Dino absent-mindedly picks up Michelle's hand with his own and explores her nails with his other hand, Adonis and the club recede, the wine swims in her system, giving the world fuzzy edges, smoothing her emotions until there is only Dino.

Adonis looks at their intertwined hands and sniggers.

'I need the gents.' Dino lets go of her fingers, kicks his chair back, and stomps across the room. His sudden departure leaves her hand exposed, palm up on the table, her mouth open.

Adonis moves his chair closer to hers.

Chapter 12

'So how long are you here?' Adonis asks.

'Just till the end of the week.' Michelle feels ever so slightly dizzy.

'So you have cast your line and he is dangling on the hook. Will you reel him in, take him off the hook, and throw him back, or will you leave him floundering on a long line?'

'What?' Is it the wine or is what he is saying not making much sense? Besides, what has it got to do with him?

'You heard.' He smiles, but there is no merriment.

'I heard, but I find it hard to believe. What business is it of yours?'

'He's my friend and I do not want to see him hurt.'

'I have no plans to hurt him.'

'Listen, you are a commanding-looking woman. You have grace that comes only with maturity. Dino is a young man, younger than me, even though we are the same age. He will not truly appreciate what is special about you. I, on the other hand ....' He shifts his chair even nearer. Michelle splutters into her wine glass.

For a moment she is speechless. So Dino is

interested! He must be, for Adonis to be saying the things he is saying. A smile plays about her mouth but she suppresses it; Adonis is also making a play, which seems unbelievable. It's very flattering, of course, but what is to be believed from a player like Adonis? Is it from jealousy that she is taking his friend away, or from the dent in his ego that Dino has 'got a girl'? Whatever the motive, it is no way to behave. She finds her voice.

'You, on the other hand, are no friend of Dino's if this is how you act behind his back.'

'Ha! You and I are people of the world. Tourists pass through here in the thousands, one very like the next, I know. But the same for you, young men must be attracted to you often, one very like the next. All I am saying is if you want to play, I am here, but not Dino. He has had enough hurt.'

Michelle's mouth drops open and she searches around in her head for her next words, which she knows will come out with force.

'Here you go.' Dino hands them a shot glass each before looking from Michelle to Adonis and back again.

'To love.' Adonis smirks looking sideways at Michelle as Dino sits.

'To love.' Dino answers back looking at Michelle. She hesitates. 'What, you don't believe in love?' Dino asks her.

'To love.' She says it quietly and looks directly at the shot glass.

178

'*Yia Mas.*' Adonis jerks his head back as he drinks, and slams the glass on the table.

Dino follows suit, Michelle drinks two sips and returns hers to the table, half full. Dino smiles at her, shifting his chair nearer to her on the opposite side to Adonis. Adonis pulls his chair forward again too.

'You know, I think I need to go.' Michelle is not finding the attention very pleasant. It has been two years since the relief of no longer having to deal with Richard and his little games, and she is not about to be pulled into the same arena by anyone else. Life is too short, as recent events have all too clearly shown.

Dino stands as she does.

'No, it's OK. I can walk myself home. Anyway, I need the loo first.' She staggers toward the sign by the bar, surprised at how tipsy she is, and relieved to be alone.

'Not a good choice, my friend. She will use you and dump you.' Adonis leans away to the table next to theirs, taps the man sitting there on the shoulder, and mimes smoking a cigarette. The man hesitates, but the girl sitting with him complies. Adonis smiles his thanks. Her eyes shine.

'I thought you had given up.' Dino speaks without looking at him.

'Did you hear me?' Adonis presses his point. The girl passes him a light; he looks up into her eyes as his cigarette catches.

'I think with your track record, you are no one

to be preaching.' Dino inches his chair away from the smoke.

'What do you know of love? This one is old enough to be your mother. Or is that what you want?'

Dino glares, hands making fists. He clenches and unclenches his jaw. 'Shut up, Adonis.' He snarls the words.

'Soon as you left the table, she had eyes only for me, her hand on my arm, sidling up to me, our thighs touching. Just your average tourist.'

'You're lying.' Dino spits. Adonis shrugs.

'Just warning you,' he says, but he cannot meet Dino's stare. Instead, he looks around the bar, feigning interest in everything until his gaze is caught by a table where three girls sit, in a far corner.

Seeing Michelle walking across the room to the exit, Dino stands, finishes his drink in a gulp, picks a couple of choice Greek words for Adonis, and trots, in not quite a straight line, across to catch her up.

Outside the moon is bright and the stars are out in their millions. Dino slings his arm around Michelle's shoulders and she does not push him off. They begin to stroll. Their steps get slower, they stop. For the briefest of moments she wonders where Adonis is, but the thought drifts away before it really lodges. Dino turns to her. The wine mixed with the fresh air makes everything spin. Michelle wonders if she will make it back to Zoe's. Maybe slowly, in stages. She looks up above Dino's face, past the silhouetted olive tree to the ink infinity beyond.

There is a tingle on her lips, her senses swim, her eyes are blind, her ears deaf, nothing but sensations. Warmth flows the length of her body, belonging, engulfed. A shiver runs down her spine. She is sinking, her legs weakening until a silent roar comes from deep within and she surfaces out of a sea of exhilaration and opens her eyes. Pupil to pupil, nose to nose. This can only end badly.

Dino steps away from her abruptly.

'Good night then.' Adonis' distant pleasantry has a tone. Dino shouts something in Greek, his face scrunching into a growl. Michelle cannot remember the last time she was this drunk.

Adonis repeats his goodnights, but this time Dino does not answer. Michelle figures they have had words.

'Hizjealous.' Her slurring surprises her. So reckless. She needs to drink some water or coffee.

The walk back to Zoe's becomes progressively easier; the air and the movement add life to her limbs. It's not that she has drunk a lot, it's just that she is not used to drinking so much anymore. Gone are the days with Juliet getting so drunk they couldn't stand, staying out all night.

'You all right?' Dino asks.

'Yes, fine. You? What's Adonis' problem?' She takes her time to annunciate each word. There seem to be too many esses.

'He's being ... did you ... no, forget it ... *Malaka*.' He finishes, turning his head in the direction Adonis disappeared.

Arm in arm he helps Michelle up the steps at Zoe's. Kyria Zoe's light is on and her door is ajar. He treads more lightly and takes most of Michelle's weight. As he is opening Michelle's door, Kyria Zoe steps from her own chambers into the moonlight, glowing in a loose, long-sleeved, floor-length nightdress. She stretches, the moon in her white hair.

'Ah, good evening, Dino.'

Hastily he unhooks Michelle's arm from around the back of his neck and with a gentle push towards her bed, he lets go of her and closes her door after her. He does not need Kyria Zoe's pious opinions after Adonis' selfish ones.

'Good night, Kyria Zoe.' He takes hold of the ornate metal balcony handrail to ensure a steady walk to his room. He feels the years of paint, the layers that have taken away all the edges and details, smooth beneath his hand. He keeps this his focus until he reaches his door, which he opens and calls again. 'Good night, Kyria Zoe.'

Laying on his back, he feels the room spin slightly. Outside it is hot enough for the cicadas to still be rasping. Bloody Adonis. It is fine for him to be with girl after girl, each summer a new set of tourists, his playground. But the moment Dino finds someone

....

He flops over onto his stomach on the ungiving mattress and tries to peel his t-shirt off without getting up. He takes a breath with one arm still in the armhole, the rest around his neck.

Beautiful Michelle. Who is Adonis to tell him what to do? Or Kyria Zoe, for that matter? He rolls off the bed onto his feet and straightens, pulls his t-shirt completely off, and throws it in the direction of the chair but misses. He rubs his hands up and down his chest and strides to the door. He opens it cautiously. The moon is behind a tall eucalyptus tree, casting shadows along the balcony, the tree's leaves hissing in the night's stirrings. All else is quiet.

Tiptoeing, he makes his way towards Michelle's door. There is the sound of something small rustling in the courtyard below.

'Can't you sleep?' A voice creaks.

In the shadows Dino sees a mattress and a person lying on the balcony.

'If you are too hot, I don't mind if you put your bedding out on the balcony. It's the only way I can sleep this time of year.'

'Oh, er, yes, too hot. Just needed some air really, Kyria Zoe. Right, I'll say goodnight then.' His room after this seems like the safer option, but the bed is just as uncomfortable. The morning light sneaks in before his eyes close.

If self-indulgence gives her this size of

183

headache, she wants no more of it. If she moves, the room spins. Coffee would be great, but she cannot face the walk down to the harbour.

There is a tap on the door. She can tell it is a tap by its resonance, but it might as well be a gong or canon. Water, she needs water first and foremost.

'Can I come in?' Just Dino's head appears around the door, smiling. 'Oh dear, are you all right?'

Did she imagine it or did they ... Adonis saying goodnight from far away, Dino's arm around her waist. Oh my goodness, they had, they did. They kissed. Her chest trembles and her stomach twists. Horror and thrill. Pleasure and pain. There is no way this is going to end smoothly. She has to go to Athens a week from today. She won't get a chance to see Juliet, talk it over, make some sense; it is all going horribly wrong.

'Dino, we need to talk.'

With a coffee in each hand and a bottle of water under his arm, Dino pushes the door open with his shoulder. He is grinning, his hair in his eyes, his jeans around his hips. He still hasn't replaced the belt he lost on the cliff face.

'Look,' she begins. Dino opens the French windows and invites her to sit, the plastic-lidded coffee cups on the table. 'What happened, last night ....' She falters, the sun on his hair, the cloudless blue sky and dazzling sunshine pleading with her to let go of all her rules and regulated living, to seize the moment, not to end up regretting what she has not done.

It is on the tip of her tongue to say never mind, drink the coffee, and enjoy his attention. As she sits, she looks him straight in the face. He is so young. For his sake she must speak.

'Dino, I am fifty.' There, he knows.

He nods his head and smiles.

'Look, unless I had a weird dream I believe we ... that you and I ... last night, just before Adonis said goodbye, we ....'

'Kissed.' He takes the top off one of the coffees and passes it to her with a grin. She unscrews the water bottle.

'You're twenty-four, aren't you? Young, anyway.'

'How old do you feel?' He rattles the ice in his coffee. The sun is overhead. She wonders how late she slept.

'Dino, that is not the point. Look at it this way. When I am sixty, you will be in your prime. When I am seventy, you will be having a mid-life crisis, buying a sports car and trying to date girls of eighteen, leaving me a lonely old woman. Whichever way you look at this, it is not fair on either of us.'

'I think I have your coffee. There is not enough sugar in this.'

'Are you listening?'

'Yes, but what do you want me to say? It is how it is: I cannot be older, you cannot be younger.'

'It's just morally indecent.' The pitch of her

voice has risen.

He throws his head back and laughs. Michelle tries to keep a straight face, but his smile is infectious.

'Dino, please, I am trying to be serious. It is futile to start anything.'

He just grins and sips his coffee.

'Don't you care?'

'No, no really ....' He rubs his face with the palms of his hands, making circular motions with his fingers over his eyes.

'Well, you will when I am incontinent and in a wheelchair!'

He laughs even more, puts his coffee down so he won't spill it, and wipes tears from the corners of his eyes. Michelle waits till his laughing subsides.

'The one thing I know about life is it can change suddenly.' He has adopted a serious tone, but the smile remains.

'Oh, you mean like poor Dolly.'

'Not only.'

'Then what do you mean?'

'No, nothing. Yes, like Dolly. Come on, drink your coffee. Let's go do something.'

'Do you not think it is wrong, me being so much older?'

'Did it feel wrong when we kissed?'

'I am not sure that is a good measure.' Michelle wonders if Dino has had enough life experience to understand why such a thing is unacceptable.

'Look at it this way, the first time I was ever in Greece, you were at home getting your nappy changed and I was getting blind drunk in bars with Juliet.'

'Ah, you see, you were missing me.' He is swilling his ice around his coffee again.

'Be serious. When I was doing my post grad, you weren't even born. When I was getting married, you were about ten. It's just not right.'

He hands her the coffee and turns slowly to face the view of the top of the town.

'You see that church?'

Michelle nods, wondering what any church has to do with their situation.

'It was built five hundred years ago. But still each day people light candles there. Others will light them long after those people are dead. It is not the age that matters.' He turns to face her. 'And the sun that you are shielding your eyes from. Eight minutes ago that light was burning on its surface. Now, to the sun it is gone, but to earth it provides light. And last night as we kissed, above us were a million stars, and many of them already extinguished years ago, gone. But the light is still reaching us, we still enjoy them.'

He looks back to the view.

'Would you not agree that today is a beautiful day, the sun shines, the world looks alive, we are in a beautiful place, yes?'

'Yes but ...'

'Well, do you want to waste this day having a

moral argument or shall we just enjoy it?'

It is clear Michelle is not going to get any further with him, and part of her is glad. It does seem a crime to waste the day. What if she were in Dolly's place next time—would the morality of her and Dino matter then? And besides, who is to be their judge?

Dino knows he is dancing on borrowed time. At some point he has to face his father, explain that he will be staying in Greece, and then he must decide if he will spend his life on the run from the army or whether he will face his obligations and fulfil his military service. He sighs at the prospect. Two years seems a long time.

'Are you sighing because I exasperate you?' Michelle asks. Her hand slides across the table and covers his.

'No.' He finds a smile.

If she is going to Athens at the end of the week, that is only a change of location, not their situation. He will go with her. The army is a more serious commitment. But she has forgotten; it is probably better that way. They will have these days, live in the moment. Tomorrow might never happen.

'Come on, then.' Michelle pulls at his t-shirt.

There is a certain awkwardness as they walk side by side. Dino walks close to her, finding reasons to touch her arm, her shoulder, at one point brushing eucalyptus leaves from her hair. Michelle maintains a slight distance, not completely comfortable in the decision that she has not yet made. But as they wander the alleyways with no particular destination, getting lost, meeting cats, visiting tiny churches, she forgets that she is in conflict and loses herself in his smile, his charm, his ease of just being alive.

They lunch on fresh bread dipped in a pot of local Greek yoghurt, sitting on the steps of a building that has no roof, its doors padlocked to keep inquisitive children safe. They feed the leftover bread to a cat that is more interested in being stroked than eating.

Standing, Dino takes her hand.

'Come,' he says.

The lane is very narrow, single file only, and she wonders if they have taken a wrong turn, as farther ahead the way is blocked by a wall. Dino strides on with confidence. As she comes level with it she sees a recessed doorframe that has been painted in red-and-white diagonal stripes. There is no door. An arrow painted on the wall inside the doorframe points up some stairs.

'I painted that arrow,' Dino says in passing. Michelle smiles to herself. The steps have dropped at the front edge slightly so she feels that with each tread she could slide backwards. They are thickly painted in grey and the middle of each has been worn smooth, back to the wood. Michelle grips the handrail, which rattles on loose screws. At the top of the steps another door stands open to a room into

189

which light streams from floor-to-ceiling windows that overlook the port. Each pane is not large and several have cracks running across them. Two near the bottom have been boarded up. But the view through them is magnificent, the mismatched cracked windows giving the scene the impression of a stained glass replica of the harbour view.

There is a strip of mirror, also floor to ceiling, on one wall by the window, reflecting even more light into the room. Through this Michelle first sees a man's back. Tall, with neat hair, wide shoulders, narrow hips, perfectly proportioned. He is sweeping the unadorned wooden floor around a single barber's chair.

'Panos!' Dino shouts. The men clash in an embrace. They hold each other, then shake hands, their free hands cupping the other's elbow. Panos is about to speak when he sees Michelle and pulls away from Dino to be introduced.

'Welcome.' He smiles. He has beautiful teeth. All Michelle can think is that if Adonis feels he is the man of the island, he has not met Panos. His smile broadens into a grin. He has a boyish look about him, despite the thin layer of stubble.

His eyes flash backwards and forwards from her to Dino until Dino makes the situation clear by taking her hand. Panos' response is to grab her by the shoulders and kiss her on each cheek.

'*Ti kani o Markos?*' Dino asks. Michelle recognises that *Markos* is a name.

'*Kala.*' The voice comes from a curtained-off corner of the room. The material is swept aside, a tiny kitchen uncovered, and a tall man with golden-blond hair steps out. Slinging his tea towel over his shoulder, he too hugs Dino. When he spots Michelle, a questioning look passes across his face and Panos nods.

'Ahhh, at last,' he says in English and hugs her. He feels as comfortable to hug as an old friend. He pulls away and slinks over to stand shoulder to shoulder with Panos, who picks up his hand and kisses it.

Michelle cannot help but wonder if Dino has chosen these particular friends to introduce her to because they understand the struggle of non-conforming liaisons. For a moment there is a twinge of offence that Dino likens their relationship to theirs, but Panos and Markos are so easy-going, so warm, and the view over the harbour from their window so enchanting that Michelle slips once again into just living.

That evening outside her room, after another lovely dinner, Dino kisses Michelle again. He has refrained from doing it all day to give Michelle a chance to decide on her feelings, but now that it is time to sleep, he wants her to know where he stands.

The world recedes and he becomes lost, time irrelevant, his hands in her hair, the smell of her skin ….

He pulls away.

'Goodnight, Michelle.' He smiles, looking back as he walks to his room. He will not be Adonis; he will not use and discard. He has too much respect for her for that. She looks slightly bewildered, but better that than hurt. They have some time, no need to rush.

Chapter 13

Tuesday

'You know that cove we scrambled down to yesterday?' Michelle asks.

'Um hmm.' They have come to the port for breakfast, but Dino is still half asleep. His eyes have closed again.

'Well, I could see another bay along the coast with a sandy beach. Can we get to that?'

'In a boat.' Dino shifts his shoulder to get more comfortable.

'Oh, can we?'

A man at the neighbouring table turns to see who spoke so loudly.

'Can we what?' Dino opens one eye and looks at her.

'Go in a boat?'

'You tease me. After the last adventure? You would trust me?'

Michelle's smile fades.

'It was sad, but it was not your fault.'

'I was responsible.'

'No, you weren't. Don't burden yourself with that. It was an accident, no one's fault.' It strikes Michelle that her words contradict those that she

193

used on the same subject just a day or two ago. They are certainly not the words of a lawyer. She grins and looks around the suntrap of a harbour. The cargo ship is in again and the men unloading are wiping their brows on sleeves. A donkey has been loaded with floorboards. They bury the animal nose to tail and extend another meter again off each end. The donkey seems quite happy carrying its own shade.

'Look, some things you do not know.'

'There are many things I do not know but …'

'OK, we can go if I can tell you something first.' He raises a hand for water and another coffee. Michelle shakes her head.

'So tell me.' Her hair shines in the sun, her neck long and graceful. She has no idea how beautiful she is. He wonders if knowing his secret will change her view of him.

'You will no longer want to know me.' He surprises himself with the suddenness of his words. Costas Voulgaris nods his recognition of Michelle when he brings the coffee, and he presents her the bottle of water with a flourish before cruising away to invite a group of Australians for waffles and honey.

Dino bends to the floor and picks a small fragile yellow flower from a clump clustered around the wooden post holding up the tarpaulin shade. He hands it to Michelle and delights in the smile this simple action provokes. It's nice to make her smile, it makes him feel … he tries to assess how it makes him feel, but he's not sure, just happy.

'So tell me.'

The energy seems to drain out of his body.

'It wasn't my fault.' It comes out louder than he expected. He can feel tears pricking his eyes. Quite unexpected, not at all what he bargained for. How can his emotion have changed so suddenly? He blinks them back and bites his inner lip.

'Hey, hey.' She leans towards him, puts a hand on his shoulder, with concern in her eyes. He can feel a lump in his throat growing, his eyes stinging, a surge in his chest. He is not going to be able to stop it. He cannot look at her. She puts her arm around him, moving her chair closer. He looks away from her, for an escape, but his legs won't move, his head throbs, his hands shake. A sound escapes him, from low in his chest, short, sharp. A sob. He needs to leave, to be in private, to gain control. She is watching.

He breathes in and out rapidly and bites the side of his thumb whilst he conjures up the image of Michelle's smile from a moment before. He regains his dignity, but his eyes are crying by themselves, his nose running.

Michelle takes her arm from around him so she can pull out a serviette from the stack on the table. He takes it but does not use it. Wiping away the tears would be like saying his Mama doesn't matter. His nose begins to run; he is forced into action, he wipes vigorously. Focusing on the action stems the tears, he blows his nose and sits upright, suddenly, aware how much he is on display.

'She died. My Mama.' Dino does not look at Michelle but in his peripheral vision he can sense a movement, a nod of the head, sympathy. A noise distracts him, over by the cargo boat, where the donkeys wait patiently. There is the thud of something dropping on the pier. The cargo men swear.

Michelle has no interest in the boat. Her hand is back around him, and she offers him another tissue. He looks back to her.

'I would help her. I would pick the herbs for her for the cooking.' He pauses. He can see his Mama peeling potatoes over the sink and calling to him out of the window for the herbs she needed. She would name them: 'Dill, coriander, sage', one by one as he ran his hands along the tops of the plants, neatly lined up in terracotta pots in the courtyard, until he reached the one she wanted. The mix of aromas hanging on his fingers and in the air.

Clutched tightly in his fist, he would bring the bunches in, and she would take his head in both her hands and kiss the top of it. Sometimes her hands were wet from washing vegetables and the water would run over his hair and down his neck in exquisitely cold trickles.

'She would tell me tales of *Pappous*, her father. Funny tales about him and his goats.' He pauses and sniffs, experiencing again the wonder those stories

196

produced, now merging into one as a unified stream. 'My favourite was when he was taking his billy to a neighbour's farm to service their does. They both lived over on the mainland.' He nods in the direction of the blue hills across the water. 'The goat was a big black animal, with impressive horns, and much in demand.'

'It was a good five kilometres to his neighbour's and it was hot, so Pappous did not want to walk. He thought about tying the goat to the back of the tractor and driving slowly, but his tractor had no cab, so he would be in the sun. He thought about taking the bus, but he had tried that before and the driver made a fuss about the mess on the seats. So, in the end, he lifted up the goat and put it in the passenger seat of his car. He would drive him over.

'Halfway between the two farms is a village, and what with the smell of the goat and the heat of the day, Pappous decided to stop for a *ouzo*, and one *ouzo* turned into a game of *tavli*— backgammon—a coffee or two, and several *ouzo* chasers. Finally he staggered from the *kafenio* towards his car, but by this time with no memory of the goat. He was so drunk he could barely see, but he could make out the big dark shape in the car and he panicked. His farm was secluded. Without his car, life would be very difficult, and he had no insurance, so he was very worried about the car being stolen. But he was not a brave man, and even with all that *ouzo* in him, he did not have the courage to approach that big, dark man in the car. So instead he shouted and screamed that a Turk with a big knife was stealing his car, and he made such a fuss that the men from the *kafenio* came out to the square to see what the problem was. Among them was the policeman, and together they approached the car. Of course, as he got closer and saw the billy more clearly, he remembered what he was supposed to be doing. So he wished the policeman good day, and went to get in the driver's side.

'"Not so fast," the policeman said. "You know the law. It is illegal to travel with loose animals in your car." At this Pappous looked offended. "Officer, keep your voice down," he said, "my Mother-In-Law will think you mean her", and he nodded at the billy goat, jumped in the car, and drove away.'

But Dino doesn't laugh, it doesn't sound so funny today.

Michelle smiles, but it is a smile of kindness. They sit silently and finish their coffees. She does not press him.

'I cannot tell you here. Come on, if we go we can take Adonis' boat.'

'I thought you two had fallen out?'

'Even if we have, he would not begrudge me the use of his boat.'

They walk along in silence to the smaller harbour, and Dino helps her into a traditional double-ended wooden boat painted in bright colours.

They settle themselves and Dino checks that

everything is in order.

'Are you still sure you trust me to take you?' he asks.

'Dino, I cannot keep saying it—it was not your fault.'

'OK, so you must listen, I will tell you.' He straightens a coil of ropes in the bottom of the boat. Michelle makes herself comfortable, leaning back against the boat's wooden side.

'Mama and I would walk into the hills.' He speaks slowly, not sure he wants to be telling this. He points to the hills on the far end of the island. 'Take a basket and gather herbs. She would show me what to gather, and I would go off and gather as much as I could to please her.' It is becoming hard to swallow again. He blinks.

'Go on.' Michelle's voice is soft, encouraging.

'So I had the basket with our sandwiches. Mama was a hundred yards away, and I came across some fennel. She loved fennel, especially freshly picked. So as a surprise I opened up her sandwich and filled it with a layer of fennel, thinking I was doing something that would give her pleasure. We continued to gather various herbs and *horta*, wild edible plants, and then we headed back to the village. When we came in sight of the first house, over on the tops there,' he indicates the hills in the distance, 'Mama suggested we eat before we hit "civilisation", as she called it. She had brought a plastic bag, and in the bag she mixed a salad with the plants we had

199

found. I was hungry and eating fast, and I was halfway through my first sandwich when my friend Zahari came past with his Baba's herd. I wanted to go with him. I looked at Mama, who smiled and nodded, so I ran off with the animals and my second sandwich. I never ate any of her salad.'

His mouth is dry, and the lump in his throat is making swallowing difficult. He could do with a drink.

'Go on.' Michelle's voice is kind, concerned.

'That was the last time I saw her.' He sits silent for a moment looking out to sea. 'I was gone with Zahari for about three hours, until the goats had their fill and we took them home. She died on the spot where I left her, of poisoning.'

He doesn't look directly at Michelle, but he can sense her mouth has dropped open, her eyes wide.

She whispers the question. 'The fennel you had put in her sandwiches?' Her hand that is not around his shoulders covers her mouth, but there is no accusation in her eyes.

'They don't know. They said it looked as if a herd of goats had gone through the area. There was nothing edible left, so there was no way of knowing if it was the herbs I had picked, the salad, or something else, although I was sure what I picked was fennel.' His eyes flick to her face and back to the table. 'I blurted out what I had done immediately. The horror inside me was too great to keep it in. But no one ever said it was me; not the doctors, not the

200

police. Baba didn't say it either, but I could tell, he thinks it.' His head sinks lower. 'My memory of the day has faded, but Baba, he looks at me in such a way that over the years I think maybe he's right. Why would he accuse me for so long if it wasn't true? But I remember double-checking; it smelt right. I was sure it was fennel.'

The last sentences come out in a rush, his feelings so great all he has is a numbness, a weight in his chest, heavy, familiar, almost comforting in the pain it creates.

'If I had stayed?' he says and shakes his head. Tears are running down his cheeks. He puts his hand over his face, hiding from the world. Michelle's arm grows firmer around him.

'I think you not staying was a good thing. She would not have wanted you to be there.' That's it. That is all she says. There is no blame or condemnation from her. And she is a lawyer.

The weight in his chest eases a fraction, making room for his sorrow to intensify, and the tears come again with heavy sobs. He fears being sucked under, that he cannot survive the weight of the grief. His head feels light, as though there is not quite enough oxygen. He sucks in air and shudders as he exhales. He is going under.

They sit silently as the wave of emotion that grips him gradually subsides.

'Let me tell you of a case I handled,' she begins. Dino can hardly hear her for the rushing in his ears.

Her hand around him doesn't move. She finds him another tissue; he takes it gratefully and leans into her arm a little.

'It was a simple case. Over the brow of a hill there was a long straight road, and at the bottom the road curved behind some trees. A girl, let's give her a name, Sarah, was driving down the hill, and from the top she could see over the dry stone wall to the left, the view of the valley, cows chewing their cud, lambs leaping, the river curling past at the bottom of the field, the whole idyllic scene.' Michelle uses her free hand to gently push Dino's fringe to one side so she can look at him for a second.

'Enchanted by the view, she stopped her car on this long straight strip, tucking it in as close as she could on the verge, to take out her camera so she could capture the scene. This was before mobile phones with cameras.' She pauses and watches a fish nibble on the algae around a rope dangling in the water.

'To get a better view, she climbed on the bonnet of her car to take the picture. Right, so this Sarah has done nothing against the law, nor has she done anything you would consider stupid or thoughtless. It is a country road but easily wide enough for cars to be parked on both sides of the road and the traffic to flow between them. She has stopped on a long straight section, clearly visible from both directions.'

Dino looks up, his attention held by what he imagines is her 'barrister' voice.

'At that point, turning the corner at the bottom and driving up the hill, was a doddery old lady. Lady Isabella of Worfolk, no less. Coming over the brow of the hill from the top was Speedy Steve, let's call him. Late back from his lunch break. He was not over the speed limit, nor had he been drinking. They both saw Sarah on the bonnet of her car. Speedy Steve pulled out to go round her, Lady Worfolk, mesmerised by a girl standing on her bonnet, drove towards the middle line, and the two cars clipped each other. Steve, perceiving no harm done, carried on his way without slowing down. Lady Worfolk, however, slammed on her brakes, sending her passenger into the footwell of the car. Meanwhile, a good three car-lengths behind Lady Worfolk was another driver who had just turned the corner at the bottom and was so busy looking at the girl halfway up the hill, standing on the bonnet of her car, that she stopped too late and went into the back of Lady Worfolk.

Everyone was fine, with only cuts and bruises. Except Lady Worfolk, who was an exact old lady and liked to do things by the clock with etiquette and rules. This accident was not part of her schedule, and it would make her late picking up her brother from the airport. In the ambulance on the way to hospital, although there were only superficial injuries, she died of shock.

'Who was to blame?' Michelle asks.

Dino looks at Michelle, wondering what this

has do to with his Mama's death.

'Do you know who blamed themselves the most for Lady Worfolk's death? Sarah. Even though, by all the rules in the book, she was the one who had taken all the care necessary and broken no laws. She even broke down at the inquest and apologised to Lady Worfolk's family. Yet she had done nothing wrong. The driver who shunted Lady Worfolk also felt she was to blame and she was prosecuted for 'driving without due care and attention'. Speedy Steve was charged with leaving the scene and also with driving without due care and attention. But no one was charged with manslaughter.

She stops to breathe. The fish is still nibbling.

'You know who killed Lady Worfolk, in my opinion?' she asks.

Dino shakes his head. The lump in his throat is clearing, the moment is passing.

'Lady Worfolk killed Lady Worfolk. The way she led her life with its rules and procedures left no margin for divergence, so when something unexpected happened, it was a shock, and in this case, one so big she died of it.

'That is not official, by the way; it was just the way I saw it. Just like the man who base-jumps for fun and one time his parachute doesn't open, or a matador trampled by a bull, they are all deaths due to lifestyle choices. Some are almost not choices, like Lady Worfolk's view on life, probably instilled into her, but the matador, the base-jumper, your mum's foraging, were lifestyle choices.

'Just because Sarah was there to witness it and turn off the engine and call the ambulance and talk to the ladies before the paramedics arrived does not make her guilty, Any more than you being your mother's son, accompanying her in her walks and eating picnics with her, and not being there when it happened makes you guilty.'

She falls silent. The fish has been joined by another one.

Dino's eyes are fixed on Michelle. She must be awesome in court. There is a strange expansion in his chest. The colours around him seem brighter, the rushing sound in his ears has stopped. The lump in his throat feels smaller. He recognises the feeling as "pre-Mama". A world filled with hope, joy. It takes a moment before he thinks of his Baba. The glimmer of hope shatters. The joy turns black. The space that has just opened inside him fills with hate. Why would his own father heap all that unspoken guilt on him?

'Why would he do that?' He spits.

'Who?' Michelle does not take her hand from his.

'Baba. Why would he have me feel guilty of such a thing?' He can still feel where the weight in his chest had sat just a moment ago. It threatens to return, but he experiences it now as sorrow, not only for the loss of his Mama, but for the loss of his Baba the very same day; the day his Baba turned on him, left him to drown in unspoken guilt, bottomless self-condemnation, blame. Alone.

His head rolls back and he yells the worst swear word of which he can think. Birds rise from the vines and trees, the sound echoes off the harbour walls. This feeling he has had all these years, that he thought was guilt for what he had done, is, in fact, rage. Rage at his father. He knows it was fennel. Third pot from the end, smells like aniseed, Hemlock may look similar, but it does not smell of liquorice. His Mama had taught him this again and again on many of their foraging walks. 'If in doubt smell it', she would say. It was fennel. The bad word comes again, breaking open the tension in his throat, cracking open his prison.

Michelle puts her free hand over his; she leans into him, her head touching his.

Chapter 14

Tuesday

They remain motionless for some minutes. Michelle watches the fish silently feeding in the water below. A swell rocks the boat and Dino looks up. Without a word he pries himself loose of Michelle, casts off, starts the motor, and eases them out of the harbour.

Michelle senses a growing discomfort. She has no doubt that what Dino feels for her is real, and her feelings for him certainly are, but how much of what he is experiencing is mingled with the loss of his mum? For his sake, and for her own, she has no desire to be a mother substitute.

The water is as smooth as glass, clear enough to see stones and fish in the shallows. As the boat edges away from shore, the underwater world dissolves into a bottomless blue. Slowly, Michelle is released from the emotional grip Dino's history had on her. He is sitting at the helm, looking out to sea, the sadness lifting as the minutes pass. She would like to be able to say something to take away his hurt, wrap him in cotton wool and keep him safe for his whole life. She never felt that toward Richard; maybe this is a gentler form of love, more compassionate, perhaps.

Michelle reasons that she cannot be fully aware of Dino's motivations, but she is satisfied that her own are not unhealthy.

A larger fishing vessel passes a good distance out to sea. Michelle watches the waves it creates, rippling, growing bigger until finally, long after the boat has gone, their own craft is rocked, and she grips the side to steady herself. Dino smiles at her, and she is glad he is free of his miserable thoughts.

Leaning over the side, she can see the water is shallower here.

'Can we fish?'

Dino looks around the boat and shakes his head. 'No line.'

'Wow, what's that?' Some distance away a slab of grey floats just below the surface. 'Is it something dead? It's huge.'

Dino follows her gaze and when he sees what she sees he hastily cuts the engine and stands for a better look.

'What is it?' Michelle feels the need to whisper the words. The boat bobs closer. The grey slab is round and flat but with what look like fins laid flat against the water on either side. A flattened fish on its side, but with no tail. Pre-historic. It is the oddest thing Michelle has ever seen.

'Is it dead?' she repeats, but as she does so, the huge mass slides beneath the water and then it is gone.

'*Orthayopiskos*,' Dino says, but Michelle is none

the wiser.

'Was it upright or lying on its side? It was very peculiar.'

'It was sun-bathing.' He sits again and starts the engine.

'Oh, hang on, yes, a sunfish. I always thought they were extinct. Wow!'

'We are near to where you fell down the cliff.'

Michelle searches the water, half expecting to see Dolly floating like the sunfish, on her side, bloated, legs out straight like a plastic toy. Her heart fills with sadness again and she wants to cry, for the loss of Dolly, for the loss of Dino's mum, for Richard gone, for the whole sadness that can be life. Why are her moods so volatile these days?

'Look.'

A cold chill ripples through Michelle's chest as she turns to see where Dino is pointing but the ice drains away as she sees his finger pointing not at the water, but at the cliff. Her warmth returns; she is back in the moment.

'There! Isn't that where we were?'

It all looks pretty much the same to Michelle, but there does seem to be something familiar about the layout of the bushes.

'What's the darkness behind that bush there?' she asks.

'That's what I was pointing to.'

'Oh, it's a cave or something. How exciting! Let's go and look.'

'There are many caves along here. I remember this one. It is close to the sea, easy to get in. You want to climb up where you fell down?'

The cliff looks benign now, harmless. The slope that seemed so steep when she was clinging on to the bushes, desperate not to fall to the rocks below, appears from here as though it would be an easy climb. His words bring Dolly back to mind. It's going to take a long time for the images to fade. Such a transformation: life to death. Does it really matter even if she is partly substituting for the loss of his Mum? Surely best to take comfort when it's offered.

Dino brings the boat nearer to the cliff face.

'It doesn't go in very far.' He eases the boat in.

'Oh, look. That bush, you can see its roots. It would have covered the entrance before it was uprooted.' The image again of Dolly falling, bushes torn out in her descent, stones bouncing off her rump.

Michelle blinks and is back with Dino, who edges the boat up to a rock and slings a rope over it. The slight breeze pulls the boat away from the rock and puts a little tension on the line.

Dino pulls the line in with one hand and offers the other to Michelle so she can disembark.

The smell is rich, of warm earth and wild flowers. Dino leaps from the bow of the boat onto the rock in a fluid movement.

Michelle negotiates her way towards the cave. Her shoulder begins to ache; partly the memory, she guesses, and partly because she is using handholds above her head. But it is easy enough, and the thrill when she gains the cave's entrance is one she has not felt since she was a child.

'Oh, it does go back a ways, and turns a corner.' She feels Dino's hands on her hips. The space is only just big enough for them both if they huddle and crouch. Taking little steps, they edge their way in. The roof gets lower. The dark of the cave contrasts with the bright sunshine outside, and for a while nothing can be seen, but slowly their eyes adjust.

'What's that?' Michelle scoops a string of beads from the ground and inspects it. 'Is it old?'

'It's a *komboloi*.'

'Yes, I have seen the men playing with them—rosaries. Well, like a rosary anyway. Is it old?'

Dino admires the red beads tipped with silver.

'They are not new, but they are not ancient.'

'I wonder how they got here? Treasure!'

A few metres farther in, the cave makes a turn.

'Oh my goodness!' Michelle is the first around the corner.

'*Panayia.*' Dino resorts to his mother tongue.

'These *are* old, right?' Michelle confirms.

'Older than you can believe.' Dino stares open-mouthed at the line of pots arranged neatly on the ground in front of them. Gingerly he picks one up and turns it around in his hands, cupping it protectively between his palms. 'It is unbroken. Unbelievable. This is Attica-ware. You can tell by the

211

red colour.'

'You know, this is not the work of any archaeological department. This looks like shenanigans to me.' Michelle's voice takes an official tone.

'What is this "shenanigans"?' Dino asks.

'Dodgy, law breaking. I presume there's a market for this sort of stuff, private collectors and that sort of thing.'

Dino closes his mouth.

'We should report this.' Michelle would like to pick one up but somehow feels she shouldn't. This stuff was made thousands of years ago.

'Hmm.' Dino gently sets down the amphora he has been turning round in his hands. The silhouetted pictures running around it are of men in one-to-one armed combat, swords, shields and helmets clashing.

'What do you mean "hmm"? These should be in a museum, not traded to some rich collector never to be seen again.'

Dino backs out of the cave slightly. There are eight pots, quite small, but they all seem to be unbroken. Not the sort of thing that is found very often; even the ones in the museums have damage, some painstakingly stuck back together from hundreds of pieces.

'You know, things are not always as they seem in Greece.' Dino speaks slowly.

'I know law-breaking when I see it, so we must report it.'

'I cannot.' Dino looks away, unable to return her eye contact.

'What?'

'If I report it, my name goes into a computer and the army will find me, then I will have no choice.'

Michelle's lips part and seal a few times until she finds the right words.

'Yes, but I am a lawyer, I cannot turn my back on something that is going on that is illegal.'

'You don't know why they are here.'

'They are here, and they should not be. That is enough.'

'So because you are a lawyer I have to do the army?'

'No, no. Of course not, but, well, if the army is the law, you should do it, really.' Her voice softens to a whisper at the end of her sentence. It feels like everything she has ever believed to be steadfastly right is being disturbed here in Greece. Just the thought of him away from her brings tear to her eyes. She reaches for his arm, trails down until she finds his hand, and interlocks their fingers. 'Not that I want you to go, but these are the things that society is based on, consensual agreement, without it ...' Dino leans towards her, he pauses just millimetres away. Her limbs turn to liquid, a rushing in her ears, she gasps for breath as he pulls away.

'You're going to have to stop doing that,' she says as he lets go of her hair, trailing his fingers across her wet lips. 'I can't think straight when you do that.'

He grins, and sweeps his fringe to one side, a slightly cocky look on his face.

'You don't need to report this,' he says. 'Just let it be.' He is retreating out of the cave.

'Why did you become a lawyer anyway?' he asks. He is back in the sun, face up, eyes closed, tiny droplets of sweat on his brow.

She follows him out.

'Do you know, I have often wondered that.' Michelle pulls a face as Dino chuckles. 'No, I don't mean in the "why would anyone ever want to be a lawyer" sort of way. I mean I do not remember making the decision to go into law. I must have done, because I did a post-grad conversion course, but I don't remember making the decision to do that course.' She picks a pebble from the sandy floor of the cave and tosses it into the sea. A fish darts away from the expanding circles, and she wishes she had not been so thoughtless. Life is stressful enough without people throwing pebbles—even for fish. 'I did my degree in accounting.'

'Did your family come to the graduation ceremony?' Dino remembers each of his friends being surrounded with parents and siblings, uncles and grandparents, even excited dogs. He had stood alone. No one was there to support him, the occasion a hollow non-event after such intense studying and cramming of the previous weeks, the future a gaping abyss.

'Mum and Dad actually came to the ceremony but Penny stayed at home,' Michelle says.

'Penny?' Dino sits in a patch of sunlight in the cave's mouth and lies back against its wall, hands behind his head, his eyes closed.

'My sister. But I never expected her to come,' Michelle clarifies.

'A sister? Why wouldn't she go? Wasn't she proud of you?' Dino says. Michelle looks back into the cave, still wondering what to do about the pots, amazed at Dino's nonchalance over them.

'She was ill. She would always get ill with some undiagnosable problem just when the focus turned to me.' She glances at him without moving her head. 'I know how nasty that makes me sound, but I remember so clearly the first time she pulled this stunt.' Michelle stops talking. She is saying too much and wonders how she can round this topic up without obviously cutting it short. Why did she start to tell him anyway? It only makes her look bad—and feel bad.

'Well, she's not here now to take the focus from you, so you can tell me what you like.' Dino opens his eyes and pats the ground next to him in invitation. Michelle takes up his offer.

She tucks her knees up and wraps her arms around them. She remains still for a moment, but it is too hot to remain scrunched up for long. She leans back on her elbows and stretches her legs over the

215

front edge of the cave, her feet close to the water. A ferryboat is passing in the distance, on its way to another island. Michelle watches the ripples from its wake grow smaller and smaller as they snake towards her and the shore. When it seems they have long since dispersed, she is surprised as the swell hits the rock face below and the splash reaches for her toes.

'Well, her "illness" did seem very unfair,' she finally exhales. 'When I got my 'O' level results and came running home to tell Dad, Penny was in the room. Dad told me to calm down and suggested that we go into the garden. I knew why. I knew he didn't want me to say how well I had done in front of Penny, who had got only three 'O' levels the year before. So I went into the garden and waited for him, but he never came. Mum called us for dinner at six, and I realised I had been waiting for him an hour and a half in the garden to tell him my news, and he never came.' Michelle stretches her neck and runs her hand around her shoulders to release the tightness.

Dino gazes at her intensely.

'We sat and had dinner. I had a lump in my throat and could hardly swallow. Mum kept asking me why I was so quiet. When it was finished and all washed and put away, and Pen had gone off to our room, he said to me, like he had just remembered, "Oh, didn't you have something to tell me? Sorry for earlier. Penny felt quite unwell. Let's go settle ourselves in the sitting room." But I had just seen

Penny helping herself to seconds of pudding and I knew she couldn't be that unwell. I looked at Dad and he looked at me with love, but he also looked afraid, ashamed, guilty. I didn't understand. But the outcome was clear, so I thought, what's the point? I went into the sitting room and I told him my results and he acted pleased, but I felt like I was just going through the motions.'

'Ah, so she is jealous of you, your sister, and manipulates your parents?' Dino hasn't moved. With his eyes shut, he basks in the heat.

'No! Well, maybe. It wasn't seen that way. It was seen that I was always bragging, or at least that was how I was made to feel. I felt I was being uncaring to Pen and pushy about my exam results. I felt I bragged about my 'A' levels, I felt I was being a know-it-all with my degree, and then my law conversion was just not spoken about and after that whatever I did was just ignored. I hardly ever see them now.'

'Did your parents side with her all the time?'

'It wasn't that they sided with her. When she would feel ill, she wouldn't say anything, it was just this look she would get, and then Mum would notice and tell Dad, and then all the focus was on Pen. So if I was enthusiastic over my studies and she pulled that look, Mum and Dad fussed over her. If I mentioned my studies again, then I was being unsympathetic to Pen and self-centred about my own achievements. And you can't argue with illness, can

217

you? I mean, health comes first and all that …'

'She sounds like a bitch to me,' Dino says. Michelle grimaces over his choice of words.

'Oh no, she never does anything mean.'

'No, just making sure you never get credit or attention.' He drops back onto his elbows. 'It's amazing you didn't just stop studying.'

'Well, exactly! Dad was a painter and decorator, and when we were children, he would soliloquise that university was something to aspire to and how he wished he had had the opportunity to go, how we would have ended up with a bigger house where we wouldn't have been on top of each other, a bedroom each for us girls, how fantastic life could be with that sort of education, until Pen scraped through with just three 'O' levels.' Michelle makes a snorting sound. 'It was obvious after that that she wasn't going to be an academic, and God forbid anyone hurt her feelings ... Until then he saw education as one of the great gifts of the "modern age". Back then the government not only paid your tuition fees, but they actually gave you a grant to go. How things have changed. Now you have to pay for everything.'

'Oh God, and don't I know it? How many years of oranges has my education taken? So your dad and my dad did the same thing—they both pushed us into going to Uni. and guess what …?' He begins to laugh.

'What?' Michelle cannot help but smile when

he laughs; it's an infectious sound.

'They both ended up with what they feared most.' He wipes a tear from the corner of his eye.

'You're making no sense at all.' She laughs nevertheless.

'I am. My Baba ended up with his worst fear—a drop out. And yours ended up with his worst fear—a success. We should swap; then they'd be happy.' He stops laughing and sits up to look over the sea. 'They both got what they deserved. That's karma.'

Michelle ponders on this.

'Well, it gave me a very strong sense of fair and unfair, right and wrong. The whole law thing, if I think about it, started from wanting to fight the case of those not being treated fairly.'

'Reporting the vases, does that fit in?'

Michelle looks back into the cave.

'It's wrong, Dino.' How can he not see that?

'I cannot put my name on any report.'

'Fine.'

But inside it's not fine. She feels he has stepped far away, to another world, where the lines between right and wrong are blurred; a world that belongs to criminals and dirty companies. A world of lies, fakery, and ultimately hurt, to a world where she cannot follow.

'I'll go with you, though.'

'Oh!' The knot untwists. Thoughts of her father fade, and in her mind's eye, Dino steps back over the blurred line to where the air is clear. Her shoulders relax. 'I just want to have a last look.' She shuffles back into the cave. Dino steps out onto the rocks and pulls the boat closer.

The journey back seems to be much quicker.

But not quick enough, as they find the council offices have closed and will not be open again until the next day.

They wander the streets for a while, Dino sharing his childhood haunts and memories, until the sky begins to turn pink, the sun surrounded by a blaze of red which extinguishes as it dips into the sea.

After another leisurely dinner, they wander back to Zoe's, where Dino wishes her a gentle goodnight.

But this evening it is Michelle who lies awake, struggling with Dino's presence just along the balcony. The story of his mother, his reluctance to do what Michelle knows is right, has brought a fragility to the relationship, it might all disappear tomorrow, the next day, with a mood, a new bit of information. She wants to hold onto it tightly, pour glue onto it so it stays. Quietly she opens the door and steps outside. It has all gone too far anyway. If she tiptoes along to his room they would only be confirming what they both already know, cement the inevitable.

Chapter 15

Wednesday

Her door creaks as she opens it. Funny how she had never noticed that during the day. Maybe he is asleep already.

The moon is bright as she pushes open her door, and in the distance the sea is visible, glinting and shimmering, alive black silk.

What if he is a virgin?

She stops in her tracks. No, that's ridiculous. No one is a virgin at twenty-four these days. Are they? The looks he gives her are too knowledgeable. He's been to university, for goodness' sake. It is impossible. But his reserve suggests he could be. The emotion, the passion in his kisses, there is no doubt as to his desires. Could he be shy?

Another step and she is outside.

'Poios einai?' Michelle recognises it as Kyria Zoe's voice.

'Oh, er.' Why on earth would Kyria Zoe be out at this time?

Zoe is lying on the balcony in her nightdress, head propped on pillows, facing down towards Dino's door. Surely she is not sleeping there? But then again, the air is deliciously cool out here, compared to the stuffiness of the room. But now what? How to explain why she is out at this time?

'I just wanted some air,' Michelle blurts out and retreats back into her room.

A stream of garbled Greek follows as she closes the door.

Back in her own bed she giggles and concludes that perhaps it is for the best. It would be funny to share what has just happened with Dino tomorrow, but then she would have to confess what she had on her mind.

Best leave it be.

'Yes, I understand what you are saying. What are you wanting me to do about it?'

'Don't you have procedures? They need to be in a museum.' Michelle can feel her temper rising.

The girl, not long out of school by the look of her, finally heaves her slight weight from her chair, puts down her coffee and cigarette, and opens the drawers of a grey metal filing cabinet which is jammed in a corner against the back wall beside a table piled high with papers.

'You have been in Greece many years?' she asks as her back is turned.

'No, I am only on holiday.'

'Ah.' The girl sighs this utterance, as if that explains everything, and turns her attention to Dino.

Dino would rather not even be addressed. If he

222

begins to talk, she might ask his name, write it down somewhere, put it on her computer. But then again, as this girl is saying, this is Greece. The cogs here grind slowly, and even if she does stab his name into the computer, the chance of that being hooked up to a database of the army? Nil! He laughs. The girl turns and rewards him with a smile. She all but flutters her eyelashes at him. Too much makeup, and her skirt is way too short. He feels Michelle's eyes on him. He looks from the girl's leg back to her. Her mouth slightly open, her eyebrows raised.

'What?' he asks in English, but as he does so the realisation crashes upon him. He flicks his eyes up into his head, a Greek 'no', but Michelle's expression does not change. The girl's back is towards them, Dino slides over to Michelle, '*Ela!*' he whispers. 'Come on! Come off it!' he repeats in English. Surely she knows it is unthinkable.

'Here, fill this in.' The girl pushes some papers across the counter at Michelle.

'But they are in Greek.' Michelle stands tall, a little disquieted by Dino's roving eye.

Reluctantly the girl pulls them back. 'OK, date of find?'

'Yesterday.'

'Time.'

Michelle looks around for a chair. This looks like it is going to be drawn out.

'So sign here.' Michelle does as she is asked. 'And you.' The girl pushes the papers to Dino.

'He is not involved,' Michelle parries and pushes the papers back. The girl looks disappointed. Dino walks out of the office into the sun.

The girl takes the papers and places them on top of the nearest pile stacked on the table behind her and returns to her computer.

'Excuse me?' Michelle regains her attention. 'Will it ever be seen there?'

'Everything will be seen, eventually.'

'But isn't this important?'

'Lady, everything on the table is important.' She lights another cigarette, having forgotten the one burning in the ashtray.

'Well, that felt like a complete waste of time.'

Dino smirks at Michelle's observation.

'Although it had its perks for you,' she adds.

Dino grins and shakes his head, steps towards her and slips his arm around her waist, his face moving towards hers. The sky goes black, her heartbeat throbs in her throat, her ears ring, and she is overcome by the need to sit down.

He relaxes away from her; his hand slackens around her waist.

'Will you stop doing that?'

'You want me to?'

Michelle smiles. Their hands find each other, fingers interlinked. With her other hand she wipes her lips.

They begin to walk.

'Pots are found all the time, you know,' Dino begins.

'Really?'

'Found and smashed.'

'Very funny.' Michelle feels a lightness within, the sun on her face.

'Really.'

'Don't be silly, why would anyone smash them?' The way narrows and the sun is hidden by the houses on either side. In the shade Dino's t-shirt turns a dull brown.

'It's the law,' he replies. Michelle stops walking and laughs, but his shaded face looks sad. 'If you dig and find a pot, you must stop digging and the archaeology authorities must come.'

'Well, that's as it should be.' Michelle smiles.

'But they have few people and there are many digs and each one costs a lot of money.'

'But the government's duty is to preserve the country's heritage.'

'But it is not the government who has to pay, it is the landowner.'

'What?'

'And even if they have the money, they must wait. There is a backlog.'

Michelle is no longer smiling. 'Of how long?'

'Years.' Dino walks on and turns away from the port, his face suddenly in the sun. 'But mostly the

225

landowners don't have the money, so they choose.'

'Choose to smash them?' Michelle supports herself with a hand on a flaky whitewash wall as she climbs some steps.

'No, choose to have a home. They have the land, they need a house. If they stop for a pot, the money they have to build a house will be spent on the archaeologists, who will take years anyway. Better to say nothing.'

'Don't people take them home?'

'No!' Dino turns to her in horror. 'If you get caught with that stuff, you will never see daylight again. Best to smash it.'

Michelle stops to take a breath. They have been climbing from the port area for a while.

'Where are we going anyway?' It comes out in gasps.

'I want you to meet Koula.'

Michelle, still breathing hard, frowns slightly and shakes her head, a non-verbal 'who'?

'Adonis' mother,' he replies. Michelle scowls. 'As a child she was like a second mother to me. Trust me.' He takes her hand and pulls.

'What if Adonis is there?'

'He'll be fine.'

The way seems to get harder, even though it is all on the flat now.

'Come on.' Dino seems excited.

Turning a corner reveals bougainvillaea that almost covers a narrow passage leading to an isolated stone house. A figure can be seen through an open door in a rough wall that encloses a small courtyard. Dressed in black, with a headscarf and apron, the old lady puts her hand to her brow to shield her eyes, trying to focus, and as she recognises Dino a smile lights up her wrinkled features.

'Ah, Dino ...' shouts Koula excitedly. The rest of the Greek flows fast but gentle from this lady, and Michelle cannot understand a word. Koula is older than Michelle had expected, certainly older than herself, which she notes with relief. She invites them up on to the terrace where she fusses over Dino, allowing Michelle to take a good look at the garden below. But it is not the garden that commands her attention so much as the view. They are halfway up the tumble of houses that forms the town, and directly in the middle overlooking the port. It could be a painting. Below her the orange roofs step down, glimpses of whitewashed walls between them, the occasional blue or grey shutter peeping in amongst the cubist abstract. The port a deep semi-circle containing the whiter-than-white boats and bluer-than-blue sea. The whole scene in dazzlingly bright hues as the sun finds every corner.

A rustle in the garden catches her attention. Autumn leaves from last year still pile up against the walls, high walls, too high to see over. It is an oasis of calm and green. Vines cover a paved area, supported by a pergola and providing welcome shade. The garden steps down to an area planted with flowers and herbs, and then steps again to a narrow strip with a single orange and a single lemon tree, the land so steep Michelle can see the port over the top of them.

There is a rustle again. A lizard darts across the flagstones directly in front of her. Already she is used to seeing them; it causes no alarm, just curiosity.

'Michelle, you want a coffee?' Dino beckons her inside. She goes into the tiny house to discover that inside is just one room, two beds with cushions posing as sofas, the kitchen in one corner, and a wardrobe screening the shower and toilet. It is hard to believe that people are living in such little space in this day and age. She reassesses Adonis' arrogance and wonders how much comes from covering up a fundamental feeling of inferiority—or is that just a British way of thinking?

'Hello, Michelle.' The words slow and pronounced. Michelle kisses Koula on each cheek, soft and slightly fuzzy. Close up she seems much younger. People here dress older than their age perhaps, or westerners dress younger.

She turns to Dino to say something.

'She says you are very beautiful, like a queen.' He looks at the floor, hands stuffed in his front pockets. Michelle notices there is a rip in one; it must have happened on the cliff.

He speaks some more to Koula in Greek, one minute laughing, the next scowling. There is no way to guess what is going on.

'She says she wants to call Adonis, bring him here so we are all together. Are you OK with that?'

'I suppose, if you are.'

Koula pulls a mobile phone from her housecoat pocket.

'He is out. Wait, I will call him. You are still as handsome as ever, Dino, and you have a fine woman to suit you.'

Dino feels his cheeks colour. He concentrates on the beep of the phone as Koula presses the buttons. 'Let's face it; you were never going to get yourself a local girl, were you? Destined to get yourself something a bit more ...'

Another phone rings somewhere in the room. Koula pushes Dino aside to get to it, sweeping cushions into a pile on one of the daybeds and fishing down the back to produce the source of the ringing.

'Would you look!' She ends the call and throws Adonis' phone back onto the bed. 'He is always losing things. I don't know how many phones he has had and you know what he lost the other day? He won't admit it, but he cannot tell me where they are. His grandfather's *komboloi!*'

Dino shrugs. He is familiar with Adonis' attitudes.

'They were all I had left of my father. Beautiful, they were, red with silver tips.'

Dino can feel the blood drain from his face. He sits on the sole wooden chair. Michelle puts a hand on his shoulder. Her face enquiring.

'Like these?' he draws the beads from his pocket and lets them hang from his fingers.

'Oh my goodness, where did you find them? If only I had two of you instead of Adonis, bless him and love him as I do. You are a magician, Dino. One minute I think they are gone forever, the next they are in your pocket. But you must tell me, where did you find them?'

He pulls himself together. The sight of her perplexed features calls on him to soothe her, repay the kindness she has always shown him.

'It is natural, Koula. He laid them down in the boat, a wave tossed the boat, and the beads were on the floor. Could have happened to me, to you, to anyone.'

'You are a good boy, Dino.' She grabs him in a bear hug and kisses his jaw lines; it is all she can reach.

'So, where will he be?' Dino asks. 'I have some things to say to him.' He lays the beads in the palm of her hand, curls them round on themselves and bends her fingers over to cover them.

'Ach, away up on the land. You know he got planning permission? So now all his free time is spent in this fantasy of building a home for me, a proper kitchen, a separate bedroom.' She smiles and relaxes with these words. 'Dear boy that he is, he says he will live here.' She casts a dismissive hand across the room's interior. 'Not right a grown man has to sleep in the same room as his mother, not right at all. But what to do? It is all we have. But he is trying, with the little money we have.'

'You better explain yourself!' Michelle says, stuffing biscuits into her bag. Koula had insisted she take them with her, couldn't bear the idea of her leaving empty-handed. The biscuits had been presented on a little tray with a lace cloth, along with the tiny cups of Greek coffee. She had chattered away in Greek and proudly showed Michelle all the interesting things her late husband had accumulated over time: a British gun from before the Boer war, with its firing pin missing, a Turkish knife from the occupation, a Nazi helmet complete with a Swastika on one side and a bullet hole in the other, and a very old leather-bound book, which she stroked and was obviously very attached to. Dino did his best to translate, but even he did not seem to understand the significance of the book.

'Hmm?' He strides out ahead.

'What was all that with the beads? I didn't know you had taken them from the cave. They should have gone to the authorities as evidence. And why are we running?'

Dino stops. 'They belong to Adonis. He is building his mother a home up on their land. We are going to talk to him.'

Michelle does her best to keep up with him but the slope is steep and she is out of breath. Finally he stops by some scrubland. A bank of earth and some rocks stop them from seeing over the top.

'Hey, Adonis?' Dino calls

'Hey, my friend, you sober now?' Adonis calls back.

'Been fishing recently?' Dino asks the head that appears.

'No, why?' Adonis scrambles down the bank that forms the border of his land to stand on the path and face them both. He nods to Michelle, but there is no warmth.

'Maybe you are rich enough not to need to fish now, eh?'

'What on earth are you talking about?' Adonis grins and puts a soil-ingrained hand on his shoulder. Dino shrugs it off.

'Well, you are making good use of the boat, but not to fish. So what is it you are doing?'

'I think you are not used to the sun my friend, too much living in England, you have sunstroke.' He rubs his palms on his jeans, trying to clean them.

'It is not I who has sunstroke; it is you who are crazy. Do you think you can sell them and not be caught?'

'What? Ah!' He stops rubbing and stands very still, his shoulders slumped slightly, some of his vigour gone. 'No, you do not understand …'

'What is there to understand? You find the pots, you hide them away, waiting to sell them …'

'Keep your voice down! Look, my Mama

232

cannot keep sharing her house with me; I am a man now. This land is all we have. I need to build a house.'

Dino cannot keep his voice down. 'But what you are doing is wrong. Better to be homeless. They are national treasures. Have you no pride in being Greek?' He knows this will rile Adonis, and it is his intention.

'Don't talk to me about being Greek, you who have gone to live in England for an easy life. What? You don't think we could all do that?' Adonis' fists clench, his voice loud and strong.

'You are making bad choices my friend.' Dino takes a step towards Adonis.

'I am making bad choices? I am doing the best I can do without running away or leaning on anyone else.' He casts a look in Michelle's direction. 'It is you who are making bad choices. You ditch your job in England, you cannot face your army service to live here, and you ask me if I have pride to be Greek. She will leave you to return to her English life, her rich friends, and leave you behind, how clever is all that?'

Dino's knuckles are white; he is trembling. Michelle puts her hand on his shoulder trying to soothe, but he shakes it off. Greeks always seem to be shouting. How can she tell how serious it is?

'How dare you try and justify what you are doing by throwing your opinions on my life! You did your national service because you did not know what else to do with your life. You fish for women, pull

233

them from your barbs, play with them a while and throw them back before they even know what has happened. You don't care if they are hurt or if they can still swim, so how dare you condemn me.'

'It is not you I am condemning, it is her. She plays with you.'

'And you should know.' Dino spits.

'I do know and I wish to save you from her.' Adonis reaches for him.

'Go to hell, Adonis.' Dino backs off.

'You are out of your depth.' Adonis lets his arms flop to his side.

'You are jealous.' Dino points, his finger to the middle of Adonis' face.

'I am realistic.' Adonis looks down the island and out to sea.

'We have told the authorities.'

'What? What the hell did you do that for?'

Michelle steps in between them, as Adonis' voice rises again.

'She is a lawyer, Adonis, how can she turn her back on all she knows?'

'And you are a Greek man and my friend. How can you turn your back on all you know?'

'She is right.'

'You choose her over me?'

'I didn't know it was you when ….'

Adonis raises his fist.

Chapter 16

'Stop!' Michelle shouts and steps between them, a hand on each of their chests. Adonis' shirt is open and he is sweaty. Dino's chest feels familiar, but his heart is racing.

Dino pushes against her hand, glares at her and turns from them both, marching away down towards the houses, turning at a corner and disappearing from view.

Swiping her hand away, Adonis scrambles back up the bank and he is gone.

'Dino?' Michelle trots down the steps after him, but at the first crossing of paths she has no idea which way to turn. He is nowhere in sight.

Has he run out on her, or does he just need to cool down? How was she to know it was Adonis who was dealing the pots, and besides, what difference does it make? Right is right and wrong is wrong. She would like to know what was said between the two of them, but it doesn't really matter. Adonis obviously justified what he had done and had the cheek to give Dino a hard time for it.

Her footsteps slow and her head drops forward. No matter what she thinks of Adonis, he is Dino's lifelong friend. It was a bitter day when she and Juliet returned from their holiday in Greece, all those years ago, not speaking. A simple quip on the last day about Juliet's good-for-nothing husband had started the hugest of rows, which lasted until their plane landed back in England.

They lost touch for a while after that. Juliet had her hands full with her two small boys and Michelle was studying and working night and day toward her bar exams. But even after the boys had grown a bit and Michelle was established, even then, for years, the relationship was reduced to nothing but phone calls—if Michelle called. Juliet never phoned, not until recently.

She would not wish that on Dino. She wouldn't even wish it on Adonis. Maybe there is something in what Dino was saying earlier, that things are never so straightforward, so black and white. But how was she to know it was Adonis?

Poor Koula, who has nothing but a single room and a makeshift kitchen. Where on earth does Adonis take his conquests? Michelle wonders suddenly. Surely not in the garden, with Koula just inside the house? No, it is unthinkable. He probably has an arrangement somewhere, like Richard did at the Queen Vic hotel, until he had the guts to come clean. In a way Michelle was glad it was the Vic, somewhere nice and seedy for Lady Whatnot.

To be fair on Adonis, it is understandable that he wants to give his mother a proper home. Her comfort must be so much more important to him than a few ancient pots. But to sell them for gain, that is just plain criminal.

She turns and heads along a straight path that seems to cross the town, right through the bowl of houses above the harbour, neither down to the port nor up towards the hills at the top of the island. The intermittent view is astounding, visible in glimpses between the houses. Walking on the flat is not bad and this entire stretch is shaded.

Michelle stops. She has no idea where she is. The alley seems to end, and it opens onto some very steep scrubland with black stone steps set into it, climbing all but vertically towards the ridge on one side of the town. She turns to look back at the view, but there are houses in the way.

The black stones are high, and it takes a big step and pushing on her knees to ascend each one.

'Should have double-checked my facts.' Michelle talks to herself as she climbs. 'Not even double-checked, just found some facts to begin with.' The process of climbing soothes her. 'But then, it is not my job to check the facts.' She can feel sweat running down her back. The exertion is pleasant in a sticky sort of way. 'Although it is a small island.' She stops for breath and turns to see the view.

'Oh my!' It is like looking down on a Mediterranean toy town, with orange bricks for the roofs, white bricks for the buildings, sweet-wrapper blue for the water, toy boats huddling in the harbour, a yacht listing out to sea. The blue hills of the mainland form a distant backdrop, with tiny islands dotted by a child's hand across the waves. So many incredible places to see in the world. She can understand Dino not wanting to spend his youth stuck in an office. If she had it to do again, would she?

The top is close now, so she continues to climb, towards a cluster of orange tiles beyond the ridge, a telltale sign of habitation.

Suddenly she's atop the last step, and before her, oddly solid in the dry, dusty scrubland, is a stone wall. After catching her breath, she begins to circumnavigate it, trailing her hand along the sandy stone until she comes to a big wooden door propped open.

The sign is only in Greek, but it is apparent by the cross over the door that it is a church or … the penny drops. The convent that she can see from her balcony at Zoe's.

She puts her head around the open door, curious. How can anyone live so separate from society?

The outer wall encloses a courtyard, with a tiny church in the middle. A line of doors on two levels behind it are, she presumes, the cells. But her attention alights on the area between the door and the church, which has been laid out as flower beds, a mass of colour, a sea of flowers competing with each other in size and intensity, not a plant that is not blooming, not a fallen leaf on the ground. Tall, majestic green stalks with flower bells hanging from them; pale pink geraniums, dark red roses and an array of zinnias; a purple ground-covering flower that is trying to engulf everything. One bloom after another catches Michelle's eye.

'*Kalos orisate.*'

Michelle jumps. She had not seen the figure in black bending, tending to the flowerbed on her left, hidden behind the door.

'Oh, sorry.' She backs out.

'Please come. I am sorry, I thought you were Greek,' the nun says. Michelle would rather not intrude, but it seems rude not to accept the invitation.

'No, I didn't mean to disturb you.'

'It is my pleasure. Please come in.' Her voice has a strange accent, her words over-annunciated, like a character in a black and white film.

The nun opens the door wide and gestures for Michelle to enter. The care and order in the courtyard is accentuated by the contrast with the wild scrubland outside. Butterflies dance in pairs, and dragonflies hover over a small pond. It is an oasis.

'It's beautiful,' Michelle whispers.

'They are all gifts.' The nun smiles, making a self-deprecating gesture with her arms. 'I think water would be a good idea. Please.' She indicates a slatted wooden bench set in the shade by the church. 'A good spot to think.' She laughs, an easy sound.

Michelle sits and straightens her clothes but soon forgets herself, gazing at the garden before her.

A movement on the path between the rows of flowers catches her eye, and she watches enchanted as a large tortoise plods from the soil onto the stone path. It stops, quite still, nose up, before continuing.

'Ah, is she there, that old lady?' The nun returns with a tray on which is a metal jug and two metal beakers. 'Yes, there she is.' She looks at the tortoise as she sets the tray on the bench between them. 'She has been in this place longer than me, can you believe it? She comes and goes. I believe she just walks through these walls.' She raises a crooked finger to indicate their enclosure before pouring water and handing Michelle a mug.

'Thank you.'

'So, what brings you here?' Her voice is quiet and gentle, lowered to invite confidentiality.

'Oh, no reason. I just stumbled on you.'

She nods as if she knows a secret.

'No really, I am just a tourist, I came for a day trip ....' At this point a donkey brays, quite close outside the walls of the monastery. Michelle's head jerks up suddenly at the sound. She feels the catch in her throat again and takes a sip of water.

'Are you troubled?'

'No, it's not me. You see I saw a donkey die. We fell down a cliff and now the owner will not allow me to make it right.'

'That sounds like a great ordeal.' There is compassion in her voice. The way she speaks indicates she has all the time in the world. 'You were

240

spared and the donkey is gone.' She pauses to watch the tortoise as it turns to face them on the path. 'Is there really any right and wrong in that?' Michelle searches for an answer to this, but the nun speaks again. 'We cannot fight life itself, and with life comes death, don't you find?'

'I wanted to buy the man a new donkey but he wouldn't accept.'

'But was it a new donkey the man was wanting?'

'No, of course not, but what else could I do?'

'Indeed.' The nun takes a sip of water and then leans over the jug that divides them and pats Michelle's hand. 'Time moves on, and the things we want change.'

Michelle sighs. She wonders where Dino is, if he is all right.

'I have only been here, let me see … I arrived on Friday. Today is …?'

'Wednesday.' The nun helps.

'Wednesday. So, gosh, six days.'

'And much has happened in those six days?'

'So much. You know, I think in those six days just about every thought I have in my head has been questioned. I came here thinking about my work and keeping my crumbling old house from falling to pieces. But the house itself is such a burden and only gives the illusion of security.'

'But it is not your home.'

'Sorry?'

'You call it a house, not a home.' The tortoise is almost at the nun's feet.

'I called it home.'

The nun takes a lettuce leaf from her apron pocket and leans over towards the tortoise. It retracts its head inside.

'Didn't I?'

'What do you think makes people happy?' The nun straightens, and the tortoise slowly puts its head out and nibbles on the green leaf by her sandaled toe.

'That's a bit of a big question, isn't it? If we knew the answer, someone would have bottled it and slapped a patent on it, and we lawyers would be in business forever.'

'And would that make you happy?'

'No, of course not. Although being productive is a great part of happiness.'

'Or is it for the accolade of your colleagues?'

'No, of course not.' But the happiest days of Michelle's life come to her in a stream: school days with Juliet; one or two early days with Richard; Christmas with Juliet; and these last few days just passed. She gasps as 'the last few days' are added to her mental list, and also notes that not one of these times was 'productive'.

'Your happiest times were …?' The nun asks, her eyes closed, head leaning back against the church behind them. 'No, let me guess.' She chuckles, kindly and softly, but keeps her eyes closed. 'They were with people you love.' She pauses. 'Or with God,' she adds as she opens her eyes and smiles at Michelle. 'Who I imagine you would call Nature.' She smiles, her head framed in sunlight.

'People.' Michelle hears her own voice reply.

'Yes, that is what is missing.' The nun nods her head. 'Faith.'

'In God?' Michelle can feel a smirk forming. She tries to keep it suppressed.

'In life.' The nun's eyes close again, a smile on her lips.

Chapter 17

She could sit all day. The courtyard is so still, so peaceful. At one point, the nun glides away and returns with coffee and glacéed fruit on a plate with a teaspoon. She waves a wasp away and passes the plate to Michelle. It is very sweet, and it sets Michelle's teeth on edge. The nun calls it '*melitzanaki*', 'little aubergines in syrup,' and explains that she made it herself, so Michelle eats the rest, in tiny bites between sips of coffee. The nun offers more.

'No, thank you. I really must be going. Thank you so much for your hospitality.'

She takes a last look around, the garden so peaceful yet so full of life, a hum of bees, butterflies. She spots the old tortoise with its front legs on a dish, its head bowed to the water the nun must have thoughtfully put down. They walk amicably together to the door.

'So nice to meet you.' Michelle offers her hand to shake.

'You are very welcome.' The nun takes Michelle's hand in both of hers, patting and stroking.

'By the way, how come you speak such perfect English?' Michelle enquires.

'I learnt a little bit at school, and the rest by keeping one step ahead whilst teaching an illiterate goat-herder.' She laughs, an easy, soft sound.

'Your accent is so precise,' Michelle comments.

'I got permission to watch a film to improve my accent. After deliberation, the church sent me a cine film. I don't think they even knew what it was; it just said 'British 1945'. I must have watched it a hundred times. Celia Johnson has a lot to answer for.'

Michelle laughs.

'God works in mysterious ways, does he not?' The nun chuckles.

'Well, thank you for my brief visit.' Michelle says. She wonders if it is done to hug a nun. She would so much like to. The nun is like a perfect mother, a lost aunt. The old lady takes her by the arm and leads her to the big wooden door.

'Well, goodbye then,' Michelle says as she steps back into the scrubland and the heat.

'Sto kalo.' The nun smiles. 'Go towards what is good,' she translates. Michelle retraces her steps along the path, then pauses to look back. The nun is still standing at the gate, accompanying Michelle with her gaze. At the turn in the way, Michelle waves. The nun raises her hand—it could be in blessing. Slowly the door to the convent closes, the buzz of the bees, the colours of the flowers, the tranquillity slowly shut from view, replaced by a solid brown arch of knotted wood.

Taking a deep breath, Michelle turns to face reality. The land around her is barren, burnt dry by the sun, a sun that seems hotter on this side of the

245

wall. To her left the open ground extends to the end of the island. Down to her right the town slides away into the harbour, and in amongst those houses somewhere is Dino, hurt and angry, and all because she thought she knew best about the reporting of the pots, that her way was the only way to deal with it, because she is a lawyer. *Such arrogance.*

What does she know, really? Not about pots, but about people and about life beyond her self-erected walls of justice, right and wrong. What, if anything, does she know about Greek people, the Greek way of life, how the Greeks do things? 'Absolutely nothing,' she tells herself.

If they had gone about it in Dino's way, a quiet word with Adonis and the whole matter might have been cleared up, with no shouting. No, the system doesn't work, whichever way she looks at it. Either there is no house or there are no pots. It is a tough decision for anyone.

She cannot help with that, but she can help with Adonis and Dino's friendship. If Adonis is cross with Dino about the report, then she can make that right, heal some of the damage she has done.

The trail back down the steps is quick compared with the slow ascent. The long stretch of level path across the town is easy but quiet. Doors and windows are closed; the sound of air-conditioning comes and goes as she passes different houses, along with the smell of cooking. Tomatoes at one house, cheeses at another, oregano and onions farther on. Michelle's stomach rumbles.

The turn off the straight path is tricky to find. Her first wrong turn takes her into a backyard hung with washing, and a man snoring, stretched on a bed outside in his shorts and vest, with a cat curled up by his feet.

A second wrong turn takes her all the way around a building and back to the alley. Finally she is on the right path and she climbs to Adonis' land.

Of course, he might not be there; he might have gone home for something to eat and a sleep in the afternoon's heat. In the one room with his mother. What happens if Adonis ever does take a wife? Will Koula sleep outside, like the old man in the white vest with the cat?

'Adonis?' Michelle calls up to the bank. She looks for a way up. Farther up the path the land levels out. Maybe she could get up that way.

The ground is full of stones, piled earth, and clear trenches where, presumably, Adonis will lay foundations. Looking into the ditches she almost expects to see the necks of ancient urns sticking out of the ground, or smashed potsherds lining the bottom. There is nothing but crumbing soil, the same colour as had fallen onto and over her when sliding down the cliff face. The donkey's face is a clear picture in her mind. Life is so short. Are ancient pots really as important as people?

'What?'

'Oh, you made me jump. I presume Dino has

not come back?'

'No, what do you want?'

'I just wanted you to know it wasn't his idea—to report the pots, I mean.'

Adonis is dusty. His sleeves are rolled up and his trousers have tears in them. The slick Adonis she met before is lost inside this island boy. He is a stranger to her; there is no resemblance to Richard at all.

He tuts his disinterest.

'Look, I insisted we report the pots. It seemed like the right thing to do at the time. I assumed someone was dealing them to the black market, stealing them from Greece, maybe even you would have told the authorities if you were in my position.'

'What do you want?'

'I want you to know it was not Dino's idea, it was my fault.'

'I know it was not Dino's idea. He would not do such a thing. He understands life in Greece. But you, what do you want?' His voice is dismissive.

Michelle is caught off guard. 'I, well I … I fell out with a friend for a long time, which is sad, and I don't want you and Dino to make the same mistake.'

'You know nothing about our friendship.'

'I know you care.'

He picks up a dirty-looking water bottle, takes the top off and drinks deeply.

'You know nothing about me. You see what they all see, the outside, the face, the clothes, the

248

dance.'

'Well, if you want to get into that, it's all you let people see.'

'What should I show them, eh? The torn trousers?' He pulls at the hole at the knee. 'The broken fingernails?' he holds up his hand to display dirt-ingrained hands. 'Shall I show my house, my mother who only has one room, a son who cannot marry because he has nowhere to take his bride? Yes, Michelle, I see that look on your face like you suddenly understand everything, but you don't. Your kind never do.'

He screws the top back on the bottle and flings it to the ground.

Tears spring to Michelle's eyes. She has no idea where they have come from or why. A deep sadness arrests her movements.

'Maybe I don't.' Her nose is starting to run, but she has nothing to wipe it on. 'But …' No words follow.

'Here.' His voice has lost some of its strength. Michelle looks up. His arm is stretched towards her holding a roll of kitchen paper, the outside layer covered with rich red soil dust.

'Thank you. I'm sorry, I have no idea where this has come from.'

'What do you want, Michelle?' His tone is flat.

'What do you mean what do I want?'

'You see, I think you do not have a clue. That is why you are here and that is why you are messing around with Dino, preparing his heart to break.'

'What?' Michelle's tears dry up. 'I am not messing around with him.'

'Then what are you doing? Will you give up your life in England and live here?' He rolls his head at the island's dusty interior. 'Or are you expecting him to go back to the place he has just left and follow your rules? I have met your kind over and over.'

'Well, I …'

'My guess is you have no idea, you have not thought, you have made promises of the heart that you are not in a position to keep.'

Michelle's tears threaten to return.

'So I ask you, what do you want? Because what you are doing comes from one of two places. Either you are not happy in your life and Dino is an escape, in which case I am sorry for you and him, or the second, which I think is more likely …' He looks her up and down. Michelle smoothes out the creases around the waistband of her trousers and tucks her uncombed hair behind her ears. She feels naked. 'You have a very comfortable life back in your own country, in which case my friend Dino is just an amusement and that makes you a …' Michelle doesn't quite catch the last word, which is in Greek, but she knows it is an insult, and she bristles.

'I am not amusing myself with him. You have no idea what I feel for him.' But after the words she deflates. Something inside has shifted. She hangs her head and looks at the kitchen roll in her hand.

250

'So you are in the first category—unhappy at home—and so my question is even more important. What do you want, Michelle?' His words have lost their accusative fire and are delivered more as an enquiry.

She shakes her head. 'At the moment all I know is I want to be with Dino, and right now he is on his own, dealing with losing one of the most important relationships of his life so far. I remember how much that hurts and how alone it makes you feel.'

'So we go to him?'

'You know where he is?'

'I think so.' He takes the kitchen roll from her and tosses it after the water bottle into one of the trenches, and strides off over the rough ground.

The land slopes down and joins a path. They walk on side by side. After ten minutes walking, Michelle clears her throat.

'Is that really why you haven't married. The one room?'

'That would make me fit a more acceptable box in your head, would it?'

'Stop attacking me.'

'Stop judging me.'

They each walk a little nearer their own sides of the track.

The path continues, but they turn off up a shallow ravine, where the trees are less stunted and underneath them there is shade and almost lushness. They follow a dry streambed, which is dappled by the sun through the leaves. Up ahead is a figure sitting on a flat rock, head bent.

'Dino,' Michelle calls and increases her pace, but the boulders are tricky and once or twice Adonis catches her by the elbow to stop her falling.

'Dino.' Her breath comes in gulps. But he just sits there; he does not reply.

Adonis says something. Michelle wishes Adonis would speak English to Dino, but it stands to reason that he speaks in the language they grew up with.

'Why are you here?' Dino replies in English. His tone is gruff. But Adonis continues to speak in Greek.

'Your lady here, she wanted to find you.'

Dino says nothing. Michelle sits next to him on the rock, a hand on his knee.

'Dino, will you listen?' Adonis asks.

'I don't suppose there is much you can say that I want to hear.'

'The pots in the cave were not there to sell.'

'Come on, Adonis. You are scraping for money to build a house and then you find something that either means the end of your building and a drain of all your savings, or it can mean a big added income. I am not stupid.'

'If I was selling them, why would I put them in a cave half way along the island? Surely I would

252

need them somewhere near to hand where I could show them to the buyers?'

'I don't know your devious ways,' Dino barks and picks up Michelle's hand from his knee.

'Come on, you know me better than this.' Adonis' tone is almost imploring.

'I thought I did.' Dino's voice is calmer.

'You do.'

'OK, so why are the pots there?'

'So that one day, not now, some day, when the house is built and my mother has a separate bedroom for herself, someone will find them.'

'What?'

'Come on, did you see them? They are beautiful, the paintings of the people, they are our ancestors.' Adonis stands a little taller and closes the gap between them. 'I could not smash them, but I will not sell them, so I put them somewhere safe. One day, in the future, someone will find them and there will be no link to me and maybe they will go to a museum in Athens.'

Dino's eyes widen.

'I reburied them, but in a cave.' Adonis smiles.

'What's going on?' Michelle asks.

'He says he couldn't smash the pots so he hid them, so they would be discovered in the future.'

'Not selling them?' Michelle tries to clarify.

'No, Michelle,' Adonis slurs, 'not selling them.'

Dino remains unmoved.

'Dino.' Michelle interrupts his thoughts, 'He

really needs to build this house. Adonis told me something before we came here. He told me the reason he doesn't settle down is because he has no house to take his bride to.' Michelle looks like she is going to say more but nothing comes.

Adonis scowls and shakes his head, staring at her, as though he is either denying he said it or displeased she has told Dino.

'Come on, you tried to cover it up, but it's true, isn't it?'

'Maybe it was once, but we become what we pretend to be, don't we, my friend?' Dino speaks up, his anger not quite spent.

'And what have you become, Dino?'

'Well, I am not a gigolo.'

'Really?'

'Guys, I am here you know.' Michelle speaks up. They ignore her.

Adonis puts his hands in his pockets and looks at the ground. Dino is already looking at a stone that he is poking at with his toe. They all remain silent for several minutes.

'Look guys, you might not be approving of each other's lives right now, but you can talk about that later. What we need to do now is get that report back, then you can discuss what you think of each other.'

Adonis looks at her first.

'Come on, what time is it, will the office be shut yet?' Michelle urges.

Dino looks at the sun.

'We've almost got time.' His voice emphasises his reluctance.

'Come on then.' Adonis takes his hands from his pockets, ready to march down to the office near the port.

'I wish you had let me come with you.' Michelle picks at the Greek salad in front of her.

'No, it was better you were not there. If we got caught it would not have been as serious as catching a lawyer.' Dino sniggers and pours her some wine before topping up his own glass.

'So, tell me what happened.'

'It was the same girl, we saw her through the side window. Adonis says she is new to the island. We walked casually to outside the door, and then stopped to talk. She looked up and Adonis had his usual effect on her that he has on all women.'

'Not this woman,' Michelle grunts, Dino grins broadly.

'He smiled at her, she blushed, the usual. "Excuse me", he says, "I think we are lost. Can you tell me which way the port is?" I froze on the spot.'

Michelle takes a sip of wine.

'*Mousaka, patates.*' The waitress puts the plates on the table, shuffling them around to make more room before hobbling away in her slippers.

'Go on.' Michelle takes the forks from the breadbasket and hands one to Dino.

255

'She came out immediately and stood close to him to show him the way. She didn't even notice me. Adonis used his charm and I just walked into the office. The report was where she put it on the table. Ta da!'

He pulls a crumpled sheet from his back pocket and holds it up in triumph.

'Oh, well done.'

'And the last I saw of Adonis, he was in deep conversation with her about dance. It seems she was a dancer before the economic crisis.'

'Oh!' is all Michelle can find to say.

Dino is looking at the sunset. The islands are sailing away for another night, the sky already the richest, darkest blue.

'You know, when we were talking outside the office, he said he thought you were genuine?'

'Genuine?'

'Yes, any idea what he meant?'

'Um, not really. More wine?'

They do not hurry to finish dinner. But when there is nothing left on the table to pick at, and it is too dark to see anything but the moon glinting on the sea, Michelle judges it is time to broach the subject.

Chapter 18

'I have to go tomorrow.' The words come out slowly. 'The strike is over, and I have to be in Athens for the meeting on Friday.' Dino, turned sideways from the table to enjoy the darkening view, becomes still, his long legs crossed at the ankles in front of him, his fingers interlocked on his full stomach.

'Did you hear me?'

He nods his head once.

'If I go on Friday the boat arrives too late for the meeting.'

He nods again.

'After that I was going to go to see Juliet. You know, when the original meeting was last Monday, this week was going to be work, but now all of that will happen next week, and then I fly home.'

He nods again.

'It seems so far away. Home. Like it has nothing to do with me. In fact, when I think of it, it doesn't seem like home at all.' The wine has nearly all gone. She looks over to Dino's glass. It is full; he is not moving.

'It feels like some distant dream, or a nightmare even.' She chuckles but the smile does not reach her eyes. 'London seems ridiculous. All that pushing and shoving, for what? There is nothing in London as beautiful as this.' She looks out at the shapes on the moonlit sea that are islands. 'And my house seems ridiculous, too. There are Adonis and Koula living in one room, and I am rattling around with five bedrooms to choose from and no one to share it with.'

She stops herself speaking. The words 'share it with' sticking like a fishbone in her throat.

'Stay.'

'Sorry?'

'Stay.' He uncrosses his legs and turns to face her, clearing a space for his elbows on the table. 'I don't think you are happy in your work. It doesn't suit you. You call your home your 'house'. Who is there in London for you?'

'Well, Mrs Riley and her husband would struggle.' She laughs.

'Who are Mrs Riley and her husband?'

'Oh, my cleaner and gardener. They have been with us—me—for years,' she states dismissively.

'You go back to keep your cleaning lady employed?'

Michelle can feel her cheeks growing hot. She is glad the only light is from a candle on the table.

'Well, no, there is Grace, and Isabella and Doreen.'

'These are your close friends, yes?'

'Well, no. Grace is my boss's secretary, but we do get on, we have a quick coffee sometimes. Isabella is a colleague. We work well together, and Doreen

258

....' She does not finish her sentence. Her list already sounds sad. If she owns up that most of her daily conversation is with Doreen, the office caretaker, she fears Dino might reassess his opinion of her.

Dino just looks at her.

'There is my job. I cannot leave my job, and my house.'

'Why can you not leave your job?'

'That's a bit of a naïve question.'

'Have you ever tried doing anything else?'

'No, but ....'

'So you have no idea if there is something that would make you happier?'

'I cannot just up and leave my job, especially at my age. What would I do?'

'What do you want to do?'

'Oh don't you start.'

'What?'

'Come on, let's go. I need to walk a little.'

Dino insists on paying, and when he returns to her, he has a bougainvillaea flower between finger and thumb, which he presents to her.

'Stay,' he repeats.

'Dino, how can I?'

'Sell your house and live here.'

'And do what?'

'What did you like to do best when you were six years old?'

'When I was six? Why six?'

'They say that is who you really are.'

'I played house, gave tea parties.'

'So there you go.'

'What! I should pack in being a lawyer and stay in Greece to give tea parties?!'

'Tea parties, bed and breakfast, guest house, what's the difference?'

'A lot of work, I imagine.'

'Oh, and being a lawyer isn't a lot of work?'

'Come to England with me.'

Dino stops walking and turns to her, an astonished look, fear in there somewhere.

'England?' He leads her up a couple of steps to some flat land by a disused windmill overlooking the sea, the moon now clearing a path of light in the waves, the mainland hills black holes in the mist of stars. Without ceremony, he flops to the floor, legs crossed in front of him, leaning back on rigid arms, head back, looking up at the stars.

It takes him a while to respond.

'I got up, I went into work, I came home, I cried. I got up, I went to work, back home and cried.' He exhales and looks at Michelle, who is standing, arms folded across her chest. She squats so she is at the same eye level, and drops her weight sideways to sit, her legs curled under her.

'I saw the days passing, my life passing, and all I saw ahead of me was more of the same—not for weeks, not for months, not for years, but for decades.'

'One day I got up, I didn't go to work, and I

didn't cry. I just couldn't face going into that non-human environment. Another day of my life would drain away for no purpose, and I just couldn't force myself to go.' He interrupts his stargazing to look at her, monitor her response. She cannot break her stare. 'The next day was even harder to make myself go, so I stayed at home again.'

'By the end of the week, the phone in the flat was ringing every hour, which I presume was them asking me where I was, so I started to go out all day, trying to form a plan, decide what to do, but mostly I went to museums. Have you seen the size of the Attica-ware collection the British Museum has? More than in Greece. Makes Adonis' few pots look immaterial.' He turns his head slightly to look out to sea. Michelle shakes her head. 'Rooms of it, they've got. Rooms and rooms, stolen, not like Adonis' pots hidden away. *Really* stolen, like the Parthenon marbles ….' He sucks his teeth, suddenly very Greek.

Michelle breaks her stare to watch what she thinks must be a bat circling.

'The days merged one into the other, and I came home to notes from my flatmate, who I sublet my room from, saying my rent was due and I hadn't done my share of what we agreed to do in the house.'

'That sounds awkward,' Michelle says.

'There were more notes, and then I came back one night, really late, and my key wouldn't work. There was an envelope sellotaped to the door saying I could "discuss" my stuff if I gave him a call—but I didn't want to call.' He sighs, a deep relaxing sound. 'I became homeless.'

Michelle stops breathing until finally her body takes over with a big gasp.

On her way to work every day, well nearly every day, Michelle has passed a man slumped in what looked like a camouflaged sleeping bag, stained and torn, claiming to be homeless and in need of spare change. She has never quite believed him, thought it was some sort of scam, or that he is a person who … well, she is not quite sure what kind of person he is, but what kind of person would end up homeless anyway? Alcoholic, drug user, mentally challenged? Not a real person that she could talk to. She puts her fingertips over her mouth. Dino turns his head so he faces the stars again, eyes closed.

Michelle wonders if the man near her work is still there. She can't remember the last time she saw him. It wouldn't be so bad being homeless in Greece; at least it's warm. She chastises herself for the frivolous thought.

'I just wandered, slept where I could, tried to think of something, make sense of life, I suppose, but whichever way I looked at it, the system wants to suck my days away in some pointless pastime, work or army, for which I am meant to be grateful.'

'Where did you go, what did you do?' She thinks the last time she saw the man on the street was the day Grace told her about the reshuffle, that someone was going to be laid off. But she was distracted by the news that day. She might be wrong.

'I watched the Thames float by. I watched the clouds change. I watched the kestrel being flown in Trafalgar Square to keep the pigeons away. Anything to feel close to nature.'

The bat is flying closer, or maybe it is another one. He can't have been properly homeless, maybe just a night or two on other people's sofas. He will have had his credit cards on him. She narrows her eyes.

'So if you were homeless, how did you get back here?' she asks.

'Oh, I rang my flatmate last week and got my stuff—passport, bankcard, and some clothes, everything I have in that bag. He had sold my speakers and the rest of my stuff to pay the rent.'

They sit silently side-by-side. Michelle leans her head until it touches Dino's, and she feels him relax with the contact.

'All the time I was wandering, I could never concentrate to sort out my life. All I could think about was why my Baba wanted me to feel guilty about my Mama's death.' He looks at Michelle out of the corner of his eye for a second, then away again.

'You know what I realised?' He can feel Michelle rock her head side-to-side on his shoulder. 'I realised I feared having a girlfriend lest I kill her, just like Baba implied I had my Mama. I started to hate him then.

'That was why I became homeless. The weight

in my chest, the feelings of guilt. The whole, "Go to an English University and get a good job to look after a good wife" bit. When I found myself in the job, I knew the wife was meant to come next. Why? So I could kill her? That's how he had made me feel!' He sits up and breaks physical contact with Michelle.

'But something didn't fit, and now I know what it was. It was the lie, the lie of the guilt I should be feeling. I knew it was fennel, I am sure it was fennel, but he condemned me with his silent accusations, so my trust in him—well, there was no trust. And yet I was meant to give up my life to follow the path he had designated. No! So I quit. I didn't know what to quit, so I quit everything.'

Michelle says nothing. Dino glances at her briefly.

'I was going to stay homeless, you know.' He stands and wanders across the grass to the windmill door, which hangs on rusted hinges. There is a clonk of distant goats' bells, somewhere beyond the town and the olive groves, somewhere in the hills.

'Until one night.' His head drops. 'It was chucking it down and someone else was in my "skipper", used my boxes and everything ....'

'A what?' Michelle interrupts.

'Skipper? Street talk. It's a place that suits you to sleep, out of the wind, out of the cold, preferably out of the rain. It becomes like your own, almost like home. So I wandered for a bit, wondering where I would sleep. I came across someone else homeless who said he knew a dry place to bed down. We walked for ages. He took me to a warehouse squat. I had been to squats before.' He lifts his head, his voice gains animation. 'There are some really good ones; clean, a sense of communal living, full of creativity, trying to make arrangements with the building owners that is agreeable to all. Sometimes they do, you know. They arrange a peppercorn rent when they see their properties are being taken care of.' He exhales and his head drops again.

'But I wasn't looking for anything positive; I was drowning in my pit of guilt and despair. I wanted annihilation, blackness. Well, I thought I did.' He gives a dry laugh. 'It turned out this was a drug squat. There was no electricity and the guy led me along a corridor with his lighter. I looked in the rooms as I passed. It was like a gallery of paintings by Hieronymus Bosch. Each room lit by candlelight, a different view on how to torture lost souls. Faces and limbs in the flames' orange glows, the shadows rustling with movement of the unseen. The man I was following stopped by one room and said hello to a girl sitting on the floor. She was rocking and holding her arm. It was cold, but all she had on was a thin t-shirt and shorts. She looked up; her eyes did not focus but she smiled. The man I was with went in and sat on the floor and beckoned me. I sat, and in the flickering light I could see the toes on one of her bare feet were all black—gangrene.' He turns and leans his back against the windmill wall.

'Sand, crushed paracetomol, scouring powder, crushed glass … the dealer will cut heroine with anything to increase his profit. Any of it, all of it, will create infections or collapse veins so the blood no longer flows. Then you get gangrene. This girl could not have been any older than me, and as we sat and talked, I knew she would never go to a hospital with her gangrene. It would spread, she would lose her foot, maybe her leg. Maybe she would take no action at all until it consumed her. But you know what frightened me the most?'

He waits for Michelle to look at him and ask, 'What?' She only mouths it; no sound comes out and there are tears in her eyes.

'There was something I saw in this girl—I recognised her pain, I related to her hopelessness, like looking into a mirror. I saw me. I stood. They only half noticed. Her eyes were rolling in her head, the man I arrived with was chopping white powder on a magazine with a Stanley knife blade. How long would it be before I tried to alleviate my internal pain with a quick fix? The path so smooth, a smoke of something weak, the sniff of something stronger, the mainline to freedom ….

'I ran, Michelle. I ran from the building and headed for lights, anywhere that was bright. I ended up at King's Cross Station. I walked till dawn. I was exhausted. I sat on the floor and someone who hurried by tossed a coin at me. It was enough to make the phone call to get my life back. And now I am here.' He stretches and grins at Michelle.

Michelle feels in shock.

Getting his life back with a phone call had been harder than he expected.

The first call was to his flatmate, who refused to even give him back his passport, let alone his belongings.

His second call was to Greece. Adonis had been there for him, as always.

'Just phone this *malaka* up and say you want your stuff,' he had grunted down the phone.

'I have tried that. He won't.'

'OK, give me his number.'

He had slept behind a fancy new clothes shop that night, in amongst the clean new cardboard boxes, under a bright back door light. The next day he reversed the charges to Adonis, who explained that he could go and pick up his things from his old flat anytime he liked.

'Did he really think you were Greek Mafia?' Dino gripped the phone. He couldn't remember ever having laughed so hard since being in England. His sides were aching.

He went round to the flat and knocked on the door. All his stuff was neatly piled like he had taken his time to arrange it and rearrange it. He had begun to laugh again. His ex-flatmate apologised for the stuff that had been sold and promised that he would try to get it back. Even gave him a twenty-pound note by way of apology.

He called Adonis back to thank him for all he had done. The conversation became uncontrollable, and Dino cried with laughter. The woman waiting to use the phone hurried away to find another box. 'What did you say exactly to put so much fear into him?'

'I need my secrets,' laughed Adonis' voice down the phone, 'but I did ask him if he had seen *My Big Fat Greek Wedding.*'

'What?' Dino had no idea what he was talking about, but at the time, it seemed funnier than anything he had heard in a long time.

Michelle reaches up and takes his head in her hands and kisses him, trying to transfer all the tenderness she is feeling to heal his old wounds, to right the wrongs, to make him feel safe in the moment.

Dino responds, his arms around her waist, turning his hips to face her.

Her head spins, reality recedes; there is nothing but sensation and touch, love and tenderness. She can no longer focus. Her weak legs give way and they both lightly drop to the floor. The stars above swirl, his words soft in her ears, the smell of the warm earth, the occasional dull clonk of a goat bell, the warmth of his nearness, a shiver down her spine until she is one with him. She looks deep into his eyes. The passion there reflects her own, and again the mists shroud her thoughts, senses heightened until they are rising far above the earth, dancing in the stars. The velvet night wraps around them, lifting them until they can reach no higher, and in that sweetest closeness they cling to each other until they drift back to earth.

They lie still, the trillion stars witnessing their elation. Their hands are still entwined. No words need be said.

They watch the moon travel part of its arc across the sky until, with a shiver, Michelle finally speaks.

'How can we go back from that?' She sits up. The deep of the night has cooled the air.

Dino does not answer. She looks over to him. He sits up and moves closer to stroke her hair.

'Seriously, Dino, what are we going to do?'

Dino still doesn't speak.

'In London you will cry. In Greece I … well I have no idea what I would do or how I would survive, but in Greece you have to go into the army.'

'Thailand. I have always fancied Thailand.' Dino grins as he speaks.

'Ha, ha, very funny,' She cuddles up to him to share his body warmth. 'Seriously, what are we going to do?' Dino pulls her to her feet and turns so they can slowly make their way back to Zoe's.

'I have absolutely no idea.' He sounds completely content.

'Aren't you worried?' Michelle feels a wave of

269

panic.

'In Greece these things always sort themselves out.'

'Well ...' Michelle looks up to the sky; there are hints of dawn, lighter shades in the east. 'In a few hours I will ring my clients and make sure they have sorted themselves out for this meeting.'

Chapter 19

'No, you stay here. You will distract me.' But Dino insists on accompanying her to the phone booth.

As she looks for change in her pockets, his arms slip around her shoulders.

'Get off. How can I make a serious call with you all over me?' She is laughing and spending more effort trying to break free of his clutches than looking for change, and she drops some coins.

He is quicker to squat to pick them up then she is. He holds out the coins but insists on a kiss to release them. She is almost annoyed with him but still laughs. He likes it when she shows just shades of being cross; her sternness feels grounded, firm.

'Look, go away and do something whilst I make this call. I have to be serious now.' Dino leans against the wall next to her, smiling. Michelle dials the number and turns her back on him, so he reaches out and smoothes her hair. She whips her hand up and swats his away.

'Really? Oh, can you tell me why? Yes, I see … no, that's understandable. I don't see why it would be. Thank you, yes I will.' She replaces the receiver.

She doesn't move for a second, deep in thought.

'Everything OK?' Dino asks. Her head is down. He puts his hands on her shoulders and bends his knees to try and look her in the eye.

'I think so. In one way it is great; in another I am not so sure.'

'Tell me.'

'They have postponed for another week.'

'Fantastic!'

'Yes, but they gave a very lame excuse. They said it was their lawyer's and his daughter's nameday next week, and that he would be off on some island.'

'So?'

'Well, what is a nameday, and who drops work to go off to an island for their children? This is serious work! I think they are getting cold feet.'

'Ah, my guess is his daughter is called Eleni. Is he called Costas?' Michelle's mouth drops open slightly, eyebrows raised as she nods.

'In the Greek calendar, every day is a saint's day and people celebrate when their saint's name comes round. It's a big deal here, because instead of one person celebrating, everyone is. Next week is the biggest name day, Costas and Eleni on the same day. Many, many people will celebrate. He will be going to an island with a whole group of people, his colleagues and their wives, anyone with those names. I should know—my full name is Constantinos.'

'Oh, so Dino is short for Constantinos ... so you

will be celebrating too! How does any work get done in this country?'

'It gets done, just not at the same speed as England, where everyone rushes about just to keep warm—or dry.' He laughs and pulls her towards him.

'No, stop now, I have to ring the people huddling to keep warm and dry in England who employ me.' She turns her back again.

Dino watches her spine bend to the side as she leans against the booth. Her elegance is not only in her height, the way she moves, the length of her neck.

She stands straight, Dino can hear a loud voice down the phone.

'I've done all I can. No, no I don't think they are stalling. Look, it's different here. It's the lawyer and his daughter's nameday, and they'll be celebrating. No, a bit like a birthday or Christmas for us.'

'There's been a bit of trouble with the internet. Of course I've tried. No, I understand. I take it you expect me to stay on for the meeting? Well, there's no way of knowing if they are going to cancel again. No, I'll keep in contact with them every day until then. Yes, no problem, OK.'

'Not OK this time, I take it?'

'Not OK.' Michelle wipes her forehead on a piece of tissue she just found in her pocket. 'I need a coffee.'

The rich waiter Costas Voulgaris serves them, winking at Michelle.

But Michelle feels too frustrated to even care.

'First they don't understand how such a thing could be put off—not once but twice. If they were here for even a day, they would see time is different here.' She sounds cross. Dino chuckles.

'It's not funny. He mentioned again how the economic climate in England means everyone has to account for their job; it was a threat.'

Dino stops laughing and leans back, crossing his ankles and sipping his coffee.

'Then he lectured me for not dealing with an email he sent me. He doesn't know I took a jolly the first weekend here, nor that I've been stuck here ever since with no internet and my laptop back at the hotel in Athens.'

'What's a "jolly"?'

'You know, when you do something for the fun of it, not work related.'

He nods and bites into his biscuit, licking the crumbs off his lips, distracting Michelle.

'So whatever happens, I have to go back to Athens to get online.'

'I thought your original plan was to go to Juliet's in the village this next week coming?'

'I was, but this postponement has scuppered that.' She huffs and sinks in her chair.

'Why?'

'I have to get online.'

'Do you need your own computer?'

'No. Oh, ah, you mean get online at Juliet's?' She perks up a little.

He nods.

'I don't know. He was asking what I'd been working away at all this last week gone. I sidetracked him, but he's right; I should have been working at something. It's just Dolly's death really shook me. I mean, how do I explain that to him?' She puts on a silly voice: 'I took the weekend off to go to an island, boss, and fell down a cliff on a donkey, bit shook up, staying on until the transport strike is over.' She throws her head back and lets out a dry laugh. 'It's all beyond anyone's imagination, let alone belief, sitting in a London office with not a donkey or an island in sight.'

She steadies herself, takes a sip of coffee. 'If I don't buckle down this next week, there may not be a job to return to.'

Dino grins. 'So just because being stuck in a hotel in Athens with your laptop feels more grim than at Juliet's, does that mean you will get more work done?'

'Well, I might, probably would—although Juliet will be working too, so maybe not. At least I never called Juliet to cancel. I meant to but forgot.'

'I told you Greece will sort things out for us.' Dino has shut his eyes in the glare of the sun.

'It's not Greece, is it? It's just a big mess.'

Dino shrugs as if to say, 'have it your own way.'

'Is the strike still on?'

He nods again, eyes still closed.

'Is there any way off this island?'

'We could take a water-taxi straight across to the mainland, but then there is no transport the other side.' He shuffles up in his seat and opens his eyes to look across the water.

'Hey, you want transport on the other side?' Costas fills his tray with their used cups. Michelle's hair swings with the speed she looks up. She had not seen him approach. 'I'm going across; my car is parked over there. How far do you want to go?'

'A village near Soros.'

'Sure, I can drop you near. Come back when you are ready. Excuse me.' He lightly trots to a group of undecided Germans. He chats easily to them in German until they make the decision to sit down.

'You're not kidding about Greece sorting things out,' Michelle says to Dino.

'I met some Greek Americans once who had come over to try and trace their ancestry. They arrived in Athens with no idea of how to begin and no idea or even where their pre-booked hotel was. So they asked the first passer-by if he knows the hotel. He said he would walk them there, and he asked if they were on holiday. They explained the purpose of their visit; he was their first cousin.'

'No!'

'Yes'

'I don't believe it.'

Dino lifts his hand, giving her the right to believe whatever she wants to believe.

'Right, we'd better go, pay Zoe, get your bag.' Michelle stands. Dino seems in no hurry to move.

'You are back on British time, marching to the beat of London again. No hurry. Costas is here. He is not going anywhere without us.'

'Yes, but we cannot keep him waiting.'

'He isn't waiting, he's working.'

'Well, I'm going.'

Dino twists himself reluctantly out of his chair, and with a few easy strides, catches up with her.

'A week's reprieve.' His hand hangs comfortably around her shoulders. She leans into him.

'It has only deferred the problem.' She lets her head nestle into his neck; he is only slightly taller than her.

'It is not a problem. A problem is something you want to get rid of.' He swivels his head and kisses her hair.

Their march slows to a walk in the heat, the sea sparkling to their right, people swimming off the rocks. The walk becomes an amble.

'How am I going to do it?' Michelle asks. 'Go back to that life, without you?'

'Stay.'

'Can't. Anyway, you have to do the army. The

277

alternative sounds untenable.' Dino's arm slips from her shoulders, his hand running down her arm until he finds her hand. 'You are going to do the army, aren't you?'

Dino pulls his hand away and puts it in his front pocket and looks up at the sky as he walks.

'Dino?'

'Two years, Michelle. Well, eighteen months. How can I give that much of my life away?'

'In order that you can do whatever you like with the rest.' They turn inland towards Kyria Zoe's. 'That's how the law works. We all agree to something and that makes society work. If we all don't agree to it, we have war, anarchy. If one person does not agree but the rest do, then they have to accept the consequences set by the others.'

'It's just not right. I don't want to learn to shoot guns.'

'So you can conscientiously object. Serve your term some other way,' Michelle says.

'It is a criminal offence. There is man who has objected. They have given him a substitute service seven and a half times longer than his service would have been. He refused to do it because of its ludicrous length, so they have taken him to court again on the same charges. They try to intimidate you with prison or lengthy alternatives to make you comply.'

'But that is in breach of the European Convention of Human Rights. I read it, quite recently in fact, on a legal website. The UN Commission on Human Rights Resolution 2002/45 says that states should refrain from using the legal system to force conscientious objectors to change their convictions.'

'Tell the Greek government that.'

'We could challenge them.' Michelle's sense of right and wrong bristles, her energies rise, ready for a fight.

'Yeah, sure, I cannot even face my Baba and you are suggesting I stand up and fight the Greek government!' His hand rises to his mouth, and chews on the side of his thumb.

'Eighteen months is not long, Dino. Maybe you can apply to do something that does not involve guns?'

They have reached Zoe's.

Zoe wishes them well, independently of each other, before waving them away.

Dino slings his big bag over his shoulder. Michelle wishes her own life were so compact.

'Do you really object to the guns, or is it just that you don't want your liberty taken away?'

'I don't want to have anything to do with guns, but it is also the liberty.'

'If you really are a conscientious objector, I will fight in your corner. You won't need to engage anyone.'

'It would be a Greek court. You don't speak Greek.' Dino chuckles.

'I mean it, Dino. I would find a way, but maybe

they would give you an equivalent term in jail instead. Would that be preferable?'

They have reached the coastal path and turn towards town. Both of them turn to see the sea view the other way, with the islands scattered to the horizon, the same view as from 'their' *taverna*. They reach for each other's hands and their eyes meet before they walk on.

'Greek jails are over-crowded and no money is spent on updating them. They are places only fit for animals. There are many bad stories. Violence rules. No, better to hold the gun than have one pointed at you.'

'Interesting view,' Michelle contemplates.

'Why do we have nations anyway? It is such a primitive idea.'

'Don't tell me you are not proud to be Greek, because I won't believe you.' Dino lets go of her hand to change shoulders with his heavy bag. 'Besides, I'm sure if someone came and threatened your mama when she was alive, just because she was Greek, you would defend her.'

'Of course, but I would defend her if it was for her money or anything else.'

'But you had the Turks here for four hundred years, would you not have defended the Greek way of life, the Greek traditions?'

'I would have defended the right to have the Greek way of life. I would have defended liberty, not all things Greek.' Dino changes the bag back to his other shoulder again and takes up her hand.

'But you will not go to prison to defend that right?' Michelle asks.

'Who does that benefit? I would suffer in jail, the tax payer suffers to keep me there. It makes no sense.'

'So by your own rules it is better to do your military service?'

He tries to shrug but the bag is too heavy, it begins to slide off his shoulder, he lets go of Michelle's hand quickly to catch it.

'What's in there anyway, Dino, the kitchen sink?'

'Clothes mostly, and some mementoes that I keep with me, some books.'

'I wish my life fitted into one bag.'

'Right now it fits into even less than that; all you have is what you stand up in.'

Michelle checks her money belt for her wallet, passport, and toothbrush; the three things that survived the donkey ride. She looks over to the sea. Somewhere at the bottom is her little rucksack with her guidebook. It seems like weeks ago since that day.

The harbour comes into view. Her desire to see Juliet, talk things over with her, just to spend time, no longer seems as urgent as it had when she arrived. She still has no answers to her self-made trap in London, but somehow a contentment has settled inside her. Trusting in life, perhaps?

281

Looking up to the convent she smiles. 'Dino, how did Adonis know where to find you when you were up the stream bed?'

Dino walks on, almost as if he hasn't heard her. She waits.

'It was where we had our picnic, the day I went with the goat herder and the goats.'

'Oh. I am sorry.'

'Adonis knows I go there to think, to talk to her, ask her views.'

Loss through death has never touched Michelle's life directly; she has no idea what to say.

'You know if we go to the village you will have to face your father. It's not big enough to avoid him.'

He nods.

'Will you be OK with that?'

'It's on my list: face Baba, decide what to do about the army, marry Michelle.'

'What? Ha, ha ha, very funny!' She swallows hard, plucks her tongue off the roof of her mouth and tries to breathe, slowing her pace to steady herself. The hairs on the back of her neck are standing on end and she is grinning.

'I am serious.' He drops his bag and turns to her. 'Marry me?'

'Don't be silly, Dino, and pick your bag up or we will be late.' Her hand strokes across her stomach, soothing its back flips. Her heartbeat throbs in her temple, in her chest. Her breathing has increased and there is a rushing in her ears. Blinking helps to

282

restore her focus.

Picking his bag up, he straightens. 'I am serious.' His voice cracks, full of emotion.

Michelle glances sideways at him. He cannot be serious, but are those tears in his eyes?

Foremost in her mind is his age, so young to make such a commitment.

'I'll tell you what, ask me again in six months' time and I will take you seriously.' She hopes this will soften her direct blow. She laughs, tries to make light of it. He smiles in response, and she pecks him on the cheek to show him that her feelings have not changed.

'Isn't that Costas standing there? Look, the guy with a bag by his feet. Come on.' Michelle increases her speed. Dino continues his steady pace.

'You act like you can't wait to get off the island, back to the village.'

Chapter 20

She might as well have just punched him in the stomach. So tactless, but he had caught her so off guard. She could never in a million years have seen that coming. What do you say to such things? She is not at a stage in her life when she can offer a spontaneous response; everything these days needs consideration, find the implications, the resulting ripples. But marriage!

Dino pulls his t-shirt straight from under the bag on his shoulder. It was not a real response, because she was surprised, but no more than he was. If he had known he was going to say such a thing he would ... well, he is not sure what he would have done differently, but perhaps not tag it onto the end of a sentence like that. Bought a ring maybe, gone down on one knee, done it properly. Now she thinks he isn't serious. Well, he said it, so it must have come from some deep desire?

They continue to walk along towards Costas, Dino lost in his thoughts.

What would marrying her really mean? It wouldn't change anything; she still has her life in London, and he still has to either return to London, if they will let him out of the country, or do the army if he stays. There, that is it! If she is married to him she has to wait whilst he does his service, be there when he is released, visit him on the free weekends, and the weeks of home leave, she will be there for him.

'Hey, there you are. Deep in thought, Dino? Nothing wrong, I hope.' Costas greets Dino with a firm hand on his shoulder and Michelle with a smile and a glint in his eye.

Dino tries to snap out of his thoughts, but they linger heavily in his mind.

'I just remembered something, I'll be five minutes,' and off Costas trots back across the flagstones, between tables, under the canvas shade into his café.

'Have you said goodbye to Adonis?' Michelle asks.

'No, I'll go now.' He sets off, taking Michelle by the hand.

Round the corner from the harbour, the café is open. Mellow music drifts out onto the street, the outside tables are full. Adonis surveys the sea of customers, alert for a beckoning raised hand.

'*Hey file, pos paei?*' Adonis says in his mother tongue. It is easy to forget that Michelle doesn't understand, so Dino returns the greeting in the same language.

'I'm going up to the village, face my Baba.' He stuffs his hands in his front pockets.

Adonis' own hand is quickly on his friend's shoulder, supporting, encouraging. 'Oh, my friend, I wish I could be there with you. Maybe it won't be as harsh as you are expecting?'

Dino swallows and just looks at his friend.

'There is no greater fear than fear itself.' Adonis smiles, his hand slips back to his side. 'She going with you?'

'Yes.' He hesitates. What would Adonis say if he knew he had just proposed to her? Would he laugh, would he warn him off, would he give his blessing?

'I think underneath her judgemental attitude, her heart is good. Someone like you will only improve her.' He smiles.

Dino senses that Michelle knows she is being talked about. He lets go of her hand and puts his arm around her.

'Good luck then,' Adonis says in English.

The water taxi takes twenty minutes to get them to the mainland, and Costas' car looks abandoned, covered with dust, next to the tiny jetty. Opening the doors lets the heat from inside force its way out, making each of them step back. There is a biro on the dashboard that has bent with the heat, and a bottle of water on the back seat which is too hot to touch.

Costas insists Michelle, being the lady, sit in the front, and it is not long before a gentle rhythmic breathing is heard from Dino in the back, which is fine as Costas is intelligent, amusing company. They talk on many subjects until Michelle begins to recognise the roads, and finally they are just outside the village.

'Can you drop us here? I would love to walk into the village, take it slowly, remind myself of everything.'

'Sure, but be sure to stay in touch, come visit, or if I come to London I would like to take you to a West End show.' He grins. Michelle feels she has found a friend.

Dino wakes with a start and is disorientated until he looks around him as he climbs out of the air-conditioned car into the full blaze of the sun.

'It's not as hot here as the island, is it?' Michelle comments.

'It is all stone and paved streets on Orino. There is nowhere for the heat to be absorbed. Here there are the orange groves.' She can hear a tension in his voice. For him, coming here is not a happy prospect; for her, she cannot wait to see Juliet.

The lane narrows; it is pitted, the tarmac non-existent in places, buildings nestled into the landscape ahead. As they near the village, Michelle recognises things: the school on a corner, the railing around it, each upright painted a different colour; a curve in the road, then a long, straight street with well-tended gardens in front of traditional houses on either side. Blue shutters, crumbling greying whitewash. An old-fashioned garage. Michelle remembers it from the petrol pumps: they look like a poster for nineteen-fifties America, block tops and tapering bases. Looking ahead she recognises the square. Walking slowly, soaking it all in, she feels very different about Greece, about herself, compared with the last time she visited.

The *ouzeri* where she first set eyes on Dino last Christmas is open. A woman in a floral dress sits outside and a man stands next to her, with one arm around her, the other sleeve of his shirt tucked, empty, into his waistband.

Michelle turns to look at him as they pass, trying to recall her impression of Dino on that first meeting. The woman in the chair, unaware that she is being watched, stands and wraps her arms around the man's neck and kisses him.

Opposite is what looks like a sandwich shop. It is only tiny, but Michelle does not remember it; maybe it's new. The square opens out. The fountain, painted blue inside, is not working, and there are Indian men still sitting around it. The kiosk is exactly as she remembers it. So, too, is the high-ceilinged, unadorned *kafenio* at the top. The farmers have brought their coffees and their rush-seated, wooden chairs outside onto the square and are watching football on a big screen in the *kafenio* window, the waiter sauntering backwards and forwards across the road. The chairs go so far back they almost mingle with the Indian men around the fountain, but there is a definite line that divides the two.

And on the other corner should be the little

288

shop that sells everything.

'Oh! What has happened to the shop?' Her hand comes up to her mouth.

'Haven't a clue; looks like they are rebuilding it,' Dino replies.

'Don't you know? It's your village.' His lack of interest amuses her.

'When you are homeless, it is very hard to get mail without a computer or an address.' He is smiling as he talks, but the tension in his voice is still there, thinking about his father no doubt.

They turn right at the top of the square and walk in front of the screen. No one seems to mind the seconds of football they miss. Michelle looks back past where the shop once was. She can see the church beyond; she had been to a wedding there, of the owner's daughter. She had gone with Juliet and her boys. Wasn't that the same day they went for chips and met Dino and his dad?

She shrugs to herself and faces forward again. They pass the public fresh water taps and turn left into Juliet's road.

Dino exhales loudly.

'You OK?' she asks, as it is an unexpected sound, the release of the tension, but he assures her that he is fine now that he is out of the main square. Michelle understands: he wants to meet his father on his own terms, not be caught unawares.

On the narrow lane to Juliet's, Kyria Georgia is in her neat garden deadheading some of her myriad flowers. She has a misshapen wide-brimmed hat on, and an apron down to her ankles that looks like it has never been washed, over her clothes of mourning. Her husband died — what was it — twenty-two or twenty-three years ago? Michelle has been told by Juliet, but she cannot recall exactly. Georgia's concrete yard is a riot of colourful flowers in pots, leaving nothing but small walkways to sidle between to water them. Some of the bougainvillea tower over her little cottage. She looks up as they pass.

'*Oh Panayia,*' and off she goes enthusing in Greek. Michelle has had Juliet explain to Kyria Georgia many times that she does not understand Greek, but it doesn't stop the flood of exclamations. On and on she talks, encouraging Michelle to laugh when she does and look grave when appropriate.

They kiss firmly on each cheek. Georgia greets Dino in the same way and then points, first to Michelle and then Dino with a mischievous glint in her eye. Dino says nothing.

After what seems like an age of not understanding anything, Georgia holds up a commanding finger for them to wait. She goes into her tiny cottage and returns with a handful of eggs.

They continue up the lane, now laden with eggs, and Michelle remembers she has not brought any wine.

The house next to Georgia's is seldom visited now as the owner, who runs a shop in Athens, has acute diabetes. His grandsons sometimes visit, bringing their latest girlfriends, Juliet has told Michelle. The place looks very uncared for.

Then there is the deserted barn with the unused land, and at the end of the rough road are the double metal gates with the arch above, covered with wild roses.

Although this is only Michelle's third visit, it feels like coming home.

Dino pushes open the gate and is greeted by two cats winding around each other, the gate, and his legs.

He shifts his bag further onto his shoulder so it won't fall as he bends to stroke them.

The front patio looks so inviting; the pergola over the top hangs with leaves and tiny buds that will be grapes. Juliet has a sofa that she leaves outside all summer, old and sagging but so comfortable. This year, next to the table and chairs, where they ate most of their meals, she remembers, she has slung a hammock between two of the whitewashed pillars that support the pergola.

Michelle knocks on the open front door and savours the cool of the interior; she had almost forgotten how hot it is outside.

'Juliet?' she calls. The room is all white: old white floor tiles, another sagging white sofa, a wall lined with books, open plan to the kitchen, all old cupboards and wood. The fridge is a little incongruous in the organic environment. Everywhere dust dances in the strips of sunlight, which highlights the corners of the room.

Michelle breathes out and Dino drops his bag in the doorway.

'Hey,' Dino calls from outside, 'look what I have found. This yours?'

He has returned outside and is manhandling her suitcase.

'Ha, they must have sent it from the airport! Where was it?' Michelle asks.

'Just out here against the wall.' Dino replies.

Michelle helps lug the case indoors.

'Juliet?' she calls again, but there is no answer. She quietly opens Juliet's bedroom door to see if she is sleeping, but the bed is made, the shutters closed. It is the coolest part of the house, the stone walls several feet thick near the base.

'I think she's out.' Michelle puts the kettle on and makes some tea, no milk, and they go through the kitchen door to the back and sit looking out over the garden. Juliet has worked wonders; she has added a pond since Michelle's last visit. It looks as if it has always been there, just to the right of the twisted olive tree, tall grasses growing around the edges. Juliet still has not walled the garden in, leaving in place the rusted metal fencing which time has worn almost invisible, opening the garden to the orange orchard on two sides and the disused barn and its own piece of rough land on the third. The fruit trees have grown and the flowers look well established. The lawn is patchy, but then in this heat, what could be expected?

'Isn't it perfect?' Michelle sips her tea. The director's chair she is sitting on feels far from firm; she tries not to shift her weight.

Dino is sitting on a couple of breezeblocks looking at his phone.

Dino pulls his t-shirt down and smoothes it out. He turns on his phone to see if there are any messages from his Baba. He wants to make the decision about when they will meet. It will have to be sooner rather than later, as many people have seen him walk through the village centre, and one of them is sure to congratulate his father on his son's return to the village. He will come looking if Dino does not forestall him. But he has made a decision. Life cannot be 'on hold' any longer. If he had already done his service, Michelle would have taken his proposal more seriously.

After eighteen months he will be free, and then he can get a job and will marry Michelle. The decision fills him with a feeling of power. He stands tall and puts his phone away.

'Juliet!' Michelle calls when she sees the car at the gate. She lurches out of the deep outdoor sofa and runs lightly to greet her friend.

Juliet jumps from her car. Dino cannot hear the words they are saying, but he can see the broad smiles on both their faces. Juliet is the smaller, her hair golden compared to Michelle's dark shiny bob. He can imagine what they are saying and is pleased for them both. They take their time to finish their initial explosion of talk and wander back to the patio, the car left with its door open outside the gates.

Dino and Juliet shake hands, and their conversation is easy.

Dino pours Juliet a cup of the tea Michelle has made. Juliet says she will get biscuits. Michelle, feeling a wave of emotion, says she needs the loo. A moment or two by herself will stabilise her. Juliet has brought past memories and feelings to the surface just by her presence.

She loves Juliet's bathroom. It has a curvy wall that separates the shower area from the rest of the room, but there is no shower basin. There is a drainage hole in the shower area and another by the sink, a 'wet room'. The sink is a bowl with a hole in the bottom that Juliet brought back from a holiday in Morocco. Painted in Eastern blues, a lacework of design, it sits on a wooden plinth she had her 'gardener' make for it.

Her gardener! Just last summer Michelle had been intrigued, and then just a little horrified, to find her friend had formed such an unlikely friendship. Her 'gardener' was an illegal immigrant from Pakistan. She had teased Juliet at the time, but Juliet never did name what their relationship was. Michelle understands it better now; the relationship was not always easily definable.

Juliet seems to always be having adventures. Michelle's life is dull by comparison, a black-and-white existence of all work, no play, only one way to go—push forward to get the qualification, get the job, get the security, and please her dad.

She blows her nose and drops the paper down the loo.

When she realised she was never going to please her dad, she can remember the momentary pause. Her life had stopped, then out from the shadows stepped Richard, as if he had been waiting for her. Rather than change her world-view, she just changed a name: Dad to Richard, Michelle Marsden to Michelle Brideoak-Grey. Life continued to be black and white. But with Richard instead of Dad dictating the path, the rules, the conversation.

This thought causes her to sigh as she washes her hands. She picks up one of many little hand towels Juliet has folded and placed under the sink.

That had been the biggest difficulty when he declared he was leaving her. It was not the loss of love, or even a friend; it was the big, wide-open place with no one declaring the rules. Thoughts about becoming a judge seemed to create her own black and white for a while. She looked into the process and saw it would be all work and no room for play. Even from the start, her heart was not in. Now she just doesn't have the enthusiasm for any of it anymore; not the work, not the house, not the whole

English possession-orientated thinking.

She sits on the closed toilet lid.

It feels beyond her control.

But Greece, or maybe even just Dino, or perhaps Adonis' pots—something has shown her that life is not all black and white; there is a whole spectrum of hues. To have it any other way is depriving herself of so much more than just colour. However, she is trapped.

She begins to dry her hands but stops. She thinks she hears raised voices. She puts the towel down. That is Dino's voice. She grabs at the latch to open the door quickly, but she fumbles. Juliet's voice. Dino and Juliet shouting at each other?

Chapter 21

The latch unsticks, freeing her, and she all but runs out to the patio. There is a vaguely familiar man standing by the gate, legs apart, fists clenched. The first thing she notices is the curl of his upper lip, a sneer of disrespect. She looks at both Dino and Juliet to find whom he is addressing. Juliet looks furious and just a bit surprised, Dino is menacing and dark. The man walks with authority through the gate, the drab, shabby, browns of his clothes almost merging into the boundary wall of the disused stone barn behind him.

'What's going on?' Michelle comes up beside Dino and puts her hand on his forearm. He is standing, facing the man, his chair between them. He has the advantage of height given to him by the raised patio. Juliet stands on the step between patio and gravel drive, hovering between the two men, ready to intervene.

'Themis, please leave.' Juliet says in English.

'You cannot hide him here.' The man's English has surprisingly little accent.

'We are not hiding him.' Michelle spits the words out. She can feel energy surging through her limbs — if this is Dino's father, he has a lot to answer for.

'Baba, I do not want to have this conversation. Whatever I say you twist it; you turn my words against me, you always have.'

'You are the woman he has been with?' Themis ignores his son and looks Michelle straight in the eye. Michelle doesn't like the implication, but he continues, 'Give me my son back, give me him for three days, and then he can make his own decision.' His tone straight, like this is a business transaction.

Michelle is speechless.

'Baba, you do not understand. It is unbelievable. It is like being in prison, but with no release date. The place is sterile, there is no sun, no sea, just brick and cement and neon lights. It is like being robbed of all freedom, and there is no joy left to life, just hand-to-mouth drudgery doing something I don't enjoy. It demands nothing intellectually and brings me in enough money to pay rent, buy food, and get the bus the next day to do it again. I cannot do it!' Dino's hands grip the back of the chair he stands behind, his knuckles losing colour. He mutters something in Greek.

'Speak English,' his father snaps.

Michelle is lost for words. She looks at Juliet, who is standing mouth open. Dino is glaring at his father.

'So you want to move back to here and do what?' There is just a hint of a genuine question in the way he says the words.

'I can get a job in the council, or the bank,

anywhere, just to see the sun, see my friends, to be in Greece. The Greeks, Baba, have *kefi*, an excitement about life, the English don't, or if they do, it is seldom and only for a good reason. Maybe it's the sun, maybe it's an attitude.' Dino gives Themis no time to interrupt. 'They work in boxes in England. Do you know how unproductive that is? Soul sapping. Every time I went to the toilet at work, the cubicles were full, the sounds of phone games pinging and tweeting from each stall, everyone trying to escape to another world. In Greece we don't need such division; there are no physical boxes around us or on our time. No one shouts if you are a few minutes late, and no one goes home on time. In England it is all about fame or riches or being in misery wishing for them—in Greece it is all about satisfaction, relationships.'

'And when you marry and you have no hope of a pay raise in your Greek job, and your wife needs new shoes for the little ones, will the sun and the sea provide that? Will your friends buy these things for you? These days in England are the beginning for you. The job being menial will not last forever. You must stick it out; you are on a ladder and each rung provides more for you until you can afford a wife, and she will be able to buy your children shoes. You will not live in a one bedroomed Greek house where you and she sleep on daybeds in the kitchen, and the children are packed into the one bedroom—you will have a proper home.'

299

'If I get promoted I will be so desperate to get out of that shoebox of a room I live in, all the raise will go on better accommodation, the rest will go on food and travel, and again I am in the same position—just with a bigger room. It makes no sense.'

'It is not like that forever ….'

But Dino interrupts his father. 'Michelle how long have you been working in your job?'

Michelle hesitates; she didn't expect to be asked to play a part.

'Oh, er, twenty-five years now.'

'And do you have a life? Do you have fun? What do you spend your money on?'

'I don't go out much because I'm usually working, but the money is good and it's enough to keep house ….'

'Do you love that house?'

She cannot answer him. To say out loud how she feels about the house seems wrong. It will make her a traitor to all she has been working for, her beliefs since they bought it. It will make her a fool in her own eyes.

'A house, what has a house to do with this? Buy them, sell them, you have the choice if you have the job, if you have the money,' Themis barks.

'And this is the home that I bought, and I do not wish there to be shouting here. Please leave.' Juliet finds her voice, but she is ignored again.

Michelle tries to restore order by talking in a

reasonable voice about the topic. 'Yes, that would make sense, Themis,' She steps toward him, takes his attention from Dino. 'But it can be a bit of a catch twenty-two, you see. I don't really feel I have the time to organise selling my house and finding a new home because of the amount of work I do. And I don't feel I can stop the work because the house needs so much maintenance.' She can see he is calming. He is looking at her now, not Dino. His breathing is becoming shallower, but it only lasts seconds before Dino shouts again.

'You see, Baba, it's a trap, and we are the ants in that trap and it is only good for the system as a whole and not the individual ants.' Dino is sweating. Themis' eyes flash and Michelle know she has lost him. She steps back; it feels unsafe.

'Boy, you need to grow up. Everyone needs to work.'

'I agree, Baba, but not that ....'

Themis turns back to Michelle.

'Give me my son back. Give me him for three days, and then let's see what decision he makes.' Themis' voice booms. 'Give me three days to remember who he is and then he is yours.'

Michelle frowns as she takes in these words. She can feel her blood coursing through her veins, adrenaline being released, but she has no desire to take flight. Instead her fists clench as she finds her voice.

Her voice is more powerful than she expects.

'I'm sorry, what do you mean "mine"? He is not mine. He is not anyone's, as far as I am concerned. He is not an object. Ask *him* for his time, not me.' Michelle's feet are rooted. She looks Themis directly in his face.

'But I *am* asking you.' Themis speaks slowly and deliberately, as if it is a threat. 'Give me three days.'

Michelle's fingernails dig into her palms, her arms shaking. How dare he? Richard thought he had that sort of power over her. She had overheard him telling her boss, Sir Sloughlow QC, in the barristers' bar that he would only need a couple of days to bring her thinking in line with something Sloughlow was proposing. Sloughlow had guffawed and muttered something about women.

'Mr Themis, you have had twenty-four years to say all you have to say to Dino. I have known him a couple of days. I somehow think that if you had anything worthwhile to say to him, you would have said it already. I, on the other hand, have a whole world of new experiences that I could share with him. It is neither up to you nor me to decide who Dino wants to listen to, or indeed what he wants to do with his life. It is his basic human right to make his own choices, for better or worse. It is not about finding out who he is—it is about deciding who he wants to be.' She bristles and unconsciously raises her hand to grasp her lapel but finds she is wearing a t-shirt and so grips the neckline instead.

Dino's mouth drops open at the tone of her delivery.

She turns to him. 'Dino, I care for you; I care for you deeply. But you must go, away from him,' she throws a scornful look at Themis, 'and away from me, too. You are young. Your life is ahead of you. Go! Go and make your own mistakes. Don't let him bully you into reliving his or stay with me to relieve me of mine.' Michelle says the words in a clipped tone. Her vision begins to swim; she would rather lose him than hold him back like his father is doing.

'Dino, come, we will talk.' Themis takes a step towards him, his hand outstretched in a friendly gesture. Juliet steps in his way and Michelle turns on him. She is ready to tear him limb from limb.

'Ha!' Themis shouts. 'You need women to protect you! You are not ready, my son, to be a man. Come. Come home, we will talk. If you do not want to return to England, we can still talk. Come.' Themis lowers his voice to sound reasonable.

'Why, Baba. Why do you do this?' Dino implores.

'I promised your Mama. I promised her the day we were married that I would protect you from the world. That was my promise as your father.' He holds his chin high.

'You promised what, exactly? What did you think you had promised?'

Themis' eyes open wide. He studies Dino's face. Michelle and Juliet both turn to look at Dino, too. The tone of his last question says that there is something hidden behind his words.

'What?' Themis suddenly seems unsure. Michelle feels that they have all suddenly stepped onto ice. It is going to crack somewhere, but who is going under? They are all looking from one to another, except Dino, whose gaze is fixed on his father.

'You know what I think?' Dino's hands have released their grip on the back of the chair and become fists; his knuckles gain no colour.

'I think you promised to yourself that I would not become the brother you hated!'

Michelle frowns. Juliet looks from one person to the next, sensing a missing a piece.

Themis' face drains white.

'I think you hated him because he made her joyful, he made her happy. Not constantly, but when he had a mind to, he made her feel light. She loved him. She never loved you. You hated him for selfish reasons.'

'You know about him, who he was?' There is a tremor in Themis' voice.

Michelle and Juliet look to one another, mystified by what they are witnessing.

'I know. He is my blood father. I have known since I was old enough to know.'

Both Michelle and Juliet gasp.

'Who told you?' His voice is small, his shoulders droop.

304

'Mama. She told me. She told me all about him as I grew up. She told me tales about him just like she told tales about grandfather and his goats. Some I believed, some I did not. But she never wanted me to be ashamed of him.'

'Why did she not tell me she told you?' Themis seems to be talking to himself.

'Why? You need to ask? Look at you, coming here to someone else's house and shouting at me, giving no respect to anyone around you. She made me promise I would never tell you that I knew. She did that for you as my father and because she didn't want a fight, but you give me no reason to keep that promise. You are no father to me.' Dino unclenches his fist.

'I gave her respect. At least she deserved it.' Themis replies, his voice losing strength.

'You wanted to keep her in an ivory tower, but she escaped by walking in the countryside, picking her herbs and flowers with me.'

Themis's head dropped and he looked at the ground. 'She disliked me?'

'No, she did not hate you, she hated no one, but she loved life and you did not offer that. You offered her a house and safety for her and me—if she didn't tell the secret you wanted to keep. She feared you would throw her out, so when I was old enough, I said we should go, but she stayed for me and I stayed for her.'

Themis begins to sob.

305

Michelle steps to Dino and puts her hand on his arm and gently shakes her head. The distress is too much to witness.

But Themis is not spent. He raises his head and finds strength.

'You see, you are like your father—you cannot keep your promises, you cannot take the responsibility of a job in England, and so you come back to Greece. But here there is the army. Your father ran away from the army, and your mother never saw him again. You are just like him. You do not have the guts to take orders, but you cannot run. Now the borders are secure, that gate is closed. You will have to hide—hide in our house, on our land.'

Dino gently pulls his arm from Michelle's grasp and steps towards his Baba. He draws a slip of paper from his back pocket. Themis focuses on the white paper.

'This is from the army. It is the number I call requesting to do my service. I have called them.'

Themis' mouth drops opens. Then he closes it to swallow. He looks suddenly old. Dino turns to Michelle.

'Michelle I will do the army—as you say it is the law—and then I will be free.'

Michelle tries to keep control. Her vision blurs, she swallows several times. He is going to do it for her, but she doesn't want him to go anywhere. She feels Juliet behind her, her hand on her shoulder. Dino's eyes are on his father. He unclenches his fist

306

and walks rigidly, straight past Themis to the gate. He holds it open and indicates Themis should leave.

Dino ignores the old man's hesitation, his wish for a last word.

They all watch as his hunched figure becomes smaller as he drags his way down the lane until he turns the corner and is lost from sight.

Dino is the first to move. He turns to Michelle.

'You know I have to go, don't you?'

'Of course you must go; to do otherwise would be ridiculous.' She smiles, he takes her hands. 'I didn't know you had rung them though.'

'I haven't yet. I will do it now.' He takes out his mobile and wanders into the garden, making his call while looking over the rows and rows of oranges trees that merge into a mass of green.

'Could anyone else use a drink?' Juliet asks and marches indoors.

Chapter 22

Saturday / Sunday

'You OK?' Juliet asks Michelle in the cool of the kitchen, taking a plastic bottle of red wine from the fridge. One of the cats jumps up onto the draining board and Juliet hisses at it, chasing it off.

'Not really.' Michelle leans against the table.

'Well, it's been a dramatic entrance. You turn up with a man half your age who has clearly become more than a friend, and then his dad, who isn't his dad, turns up for a showdown. Anything you want to tell me?'

'We just hooked up as friends, but after we fell down the cliff face, something changed.'

'Ah, you mean you got Stockholm Syndrome … I thought I heard a bit of that in your voice when you rang me from the hospital.' Juliet pours two big glasses. 'Will he want any?' She taps a third empty glass with the bottle.

Michelle shrugs. 'It's not Stockholm Syndrome; that's when you side with someone who captures you.'

'Exactly.' Juliet laughs.

'Plonker.' Michelle smiles and they touch glasses before they drink.

Juliet drinks heartily before putting her glass down.

'So, what's the deal? You in love?'

'She'd better be.' Dino comes in from the garden. 'I go into the army on Monday to make her proud.'

'Please—no! Don't go for me, go for yourself.' Michelle puts her own glass down, her smile gone.

Dino laughs but doesn't say anything.

'Dino?'

'Relax, the die was cast when I re-entered the country, wasn't it? Having done homeless, I know for sure that I do not want to be homeless and on the run until I am too old to be eligible for the armed forces.' He is grinning. 'Go on, say you are pleased I stood up to him.'

'Homeless?' Juliet asks, but her voice is unheard.

'I'm thinking I don't know you.' Michelle faces him. 'First you drop the bombshell that he isn't your father anyway, and now you drop the second bombshell that you have already made the decision to fulfil your army obligation. In all honesty, it sounds like you've already mapped out your path and I was just a distraction along the way.' Michelle turns her head away from Juliet, who looks at her over the top of her glass before gliding noiselessly out of the back door.

It all suddenly seems too fragile, their knowledge of each other, the strength of their feelings, her feelings—no—his feelings. Has she really just been a distraction? The proposal of marriage; was it just a game, a jest? She is glad she never answered him.

'Michelle.' His arms slip around her waist. She knows what is coming, his eyes looking straight into hers, the closeness of him, a rushing in her ears. She closes her eyes and the world recedes, life coursing through her veins, her senses heightened, shivers down her spine. Her hips move in turn, she can feel him against her.

Drawing away, he gives her a lingering look.

'OK, Dino, so you do something to me, but I am a big girl and I will get over it if you tell me I was just a distraction.'

The laughter in his eyes reaches his lips. 'Yes, Michelle, you are just a distraction!' Her stomach drops out of existence, leaving nothing but an empty hole. She tries to wriggle from his arms.

'Oi! Stop it! I am kidding.' Dino holds her tighter.

Michelle stops still and looks at him.

'I love you, Michelle. I want to marry you.' He lets go of her and drops to one knee. 'Marry me?'

"Oh, am I interrupting something?' Juliet smirks as she comes in, her glass empty.

Michelle can feel her cheeks grow warm.

Juliet doesn't wait to fill her glass, she just grabs the bottle and leaves again.

'Get up, Dino.' Michelle hisses.

310

'That's no answer.'

'Get up and I will give you an answer.'

'I am up, so what is your answer?' His arms are round her waist again.

'My answer is: go do the army, do it by yourself, take leave with the friends you make in your barracks, or wherever you stay, and if you ask me again when you are out the other side, I will take you seriously.'

'There's no pleasing you, is there? If you think I am playing with you, you are offended; if you think I am serious, you treat me as if I don't know my own mind.'

'That sounds like Michelle.' Juliet is back, she takes a hat from a hook by the back door. 'What?' Juliet says to them both as they stare at her. 'It's hot. I need a hat.' She leaves.

'She's right about me, isn't she?' Michelle asks.

Dino nods. He runs his hand through his hair, brushing his fringe sideways. He is still smiling, so hard to offend. He makes her feel as if life is just an adventure, that it should be lived for fun. The idea sticks in her guts. The prospect fills her with fear, the invitation to let go of the grip she permanently has on her life. What will hold it together if she relaxes?

'So, do I have to wait for my answer?' He picks up the empty glass and looks around for the wine and then looks to the back door through which the sun is streaming.

'I still have a job in London.'

'Excuses, excuses. Think about it then, because I am serious.' He takes her hand. 'Come on, let's go track that bottle of wine down before it has all gone.'

Dino is lying in the hammock sleeping in the shade in the afternoon's heat.

Juliet tugs at Michelle's sleeve, and they stand and walk around into the back garden. The temperature has not dropped, even though evening is drawing in. They had all fallen asleep in the heat, but a cat jumping on Juliet's stomach had woken her, and she kicked her legs out in response, making firm contact with Michelle's knee. Michelle had been asleep on the sofa next to her, head lolling back, mouth open, arms across her chest, until her rude awakening.

Outside the garden looks abundant with growth.

'So what's this with Dino then? Was he on one knee, or was he on one knee?' Juliet giggles.

'He was on one knee.' Michelle sighs.

'You have smitten him. Was he being serious?'

'He said he was.'

'What fun! Did you answer him?'

Michelle shakes her head.

'Oh, good for you, keep him dangling.'

Michelle stiffens. 'I am not keeping him dangling.'

Juliet smiles kindly.

'Do you know who this mystery dad is then?'

Michelle asks.

'I have heard the rumours, but I always thought it was just gossip.'

'So who was he?'

'Well, the rumours have him as a bit of a flirt, really good looking and charming, but by the time he was eighteen he had broken all the girls' hearts, except one—Dino's mother. Themis had feelings towards her too, they say, but she did not return them. Anyway, in the first version I heard, the brothers had a big argument, and in retaliation, the elder brother began to flirt with this girl.'

'Bit of a mean trick.'

'Maybe, but in the way I heard it, she never thought much of Themis anyway.'

'I can see him as a stalker.'

'Well, maybe not to that degree, but I know what you mean.'

'So they got together then?'

'Well, I understand that the elder brother, sorry I don't know his name, played with this girl, led her on, did "the deed" and left her pregnant, and then dropped her.'

'Doesn't sound like a good start. I wonder if Dino knows all this?'

Juliet shrugs. 'He will know his mother's version, I suppose.'

'So then what happened?' Michelle asks.

'Ah well, this is where I've heard at least two versions. One has Dino's real father being called up to do his military service; the other has Themis calling the authorities to say his brother intended to avoid the military service. Whichever it was, the army is meant to have come to escort him to the barracks. It sounds very unlikely to me. If they did that for every person who didn't want to serve, the whole army would spend its time hunting people down. It makes the whole thing hard to believe.'

'That might be why Dino doesn't want to do his service, though.' Michelle voices her thoughts out loud.

'Doesn't he? Well, like father like son then, because his real dad is meant to have run away, left the country out through Bulgaria and was last heard of in Romania where the revolution was going on at the time.'

'So he is dead then?'

'Who knows? But what I heard is that Themis pressured Dino's mum to marry him for the sake of the child needing a father. That and the fact that she would be an outcast as a single mum, and so she married him.'

'But, to be honest, I always thought it was just village gossip. This all happened down on the island, so it's not as if it is first-hand from anybody.'

'Rumours or not, it must have been very difficult for Dino growing up with all that around him.'

'To be honest, I think his mum dying would have been worse. The gossip there is that she killed herself. Did he say?'

'No!'

'Poisoned herself because she couldn't stand Themis any longer, but I find that one hard to believe. What mother would leave behind a fourteen-year-old boy to fend for himself? No, I think that is just idle people with nothing better to think about.'

'Like you.'

Juliet turns to face her sharply, relieved to find Michelle is smiling.

'I just thought you should know everything.' Juliet defends herself.

'It's good to see you,' Michelle says.

'It's good to see you too,' Juliet answers.

'It doesn't feel like it has only been a couple of months.'

'I know. You've been out here three times in less than six months. Has work taken the hint yet?'

Michelle is distracted by the flowers Juliet has planted around the pond.

'Don't talk to me about work.'

'Why? What now?' Juliet bends and deadheads a flower, throwing it over the fence into the orchard.

'Actually, I wanted to talk to you about work. That was part of my reason for offering to attend this meeting.'

'Go on then.'

'But so much has changed since then. Not with work, more with … well, the way I think, I guess.'

There is a plop and Michelle watches ripples

growing from a point in the pond. 'Was that a frog?'

'Yes. They're really lovely. You know they really like being handled.'

Michelle pulls a face.

The bedroom is cool. Juliet's computer sits on a desk in front of a window that overlooks the whole of the back garden. She can see Juliet with her broad-brimmed hat, strolling from plant to tree, nipping here, snapping there, a cat following her.

The computer blinks into action. The list of her emails seems endless, several from Sloughlow and Grotchet, a few from the firm in Athens, but nothing urgent. She scrolls down. One from a roofing company with an estimate to replace some lead flashing where it is leaking into the guest bedroom; another estimate for re-pointing the wall on the north side, which really needs to be done before next winter. Not a single email from a friend, unless she counts the chatty one from Doreen to give her notice that the ladies' toilets will be out of action for at least a week, and so they are assigning one of the men's toilets over to the women.

It all seems a million light years away. The cold, grey metal sky a memory that seems impossible in the sun. She looks back out. Juliet is lying on her back on the lawn, holding a cat at arm's length above her, the cat batting the edge of her hat.

Juliet might not be surrounded by a big circle of friends, but if you are going to be single, why not do it in the warmth of Greece where at least the weather is clement enough to go out to meet people? Michelle scans a few more emails, deleting them as she goes.

She looks out to Juliet again but there is no sign of her.

The computer pings and a new message comes in from Sloughlow and Grotchet.

It's the weekly 'newsletter' from Sloughlow himself. It's the usual 'work hard as a team' and 'we have done really well this week, but' message, but there is something new too. Previously only circulated amongst the partners in private memos, it seems he is going official about the need for redundancies—'as the economic climate remains harsh, we may need to release underproductive members of the team ....' This is followed by a lot more padding until the bottom line, which states, almost without camouflage, that the least productive man or woman will be out. But Sloughlow is never one to give up easily, or one to not take full advantage of the situation. There is a further paragraph saying that the firm is open to people offering to take wage cuts or committing to overtime hours for free. Anyone interested will need to apply for this overtime, as they expect the full squadron of partners to offer their time.

Michelle sits back and swallows hard. She wishes she hadn't opted for the Athens meeting. It is not as if she is exactly being productive sitting here.

She opens the email about the re-pointing again; she cannot believe the price, she must have remembered it incorrectly. No, she is right.

Her eyes glaze over and she falls into a stare.

She can hear dogs barking somewhere in the village, a tractor on the hill, and a distant donkey cries plaintively.

She snaps out of her meditation with such a jump her elbow slips off the desk. Looking again at the email from the builders, she opens a new window and types away with fury. She fires off two more emails before Juliet's head appears over her shoulder.

'Are you really going to commit to that?' She says, leaning over her shoulder. Michelle stabs at the button marked 'send'. 'Will you be relating this restructuring of your life to Dino?'

'No, absolutely not, and I don't want to talk about it. OK?'

Dino doesn't wake up from his siesta on the hammock. Juliet says she has seen the same thing in her boys when they were emotionally stressed; their need for sleep was several-fold. The best thing is just to leave him.

Michelle feels lonely, even though he is just yards away, because he is asleep and he is going to start his military service as soon as he can, to get it over with, he said. Michelle admires his attitude but was shocked when he announced he would leave on the first possible train. The bottom fell out of her world then.

Juliet tries to take Michelle's mind off it by suggesting they go out to eat, which is tempting, but these are the last few hours before Dino will go away to some unpronounceable place, and they seem too precious to leave him, even though he is asleep. She doesn't want him to wake up and her not be there. She doesn't want to miss a minute of time with him if she can help it.

Juliet is easy going. Eating at a *taverna* is commonplace for her anyway, so they lounge on the grass for a while, sit with their feet in the pond for a bit, slowly put a meal together, at which point Michelle is wishing hard that Dino will wake, but he doesn't.

They have drunk most of a bottle of wine before the food is cooked, and they start to get silly. At one point they climb up a ladder onto the flat roof of Juliet's tiny extension, which houses the washing machine and most of her books. The view is breathtaking. The village before them huddles at the bottom of a hill topped with pine trees. The orange groves around the houses march off to the foothills that circle the flat plane of the valley, the sea creeping as far as it can inland.

It all feels too perfect to be spoilt by Dino's imminent departure.

The clean sheets on the guest room bed smell fresh when she wakes. She pads into the sitting room, and through the windows of the double door she can see Dino's shape unmoving in the hammock. The coffee smells good. Juliet is humming to herself in the kitchen, the cats meowing an accompaniment as they wind around her legs.

The morning progresses and Dino finally wakes in disbelief that he slept through till the morning, and chastises them both for letting him do so. He is smiling, but Michelle can feel a heaviness about him. Today he must take the train.

'You should tell him.' Juliet hisses in the kitchen, looking through the open door to Dino, who is prodding a stick into the pond.

Michelle chooses not to answer.

'It's only fair.'

'Fair for who? Me or him?'

Juliet picks up a tea towel to dry the pots. Michelle goes to him.

The hours spin past and Juliet calls them.

'I have just called the taxi. It will be here in ten minutes.'

'OK.' It is Michelle who turns to answer her. Juliet takes the opportunity to mouth, 'tell him,' whilst jabbing her finger in Dino's direction. Michelle glowers at her.

'Shall I come with you to the barracks?' Michelle asks.

'No! I don't want you to come any further than

the taxi door.' He smiles and takes her hand.

'What? You mean not even come with you to the station?'

'I want to remember you here with Juliet.' His smile fades. 'Michelle please write to me, give me hope that you will see me on my weekends off. If you don't, I shall go AWOL and come find you.' He grabs her hair, and forces her to look in his eyes.

There is a toot of a horn, and Dino releases her, their smiles fading at the sight of the taxi.

'Tell him,' Juliet says, bringing out Dino's huge bag.

'Nothing.' Michelle answers.

Juliet gives Dino's big bag to the taxi driver who puts it in the boot.

'Not going till you tell me,' he says softly. Juliet waves her goodbye and retreats indoors.

'OK, the meeting has been postponed again and I may be here a little longer.'

'Oh!' Dino replies. Michelle is aware that he will be confused, as this news can have no effect on him, but better a small lie than the truth.

'What are you doing?'

'Well, it is my computer.'

'Yes, but that is not your email.' Michelle cannot raise a smile, even though she is teasing. She couldn't give a hoot about her email. Where her lungs once were is a bottomless hole, and in the dark centre is a heavy weight that is extinguishing her life.

Dino has gone.

'Oh, don't get mawky, he has only been gone two minutes,' Juliet says. 'I love this bit. Actually, I love it all. I take it we can talk about it now he's gone? "Dear Sloughlow and Grotchet",' she affects a more refined accent, '"With regard to your last 'newsletter', I have a solution for the chamber's economic crisis. In my opinion, the partners are all cost effective and have earned their places on the board with merit. It is uncalled for to put them under pressure to prove their worth, as they all did at the beginning of their careers."' Juliet pauses. 'I hope you sent this to all the associates as well?' she asks.

'No, but I copied in Doreen, which is the same thing; the partners will know about it before it has got past Sir Sloughlow and Lord Grotchet's secretaries.'

Juliet straightens her back to read on.

'"My solution to this problem is to tender my resignation with immediate effect. I will of course attend the meetings in Athens and pursue the claim, and will work a month's notice if required."'

'I mean, could you have made it sound any more pompous?' Juliet starts to laugh. Michelle throws herself across the bed. The cotton sheets feel cool.

Chapter 23

July

'I found Yanni's number and rang him for you whilst you were in England,' Juliet says as she passes Michelle.

'Yanni the donkey man?' Michelle calls to Juliet from the drive.

'Yes. You weren't mistaken. He didn't want your money. But I understand; it's very Greek. So I talked to him and explained how it was only right and he understood what I was saying, but it didn't make any difference to him and so I suggested he take the money to make you feel better.'

'Good move. What did he say?' Michelle goes into the house as Juliet returns to the drive.

'He said he would think about it, so he did, then and there whilst I was on the phone. He went so quiet I thought he had hung up.' Juliet laughs, passing Michelle again.

'Yes, he went quiet like that when he realised Dolly was dead.' Michelle's voice drops off at the end of her sentence.

'Anyway, he says OK, but he will not take the money itself from you. Instead, he will come up to the donkey breeding centre, which isn't far from here, and that you must choose the replacement, and then you can pay them.' Juliet stops to breathe.

'For goodness' sake, what do I know about donkeys? And besides, what difference does it make if I hand the money to him or the donkey breeder?' Michelle stops shifting boxes too.

'His pride. He said he didn't want to take the money and for you to think he was spending it on something else, taking advantage.'

'But I wouldn't.' Michelle sets off into the house, another two boxes in her arms.

'I know that, but he doesn't. Anyway, it will be a good day out, so I said we would go.'

Michelle shrugs, exasperated. 'OK, we'll go.' She takes another three boxes into the guest room.

'Don't put them all in there. There'll be no room for you.'

'Yes, but there are loads more. You don't want them all over the living room.'

'It's not for long,' Juliet beams.

Michelle carries in a box of shoes but wonders why she has brought them. They will be too hot for Greece.

'Coffee or wine?' Juliet asks, putting the box on top of the fridge.

'Wine? During the day?' Michelle picks up her guidebook, wondering where to put it.

'Get used to it, girl. You are in Greece now. Oh, by the way, Christies also called …'

'Oh, yes? Do you know what they said, by the

way, when they came round? They said that they have a lot of foreign investors taking advantage of the slump in the economy and they thought they could sell it relatively quickly, especially as it's furnished.' Michelle puts a box of gloves and scarves under her bed and tuts at herself for bringing them. 'Oh that fits then. They said they had lined up five viewings already, all overseas buyers. But here is the best bit. They just happened to mention one was Greek, from Orino. How funny is that!' Juliet pours the local wine and takes the two glasses outside. The pile of boxes dumped on the driveway doesn't look to have diminished by much.

'What is all that?' Michelle asks as she sits, still holding the guidebook, looking at the stack of her boxed things in the sun.

'I don't know. You packed it and brought it over. You tell me.'

'The thing is, if I don't know what is in any of them, then I'm not missing the stuff, and if I'm not missing the stuff, then why not just dump it?' She puts down the guide to pick up her glass.

'Ah, you say that now, but in a few months' time when you want your automatic electric cheese dicer dispenser, you'll wish you'd kept it.'

'Ha ha, very funny.' She sips the chilled red wine. It seems normal to chill red wine now.

'So when do you sign?' Juliet asks.

'I decided to use an estate agency. "Dreams of Greece," they call themselves. How tacky is that?

Anyway, the bloke who runs it seems very professional. He knows all the pitfalls. He says I could sign at the end of month.'

'Fantastic. I had a word with a builder in the village, and he reckons a team could have it done in a month.'

'A month!' Michelle sounds incredulous.

'He thought your biggest problem will be pinning down an electrician. Apparently they are like gold dust. Oh, and a chippy to build you some doors. Those that are left are just rotted.' She sips her wine. 'Wow, it's going to be so great having you as a neighbour. Here's to you and your barn conversion!' Juliet raises her glass.

'Here's to you having the sense to move into a place with a disused barn next to it!' Michelle touches glasses, which ring.

'Oh yes, you said you had come up with an idea of what you were going to do over here. Come on, spill the beans.'

'Umm.' Michelle stops drinking in her excitement and puts her glass down. 'Once the house in England is sold, apart from renovating that,' she nods at the stone barn next door, smiling, 'I thought I would buy a guest house or a small hotel on Orino.'

'Really? It's a fair run to there. Why not get one in Saros?' Juliet nods toward the gate that leads to the village centre and the coastal town beyond. 'Besides, would you really like introducing lots of tourists to Greece on a daily basis? I couldn't think of anything worse.'

'Oh no, I wouldn't run it.' Michelle sounds absolute. She is still thumbing through the guidebook. 'Oh, look, it has a Greek philosophers' quotes section in this guidebook. I never noticed that before. How about this one? "There is only one way to happiness and that is to cease worrying about things which are beyond the power of our will." Epictetus.'

Juliet narrows her eyes. 'So who would run it?' she asks.

Michelle looks up from her guidebook, raises her hand so she can see Juliet against the glare. In the sun, everything is so full of colour, prisms of life dancing in all she sees. Juliet is waiting for an answer.

Michelle shrugs.

And smiles.

She looks up to the sky, blues as far as she can see, not a cloud in sight. She touches her shirt pocket where the letter with the Greek stamp is nestled. The letter that arrived in England the same day she did, the letter that she has kept in her left shirt pocket ever since.

Made in the USA
Lexington, KY
28 March 2014